I WISH YOU MISSED ME

A Selection of Recent Titles by Bonnie Hearn Hill

The Kit Doyle mysteries

IF ANYTHING SHOULD HAPPEN *
GOODBYE FOREVER *
I WISH YOU MISSED ME *

The Star Crossed Series

ARIES RISING
TAURUS EYES
GEMINI NIGHT

* available from Severn House

I WISH YOU MISSED ME

A Kit Doyle mystery

Bonnie Hearn Hill

This first world edition published 2016
in Great Britain and 2017 in the USA by
SEVERN HOUSE PUBLISHERS LTD of
19 Cedar Road, Sutton, Surrey, England, SM2 5DA.
Trade paperback edition first published
in Great Britain and the USA 2017 by
SEVERN HOUSE PUBLISHERS LTD

British Library Cataloguing in Publication Data
A CIP catalogue record for this title is available from the British Library.

ISBN-13: 978-0-7278-8679-8 (cased)
ISBN-13: 978-1-84751-782-1 (trade paper)
ISBN-13: 978-1-78010-851-3 (e-book)

All Severn House titles are printed on acid-free paper.

Severn House Publishers support the Forest Stewardship Council™ [FSC™],
the leading international forest certification organisation.
All our titles that are printed on FSC certified paper carry the FSC logo.

Typeset by Palimpsest Bool
Falkirk, Stirlingshire, Scotla
Printed and bound in Great
TJ International, Padstow, C

For Stacy Renée Lucas, talented writer, cherished friend

ACKNOWLEDGMENTS

Thanks to everyone who helped me with this book, most of all, my brilliant literary agent Laura Dail. I'm grateful to the following, who provided ideas, support, and inspiration: Hazel Dixon-Cooper, Christopher Allan Poe, Jen Badasci, Ann Brantingham, John Brantingham, Stacy Lucas, John Milburn, Kara Lucas, Unni Turrettini, Larry Hill, Rochelle Kaye, Michael Ko, Brenda Najimian Magarity, Kay Rutherford Adams, Tom Adams, Terrie Wolf, Margaret Mizushima, Lisanne Harrington, Alice McCord, Janice Noga, Cyndi Avants, Jeani Tokumoto Brown, Dianne Swain, Cece Hawkins Avila, Dee and Jon Rose, Elbie Groves, Jeannie Groves Erdman, and my talented friend Kim Stephens, the Awesome Anchor.

ONE

Megan puts on the large, white-framed sunglasses, even though it's starting to get dark out. The dress Will insisted she wear is too low cut for an evening in a pub and too sexy, even for her. She ties his red bandana around her neck and makes a double knot, turning it into kind of a cowboy kerchief.

'You ready yet?' Will calls from outside the cabin. Then he walks inside and his boots squeak to a stop on the wood floor when he sees her. 'Nice.' He circles her slowly and then stops so they are eye to eye. 'Very nice. But take your hair down, will you?'

'I thought a ballerina bun would look better with this dress.'

'You're not paid to think.' He grins and swats her on the ass. 'Come on, beautiful. Time's a-wasting.'

She shakes out her hair, pulls it behind her ears and over one shoulder. The cracked bathroom mirror makes it look as if she has five eyes. Megan blinks all of them and says, 'Let's go.'

He's promised this will be the last one and she believes him. Will is many things but not a liar. Not to her, anyway.

They pause at the top of the stairs and the sound of the creek in back, combined with the redwood scent of the deck after a morning of rain, reminds her why she came here with him and why she stays. Not that she needs reminders.

'What are you thinking?' he asks.

Just like that, she remembers something. 'I was supposed to help Priscilla and the other women make blueberry jam tonight.'

'Like she will care if you don't show up?' He starts down the stairs. 'Priscilla. Michael. I'll never figure out these people.'

'Good people,' she reminds him. 'They took us in with no questions.'

'And they leave jars of jam in those little stands with no one manning them. Like anyone would actually leave money in the freaking jar.' He reaches the ground ahead of her and puts out his hand.

'But they do.'

'You've got that right.' He helps her over the space at the bottom where the last step is missing and then puts his arm around her waist as they walk to the driveway. 'Why would anybody leave money when they take jam from a stand with no one in charge? Once I'm back in school I'm going to write a paper on that one.'

'Me too,' she says, and they laugh because they both know that only one of them will be returning to school.

'Ready?' he asks when they reach the car, and she tells him the truth because she is sure he knows it anyway.

'Ready to get it over with.'

TWO

Sometimes driving was tricky but today Kit Doyle had managed fine. The breeze through the window of her car carried the promise of spring rain, but she knew better. Soon enough, summer in Sacramento would arrive in all its brutal reality. As early as June, the unrelenting sun would spread its thick, muggy heat over the city. On nights like this, Kit missed living in Seattle and, as always, she missed her mom.

You can't live in the past. All you really have is now. She could almost hear Elaine Doyle, her adopted mom's no-nonsense voice, so vital and confident when she was alive. Her message of mindfulness – not that she would have ever called it that – was echoed by the mediation group Kit had tried to join and then dropped. Her head was still too full of noise and memories to fully relax.

As Kit drove away from the shelter, she thought about how good it would feel to get home, escape into the shower and wash away the hopelessness of her day. Volunteering there had been her way of giving back and maybe even an attempt to heal, but most of what she had witnessed in almost four months offered little redemption. Although she knew she wouldn't *bounce back* – a term her friends liked to use – from what had happened right away, Kit hadn't counted on losing her passion for everything.

She couldn't listen to John Paul and Farley on the radio segment that she and Farley used to share. The stories they discussed reminded her too much of her own. Only watching the kaleidoscope of young lives that passed through the cots and kitchen of the temporary reprieve of the shelter brought her back to volunteer one more day.

The traffic was as aggressive as usual for a Friday. As she pulled off the freeway, dusk gave way to night and Sacramento became a blaze of headlights. A vehicle behind her came up too fast. Kit touched her brake and adjusted her rear-view mirror, but she couldn't see anything except a dark van, its windshield reflecting back the light.

So pass me.

She slowed down more so that the van could go by.

Instead, it slowed.

OK, don't pass me.

Lots of vans in Sacramento. No reason to worry. But she did have to wonder why this one seemed to be following her, though now keeping its distance. Kit turned off at the intersection, glad to be free of the glare. She let the cool breeze blow back the hair from her face. Fifteen more minutes and she would be home.

At the stoplight on Broadway, she glanced in her mirror again and saw a van merge into the lane behind her. Same one? Maybe it was heading to the fast-food place in the brick-front shopping center to her right. She squinted to see better but the streetlights reflected off the van's windshield and distorted her view of the driver.

Only one way to figure this out. Kit steered into the next lane and took a sharp left. Probably a paranoid move on her part but she already felt her heartrate slow down.

A yellow glow cut across her vision from behind. *Any vehicle.* It could be any vehicle, she thought. She slowed; so did the van. She sped up. So did it.

As she shot through the red light, Kit remembered everything that had happened to bring her to this moment and knew she had to just drive, just run, get away as far and as fast as she could.

John Paul didn't live far from here. She could call him. But first, another stoplight. Kit grabbed her phone, dropped it and realized she was shaking. Carefully she picked up the phone again and sent a text to John Paul.

Need help. Just passed Stockton and Broadway. I think there's a van following me.

His reply popped up immediately. *Come here. My place.*

OK.

Come now.

She no longer knew exactly where she was. Sweat soaked her shirt and her slick hands could barely hold onto the wheel.

Not sure how. Find me. I'll go around the block back to Jack In The Box on Broadway.

Headlights sneaked up behind her again. They looked the same and she took an illegal left turn.

Her phone buzzed and Kit looked down. John Paul. She took the call, pressed speaker and slammed the phone down in the seat beside her.

'I can't talk, John Paul. It's a van, and it's . . .'

Headlights washed over her again.

'. . . right behind me.'

The van nudged closer but she still couldn't make out the person inside it. She pulled over to the curb and waited. The van paused, then backed up and went right. Kit began to tremble. Tears filled her eyes.

'It's OK,' she said to herself. 'It's just a driver who made a wrong turn. Weird coincidence. That's all. It's OK.'

Minutes passed. She calmed down. Finally new lights illuminated Kit's car. Her phone beeped. She looked down at the text on it. John Paul.

I'm here. Found you.

Kit yanked open the door and met him between their two vehicles.

'Thanks for coming.' She stopped short of hugging him and gripped both of his hands in hers.

'Are you all right?' His smile was slow and guarded. 'Any idea who was following you?'

'Not a clue.' Now, under the bright streetlights, she felt her cheeks burn. 'I've had a bad time lately. I'm starting to think that maybe I imagined it.'

'Come on,' he said. 'Your hands are freezing. Let's get you some coffee.'

'I'm fine.' She let go of him. 'Sorry I bothered you. Guess I'm still dealing with stuff.'

'You have to be. That's normal after what you've been through.'

He didn't move. For the first time since he arrived, she really saw him. He had shaved off his short Afro again, but that wasn't what made him look different. His expression was worried. He also seemed distracted, and something she didn't understand hung in the air between them.

'What is it?' she asked him.

'Do you have time for a drink?'

'Just tell me, John Paul.'

'Not out here on the street. Get in, please.'

Kit climbed into his truck and realized that she was more afraid now than when she was trying to lose the van. Whatever was wrong with John Paul had nothing to do with her fears about being followed. 'Tell me,' she said again. 'It's not my dad, is it?'

'Mick's fine.' He sighed. 'No easy way to say this, Kit. It's Farley. He's missing.'

'No, he's not.' She sank back in the seat, relieved. 'Farley's surfing. He'll be back Sunday night.'

'Listen to me.' John Paul spoke softly. 'That girlfriend of his says he never showed up for their trip. She hasn't seen him since Wednesday.'

As the words sank in, Kit realized what he was trying to tell her but he had to be wrong. Farley had been in touch with her just today.

'What about his phone?'

'It's not taking messages.'

'And his girlfriend?' At that moment, she didn't mind using that term for Monique.

'Beside herself. She's the one who called me from Malibu. Farley was supposed to meet her there.'

'Then there's been some kind of misunderstanding,' Kit said. 'You know how often he loses his phone. You probably have an old one.' She pulled out hers and punched in Farley's new number.

Only a flat electronic ring, over and over. Slowly Kit started to realize Farley was really missing, not just off the grid. John Paul was a former cop. He wouldn't jump to conclusions about anything this serious.

She looked up into his eyes. 'What are we going to do?'

'You're going to do nothing.' He turned the key in the ignition.

'Let me walk you to your car. Then I'll follow you home, just to be sure you're all right.'

'But what about Farley?'

'I'll find him, and I'm starting tonight.'

The dismissal in his voice awakened her anger.

'You expect me to just go home?'

'Hey, maybe whatever happened is as simple as a flat tire.' John Paul gestured toward the quiet street. 'But we don't know for sure if you were followed, Kit, and we can't take any chances.'

'I told you, I think I just imagined it. I overreacted.'

'And you're doing that right now.' He opened his door. 'Come on. I want to get back and call Monique again.'

'What about your cop friends?' she asked. 'Did you talk to them?'

'Sure, but they're dealing with crime twenty-four seven. So far, nothing's actually happened to him. For now, he's just a surfer who didn't show up where he said he would.'

'Which isn't like him. You know that. Farley doesn't lie and he doesn't dodge his commitments.'

'That's true.'

They sat like that for a moment, the breeze and the now-soft traffic noises drifting through John Paul's truck. Kit had been afraid when she'd caught sight of that van behind her. Now she was really worried, not for her own safety but Farley's.

'John Paul,' she said, 'we can do this together or we can do it separately.'

'Threatening me, are you, Doyle?'

He hadn't called her by her last name since they had grown close. But that was four months ago. Right now, they could be strangers again – strangers with one friend in common. For the first time in a long time, Kit's head cleared and she could really think again, really feel.

'I'd rather do this with you,' she said.

With one hand on the door, John Paul turned slowly and looked at her. 'No, Doyle. I can't risk it.'

'If that's the way you want it.' She kept her voice flat and hoped he hadn't heard the annoyance in it.

'It's the only way. You need peace and quiet and I need to be able to move quickly.'

'Let me know if you find out where Farley is and I'll do the same.'

Before he could reply, Kit hopped out of the truck, hurried back to her car, got in and drove away.

Farley, she thought as the street signs flew past and she headed toward home. He wouldn't lie to her about where he was going. Just before she took the turn on Markham Way, Kit noticed headlights behind her again and caught her breath. Then she realized that no dark van followed her this time, only a silver pickup, and it wasn't trying to hide.

She lifted her hand, waved to John Paul and then turned onto her street. Next to her dad, who had been Farley's mentor, and now, next to Monique, Farley was closer to Kit than anyone. John Paul would start looking for him tonight, and she would do the same. Something had happened to her friend, and it was worse than a flat tire.

THREE

That night, every memory Kit had tried to bury returned. Although she had left radio to help find missing people, she was far from ready and, in spite of her defiant words to John Paul, had no idea where to start. She dozed fitfully, unable to surrender completely to sleep and whatever dreams accompanied it.

The next morning, she drove to the shelter to help Virgie, who was on breakfast detail. Not that Virgie needed help, but Kit had sponsored her for the program and Saturdays at the center were busy. Besides, she needed to distract herself until she came up with a plan. The kitchen, located in the back of the building that had once been a medical clinic, smelled like cinnamon and bacon. Wearing a white smock over her jeans, her hair in a bun that was covered by a sparkly net, Virgie stood at the sink, rinsing plates and shoving them into a dishwasher that had seen better days. When she heard Kit, she jerked around.

'Hey,' she said. 'What are you doing here?'

'I thought you might need some help.'

'You must be reading minds now.' Virgie slid a dripping plate into her hands as if handing off a football. 'A bunch of kids just got here. I need to get out there and feed them. You got this?'

'I do,' Kit said. 'You go feed the kids.'

She knew how to move through dirty dishes and desperate young people. The time flew, and once everyone was as settled as they would be in this well-meaning yet tenuous place, Kit picked up a large trash can from the back of the building and rolled it out into the alley.

Across the road, the weathered bricks of a Korean restaurant caught her eye. Kit breathed in the scent of sweet-spicy barbecue and realized she hadn't eaten all morning. Among the usual graffiti, obscenities and names of those who had passed through, someone had written *I wish you missed me*, in something that looked like a type font.

The stark statement cut into Kit. She tried to imagine the person who had labored to create art from that painful wish, and she wondered if the 'you' were a parent, a lover or someone else who mattered.

'What's keeping you so long?'

Kit turned to face Virgie, still wearing her smock but with the expression of someone in charge.

'Taking out the trash.'

'Looks like you're doing more than that.' Virgie put her hands on her hips and immediately seemed taller.

'Just taking in the local graffiti,' Kit said. 'Isn't that note sad?'

'Everything out here's sad. Including you.' Virgie motioned toward the alley. 'You came out here to get away from something, didn't you? Same thing you was trying to get away from inside.'

From the first time they met when Virgie was homeless and Kit was pretending to be, their connection had never failed them. Kit couldn't lie to her now.

'It's my friend, Farley.'

Virgie sighed and shook her head. 'What's that fool up to that's worrying you so much?'

'He's gone,' Kit said. 'Missing.'

'I thought you said he was at the beach.'

'That's what he told me but he didn't show up at his destination. I'm the last one who heard from him, and that was yesterday.'

'Then you ought to be looking for him instead of hanging around here,' Virgie said. 'Ain't that what you do? Go find missing people?'

'Not exactly. I mean, sort of. I just don't know where to start.'

Virgie yanked the trash can effortlessly. 'What'd you find in his house?'

'I can't get in his house,' Kit said. 'He moved last year and I don't have a key.'

'Since when do you need a key?' She tilted her head and gazed at Kit. 'You know what I mean?'

Then she realized what Virgie was offering. 'Absolutely not. You're finally getting your life on track.'

'Haven't lost my touch, though,' Virgie said in a flat voice. 'Let's go.'

'I said no. He lives in a gated community with a complex security system.'

'Wouldn't be my first.' Virgie motioned toward the door. 'Come on. We don't have time to talk about it.'

Kit wanted to follow her inside, to the car and to Farley's. If she really could figure out his complicated security system, Kit would risk anything to try it – except Virgie's future.

'What if someone sees us?' she said. 'You might get arrested.'

'Just say Farley gave you a key and I'll go on about how it was my fault you lost it.' She opened the door and motioned for Kit to pass through. 'That's another thing I'm good at. Lying.'

'You have other strengths – better ones.' Kit reached for the garbage can but Virgie shrugged and started pulling it inside.

'You want to find your friend or not?' she asked, and Kit had no answer.

They arrived at Farley's complex late that afternoon and drove in behind another car before the gate could swing shut. Virgie looked around at the small, simple homes with their lawns barely wider than a sidewalk and said, 'This will be easy.'

'It's not,' Kit said. 'Farley and I got locked out when he was moving and he had to call a locksmith.'

'Should have called me.'

Kit glanced over at her and couldn't tell if she were joking.

'I probably shouldn't have agreed to let you do this,' she said.

'It's your only chance.' Virgie sat straight in her seat. 'You know that, don't you?'

At that moment, Kit didn't know anything except how worried she was. She pulled up in front of the wrought-iron entry gate. Behind it, Farley's townhouse seemed to have shrunk. A small rose bush in front shriveled from lack of water. Drought seemed to be choking the life out of the city. Virgie jumped from the car and went to work with a toolkit that she had picked up as they left the shelter.

Kit stood in front of her and hoped no neighbor appeared. Then she heard a click and, when she turned, she stood before an open gate.

Virgie grinned. 'Told you so,' she said. 'Next, the door.'

As Virgie worked on the front door, Kit pulled a hose around to the rose bush by the garage door. Farley had planted it himself, and to deny it right then would make her feel even more hopeless. Standing in front of the garage door, Kit remembered how she and Farley had lifted it from the bottom the time they had been locked out. She walked over, slid her hands under it and pulled. The door was too heavy. She groaned and tried again.

'Hold on,' Virgie called out. In moments, she had the other side of the door, and together they lifted it segment by segment.

They walked into the garage and the first thing Kit saw was Farley's surfboard in its usual place on the left wall. Beneath it on a wooden shelf were his wet suit, change mat and black poncho towel.

'He really didn't go surfing,' Kit said. Seeing this proof hit her the way it hadn't before. Fighting panic, she reached for the door to the house and turned it. 'Locked,' she told Virgie.

'Not for long, but first I got to disable the alarm.' Virgie opened the gray box next to the door. 'Hell, it ain't even set.' Then she crouched before the door. 'These are the easiest.' It opened as she spoke and they stepped into Farley's laundry room.

As Kit walked past the stacked towels on the dryer and the neatly arranged bottles on the shelf, she marveled at what Virgie had accomplished in minutes – something that would have been impossible for her.

'We need to get you some kind of training,' she said. 'You're gifted.'

'Don't start trying to rehabilitate me.' She scowled at Kit and headed into the house as if she had been there many times.

'How old are you anyway?' Kit asked, and Virgie lifted her hand as if stopping the words.

'Kit, I mean it. You talking like this is a deal breaker. Come on. Where's the kitchen?'

'Left.' Kit realized that Virgie had tight boundaries and that she had better not cross them if she wanted to help this young woman, not to mention find Farley.

The kitchen and its stainless-steel appliances were immaculate. The round glass table by Farley's patio door gleamed like a mirror that had just been polished.

The front doorbell chimed and Kit's stomach sank. Virgie slammed her body against the kitchen wall and pointed to the patio windows. 'Stay against the wall,' she whispered. 'Follow me.' She inched toward the hall that led to Farley's bedroom just as the doorbell rang again.

'Let's go out the back,' Kit said. 'We can sneak through the patio door.'

'Not if someone's coming around there. I said follow me. It's safer this way.'

Kit pressed her back against the wall and followed Virgie. Maybe it was just the mail carrier or one of Farley's neighbors. Still, she had no way to explain what she was doing inside. Finally they rushed into the bedroom. Virgie closed the door quietly and turned the lock. Kit sank onto the bed and exhaled.

Virgie put her finger to her lips but Kit was too frightened to speak anyway. As moments passed and the doorbell remained silent, she calmed down and got up from the bed.

'Might as well look around while we're here,' Virgie said.

'Right, but then we're leaving. We took too big a chance.'

Virgie shoved open the sliding closet door. 'Can you tell if anything is missing?'

Kit walked over to the rows of shirts arranged by color, most of them blues and greens. 'Other than the day Farley moved, I've never been in his bedroom,' she said.

'Whatever,' Virgie replied without turning her head.

'I wouldn't lie to you. I have no idea where he keeps things.' Then she looked down at the flip-flops and tennis shoes. 'Wait a minute.'

'What?' Virgie shoved the door back the rest of the way and Kit crouched so that she could see the entire length of the closet.

'His hiking boots,' she said. 'They aren't here.'

'Is there another bedroom?'

Kit nodded. 'He uses it as an office. And he's too organized to put his clothes in there.'

'Let's check it out,' Virgie said.

They had pushed it too far already. Kit looked at the bed with its reversible black-and-white comforter that matched the color-block night table. On the table was a large plastic bag that, unlike most of Farley's life, had not been categorized and labeled. Kit grabbed it then reached inside. Some kind of price tag that must have been clipped to the clothing fell onto the bed.

'You see.' Virgie grinned. 'I told you it was worth the risk.' She grabbed the tag. 'It's for an alt. down vest, whatever that is, size large.'

'Alternative down,' Kit said. 'He has allergies.'

In the silence of the house, the doorbell chimed again.

Virgie's eyes widened and she scanned the room, her gaze settling on the narrow window above the bed.

'No,' Kit said.

'We might not have any choice.' Virgie wiped her forehead. 'Remember what I told you. I can probably lie us out of this mess.'

A knock hammered on the front door. Kit now looked at the window as well. Maybe it was their best option. Then she heard the door open, followed by what sounded like footsteps on Farley's hardwood floor. Virgie seemed to transition into another zone. She nodded to the sound of the steps, stood against the bedroom wall and motioned Kit to do the same.

The steps grew nearer and paused before the bedroom door. Kit heard a click, looked down and saw the silver knob turn. She glanced at Virgie, whose entire body seemed to tense. Kit could barely breathe. Maybe it was John Paul, maybe even Farley. She didn't dare ask. Finally the footsteps went back the way they had come. Kit heard the sound of a door closing, exhaled and realized she had broken out in sweat.

'Now,' she told Virgie. 'We are getting out of here.'

Virgie nodded but didn't meet Kit's eyes. She creaked the door open and Kit grabbed the plastic bag. Together, they ran to the front, looked through the blinds and then rushed to Kit's car.

'Never again,' Kit told her as they drove out of the complex, car windows down, warm breeze blowing in. 'I'm never going to let you talk me into a risk like that again.'

'Don't be so quick with all that.' Virgie glanced down at the bag in Kit's lap. 'At least you have more than you did before. There's more stuff in the bag too.'

FOUR

The items Virgie found in the bag consisted of only a credit-card receipt for a bottle of port from an expensive shop and an empty pink-and-blue Benadryl box. Farley's allergies were no secret, so that explained the Benadryl. Yet he drank wine only when he was forced to at business functions or trying to impress a woman. Maybe that thirty-nine-dollar purchase was for Monique. Perhaps he was just stocking up on allergy medicine and maybe nothing in the bag meant anything. Yet they were the only clues Kit had.

John Paul sent her a text: *Didn't mean to be harsh. Call if you need anything.* No reason to answer it just yet. John Paul wasn't about to change his mind about helping her. Besides, the man was a walking lie detector and she was vulnerable. In no time, he'd have her confessing to breaking into Farley's.

She also had several frantic voice messages from Monique, desperate to know if she had heard from Farley. Kit called her back and, when she got no answer, left a message saying she hadn't and to please call her the moment she learned anything.

She and Virgie returned to the shelter. Kit knew she'd have to talk to Monique on Sunday morning when she went into the radio station to work on the program logs. As they got ready to leave that evening, Virgie was bundled up in a scarf, as if for the streets, and Kit invited her to spend the night at her house.

'I have a guest room no one has used,' she told her as they walked to the door. 'I'd feel better if I had someone else staying there.'

Virgie's expression hardened. 'I got a place.'

Kit knew better than to ask where.

It was time to go home, to practice what she had been taught about living with her fears and her memories. Once alone, she could quiet the thoughts and tune down the sound on the film that ran continuously in the back of her mind.

The house had been her consolation prize in the divorce. Richard, who had proven more attentive as an ex than a husband, had replaced the broken sprinkler and hired a contractor to build a redwood arbor to protect the back patio from the sun. He and his niece Jessica had purchased a townhouse closer to her college – a sensible move, he had explained. Kit might as well have the house. It wasn't as if they had lived together there. This peaceful neighborhood, this house, would be her fresh start.

He meant well. To him, security was an arbor where strawberries already threaded their way upward. Yet this Tudor-style house he had occupied for the short time of their separation felt like someone else's home.

Farley had tried to distract her with dinner invitations, even when Monique was around, which she was most of the time. Kit knew neither of them wanted her there and she didn't take it personally. They were too preoccupied with each other and the shiny newness of their relationship to care about much else. When their eyes met across a table, their smiles seemed to match and Kit had to look away. She didn't need any reminders of how that felt.

Now, with the empty allergy-medicine box, the tag for the alternative-down vest and the wine receipt lined on her white pedestal table, Kit switched off the television she wasn't watching anyway, headed for the stove and turned the heat on under her copper teapot. Something wasn't right – maybe just the mosaic of thoughts trying to distract her again.

Deep breath. Breath is the anchor.

The banquette circling the table was stiff but cozy in a way that made her feel as if she were sitting in an old diner. It lacked only a potted palm or a neon sign to qualify as really cheesy. Maybe that's what this place was missing – something corny enough to make her smile.

The banquette overlooked the backyard, which, thanks to the new lighting system Richard had installed, would soon be visible through the open blinds. As she waited for her tea water to boil, she looked at the receipts again. The wine was from a shop on Fair Oaks Boulevard. That would be her first stop after seeing Monique tomorrow morning. She glanced out of the window at her backyard, now darker than before. Not a single light had come on. Kit got up and went to the sliding glass door, wondering if she had accidentally disconnected the switch. She wanted those lights.

As she touched the handle, the door slid open. Night air drifted in through the screen. Although it still carried the warmth of the day, it felt ice cold. Kit shoved the door shut and clicked the lock. Then she tested it. The door held firmly.

She would not have left that door unlocked. She would not have turned off the backyard lights.

The tea kettle's whine became a piercing whistle.

Someone was in this house.

The thought was as persistent as the sound of the kettle. Kit ran to the stove, yanked it off the burner and set it on a potholder.

Her phone lay on the table.

She should pick it up and call someone – the police.

And tell them what? That someone might have been in here but nothing was missing?

She glanced down at the text from John Paul again.

Call if you need anything.

The stairs creaked. Kit glanced up them, toward her bedroom, and couldn't take a step.

Certainly no one was up there, but why take chances? John Paul answered on the first ring.

'Taking me up on my offer?'

'I need you to come over here right now.'

'Good.' He chuckled. 'I was actually going to buy you some flowers.'

'This isn't funny, John Paul,' she said. 'I think someone's been in my house.'

'Don't do anything.' He spoke with certainty as if reciting a memorized script. 'Stay where you are. I'm on my way.'

Knowing that restored her confidence. Reminding herself of what she'd just survived did the rest. No one would be hiding up there, assuming anyone had been in here at all. Although what had happened a year ago had tested everything she thought she believed about herself, it had also taught her that she was a survivor. Now, though, she fought a different battle – her mind against her mind, her memory against her reality.

Breathe . . . be grounded. Kit took a breath, held it in and took another. Then she slowly got up.

Move from the kitchen to the great room and turn on the lamps one at a time. Then the overhead light that illuminates the hall and the wooden staircase with the bamboo-print runner up the center. Check the pantry, the laundry room and again the kitchen. Then the outside door. Pull at it. Check the lock.

At the sound of the doorbell she stopped, uncertain how long she had been going from room to room, turning on lights and talking herself into calmness. John Paul stood outside. Although his jacket hung loosely around his hips, she could have guessed his former job by his stance, and she had never been happier to see him.

'I checked the outside.' He closed the door behind him, his jaw tight in spite of his calm tone. 'Your side gate's open.'

'I always close it.'

'I know. Someone must have been in a hurry. What about the house?'

'I've been turning on lights,' she said. 'I mean, I haven't gone upstairs.'

'Good. You wait here.' Not a question.

She tried but couldn't stay put. Instead, she took the stairs behind him to the landing.

'How many bedrooms up here?' he called out.

'Just mine and a guest room,' she replied. 'One bath.'

He turned on the landing and the outline of his gun showed through his jacket. 'I asked you to stay down there.'

No need to remind him why she couldn't stay put in her own home. 'Do you really think someone was in here?'

'I'm not sure yet.' The double doors to her bedroom stood open, just as she had left them. He glanced at her and she nodded.

He flipped on the light and walked inside the room, jacket open, his hand on the gun.

'Is everything the way you left it?' he asked.

Kit looked past him around the room – the bed, coverlet thrown back, water glass on the bedside table beside the open book she had tried to read when she couldn't sleep last night.

A rustling from the far corner startled her. Her bedroom curtains fluttered against the wall on either side of the open window.

'Did you leave it that way?' John Paul asked.

'No. I'd never.' She started toward it and then stopped at the area rug beside her bed.

'What?' She tried to make sense of the small pink stain at her feet.

'Don't touch it,' he said.

Kit couldn't look away. Overlapping the pink, traces of green were ground into the rug.

'Did you call anyone?' she asked, still staring at the stain.

'My buddy Jasper.' He moved beside her. 'You need to report what happened.'

She made herself glance up from the rug into his eyes. 'Somebody climbed up the arbor out there and through the window.'

'How do you know?'

Her eardrums ached; her chest clenched and she had to fight to breathe.

'Kit?'

She pointed at the floor. 'That's a crushed strawberry. The vine outside is full of them.'

'Come on.' He touched her arm and she jumped.

'Sorry. I guess everything's just catching up with me.'

'Downstairs,' he said, and this time she did as he told her.

When they got to the kitchen, he sat across from her at the table.

'Whoever it was,' she told him, speaking carefully, 'whoever climbed the arbor and went in up there left through that door.'

He got up and crossed the room. 'It's locked.'

'It wasn't.'

'You touched the handle?'

'I didn't know anyone had been here.'

'Are you sure nothing's missing?'

'Nothing obvious. All I knew when I came in the house tonight was that something was different. Something was wrong.'

'Because you were worried about Farley?'

'I'm not sure,' she said. And then, because he had always been able to get the truth out of her, she added, 'I felt as if someone had been or was in here. That's what made me remember the outside lights.'

'You can't stay here tonight.' He took a step toward her. 'Want me to drive you to your mom's?'

'No.' Her voice came out too loud, too panicked. She forced herself to lower it. 'I don't want to worry her.'

'You need to stay somewhere, at least until we can take a look around.'

She started to protest and he took another step, as if not wanting to frighten her more.

'Maybe it's nothing, but that window up there was open, and if you didn't walk on that rug, someone else did.'

'I'd rather not worry my mom for no reason.'

'A friend then?' He stopped and she knew they were both thinking of Farley. Kit realized she was biting her lip. 'A hotel?' he asked. 'I can talk to Jasper.'

'Anyone can follow me to a hotel.'

'I'll drive you. This one is in plain sight. You'll be safe.'

But where would she ever feel safe? Kit couldn't form the words. She could see only that smeared spot on the rug – evidence that someone had climbed through her bedroom window. She looked out at the backyard and its lights so neatly and strategically placed that they might be ferns and shrubs as well. 'I don't know.'

'Well, I do,' he said and put out his hand. 'Come on. It's only one night. Let's get you out of here.'

FIVE

Located beside the Riverside Promenade, the suite hotel was across from Old Town. John Paul hadn't been kidding when he'd said it was in plain sight. She had passed it dozens of times. The desk clerk nodded when he checked her in and Kit knew they were expected.

'So,' she asked John Paul, 'is this like a safe house?'

'A few steps away from that and much more relaxed.' They headed through the two-story lobby to the elevator and his limp seemed less pronounced. 'You'd probably be fine at home but there's no sense in taking chances.'

They arrived at the second floor and he guided her down the row of rooms overlooking the Sacramento River and the golden lights of the Tower Bridge. At another time, they might be strolling across the vertical lift bridge the way other couples did now.

'What are you thinking?' he asked. Then he stopped, looked out at the unhurried world she had been observing and his gaze met hers. 'Never mind. I know.'

For a moment, she considered asking him to come in and talk, but this wasn't the time.

'If you find out anything at all about Farley tonight,' she said, 'you will let me know, won't you?'

'Of course.' He put in the key and, when the tiny light on the door flashed green, opened it. 'No need for me to check it out, but I will.'

He stepped in ahead of her and she waited.

His walk-through took only a minute, if that. 'Everything's cool,' he said and gave her a one-armed hug. 'Get some sleep. I'll pick you up tomorrow.'

'And—'

He wouldn't let her finish the sentence. 'I already told you. I'll let you know if I hear anything about Farley.'

Once he left, Kit had to tell herself that she was better here than at home. With her back pressed against the bed pillows and two blankets piled on top of her, she tried to make herself comfortable. Instead, she imagined how easy it would be for someone to walk into the hotel, into the elevator and inside this room, the same way someone had climbed into her bedroom at home. But John Paul wouldn't have insisted on her staying here if he hadn't been convinced of how secure the place was. Besides, if anyone had wanted to harm her, they wouldn't have broken into her home in the middle of the day. They would have waited for night when she was alone, the way she was now.

She glanced at the tightly drawn curtains and reminded herself that she was safe here. Closing her eyes, she tried to drive the images from her mind. Giving into the fear would ultimately destroy her. It was the true danger.

Farley was at the heart of this. That's why she had been followed, why someone had broken into her house. It had something to do with where Farley was and who, if anyone, was with him. Figure that out, find him, and she could put an end to this nightmare. That's what she had to do – just stop being a coward. No more fear. No more hiding.

A soft knock on the door jerked her awake. She glanced at the bedside clock. Almost eight-thirty.

'It's John Paul. You up?'

She had fallen asleep swearing off fear, and she had awakened full of it.

'Be right there,' she managed to reply.

Sunlight filtered through the drapes and Kit realized she was fully dressed, right down to her shoes. She had kicked off the covers during the night and they bunched at the foot of the bed. In the bathroom, she tried to smooth the frizz out of her hair. Then she rushed back to the bed, pulled up and smoothed the covers just in case he wanted to go through the place again. Kit took a deep breath, closed the bedroom door behind her, walked through the living room/kitchen and opened the front door.

'Good morning.' John Paul stepped inside and they exchanged glances. 'Didn't get much sleep, did you?' he said.

He hadn't shaved, and in the light of the room his weary eyes were a dull pale brown.

'Not much.' She picked up her bag from the table in front of the window. 'I'm feeling better, though. Thank you for insisting I stay. Did you find anything else at my house?'

'Everything seems back to normal. You should probably change your locks, though.'

'Even though whoever it was climbed through my window?'

'Just to be safe. I'd prune those vines too.' He glanced at her suitcase. 'I can take that for you.'

'It's fine.' She should probably offer him coffee but the place seemed to be closing in on her. 'Let's get out of here.'

'I parked across the street,' he said. 'In Old Town. A friend of mine has a little yogurt place on Front Street. He'll open for us.'

'I need to get to the station.'

'On Sunday?'

'Monique will be there. I want to talk to her.'

She stepped outside and saw the same view of the bridge, only in daylight now, its reflection an iridescent blur in the river.

'Coffee will just take a minute,' he said, 'and frankly, I could use some.'

Kit knew he had probably spent the night parked in front of her house. 'So could I,' she told him. But more than coffee, she needed to question Monique.

They took the elevator to the ground floor and crossed the street onto the wood-plank sidewalks of Old Town. The weathered lumber creaked and gave way slightly beneath her shoes as she and John Paul passed the tattoo parlor and old-time photo booth with sepia-tinged prints in the window. The place never changed. Except for the buildings in the distance rising into the sky and the border of vertically parked vehicles surrounding it, the rustic street must look the same as it had when this district was thriving thanks to its proximity to the river and its abundance of agricultural crops and gold.

'In spite of everything,' John Paul said, 'it's good to be spending some time with you again.'

'I know what you mean, and I'm afraid it won't be much time. I really do need to get to the station while I know Monique is still there.'

'Let's wait to do that that once you're feeling stronger.'

Kit lifted her face to the breeze and realized that her palms were damp. She rubbed them together and tried to remember what she'd been taught. If she didn't stop it now, the panic would attack her breathing next. John Paul would know and he wouldn't share anything with her.

'You OK?' he asked.

'I'm fine, and I'll be better once I see her.'

'Let's at least get some coffee first and talk about it.' He motioned down a side street, which had already started to fill with visitors holding ice-cream cones and doughnuts.

'I don't want to wait around here,' she told him, more forcefully this time. 'Would you mind driving me over there now? Monique left me some messages, and if we speak she might remember something she didn't tell you. You have already talked to her, haven't you?'

'Of course I have.' He stopped as a flurry of people conversing in German streamed past them. Kit had been like them once, excited about absorbing the history and secrets of this city. Unafraid.

'I'd still like to talk to her as well.'

'Not today.' Before she could ask why, he added, 'Have you

told me everything you know about Farley? Everything he might have shared with you?'

'Why would you ask me that?'

He squinted at her as if staring into the sun. 'Have you?'

'Everything I can think of that might possibly be important.' When he didn't respond, she said, 'I know I haven't acted all that stable lately, but I'm all right now and I know what I need to do.'

'Which is?'

'I'm good at finding missing people, John Paul. I think I've proven that.' She was breathing just fine now, keeping up with his long, uneven strides, intent on finding out what had made him doubt her. 'Why don't you want me to talk to Monique?'

'I don't mind if you talk to her.' He touched her elbow, as if to remind her that they were arguing in public. 'Just not right now. Not this morning.'

They reached his truck and he opened the door for her. 'Why not?' she asked.

'First of all, her boyfriend is missing. She's upset.'

'So am I. So are you.'

A tour bus stopped behind them and passengers crowded off and onto the street. The breeze grew stronger and fanned the red, white and blue bunting over the narrow shop doorways. Kit climbed inside the truck and John Paul walked around to the other side as if the conversation had made him weary.

She waited until he was behind the wheel and asked, 'What's really going on? Are you saying you won't drive me to the radio station?'

He raised an eyebrow. 'What if I am?'

'Then I'll just have to drive myself,' she said. 'You're probably busy anyway. Go ahead and take me home. I can handle it from there.'

He turned, and his eyes were once more the clear lie detectors she knew all too well. 'Before I do, isn't there something you'd like to tell me – something you haven't gotten around to mentioning?'

There was no way he could know what she and Virgie had done, unless he had been the other person in Farley's house. Of course. That's what was going on. John Paul had been at Farley's and had figured out she had been as well. He might even have followed her there.

Maybe it was lack of sleep. Maybe it was the anxiety demon she tried to destroy or at least tame. Or maybe she kind of trusted John Paul, which for now was the only way she could trust anyone.

'Once you told me Farley was missing, I went to his house,' she said.

'You have a key?'

'I broke in.'

'With his new security system?' His eyes widened. 'How'd you manage that?'

'I can't tell you.'

'Not even if I guess?'

'Especially if you guess,' she said.

'You should have called me.' He started the truck and shook his head. 'So you and Virgie broke into Farley's house? That woman must be a technological wizard.'

'*I* broke into Farley's house,' she said. 'Alone. You were there too, weren't you?'

'No.' He clutched the steering wheel. 'I wasn't at Farley's.'

Chills prickled along Kit's arms. 'Someone was. They rang the bell and knocked. Then later, someone came down the hall and tried the knob on the bedroom door.' Her voice trailed off and she knew that he was thinking the same thing she was. 'If you weren't there, how did you know I was?'

'I didn't.' The light switched to green but he continued to stare at her. 'All I knew was that you were holding something back. Like you, I'm good at what I do.'

SIX

Even though no vehicles are allowed here, everyone, including Megan, knows about the battered blue pickup hidden behind the trees for emergencies only. The last emergency, right after she and Will moved in, was Callie, the breech birth daughter Priscilla and Michael almost lost. Now that Priscilla is pregnant with their third daughter, Michael seems to spend more time working on the truck. She and Will pass the trees where that truck is hidden and they stumble over stones and broken dirt paths until they come upon the grove where he keeps the motorcycle.

'Be careful,' she says, as she climbs on the back, which is still so cold that it numbs her thighs through the jersey dress.

'You'd better hang on.' Will's laughter is the same as when they make love.

She shuts down her mind, shuts off the sounds and feeling of the short drive. A jolt tells her they have arrived, and she knows where.

Will extends an arm to help her off the bike, and she can smell his strong scent like something out of these woods, something feral. Her imagination, probably. They have one of the few showers in this place, and he took one just this morning.

Now, she's placed her feet on the ground. He's lifting her face in his hands, even though they are almost the same height.

'You know what you need to do?' he asks.

'It's the last time, right? That's what you said.'

'We're not talking about what I said.' Will puts his arm around her and nudges her forward, toward the muffled noise of the pub. 'We're talking about what you need to do right now, in about five minutes. What you need to say. How you need to act.'

'I know all that. I just want you to promise me that this is the last time.'

'Have I ever lied to you?' Standing beside the bike, he reaches out and arranges her hair around her face, her bare shoulders. 'Answer me,' he says.

The music drifts from the pub – a song, the sound of a man's voice accompanied by the rhythmic strumming of a guitar.

She takes his arm and heads toward the noise and the people. 'You've never lied to me,' she says. 'Let's go find him.'

SEVEN

K it knew that John Paul was telling the truth about not being at Farley's on Saturday. That meant someone else had been. Although she insisted that she'd be fine, Kit was grateful when he went through her house room by room one more time.

After he left, she locked herself in the bathroom and took a long shower, soaking in the sun from the skylight above. Time to talk to Monique.

Standing at the full-length mirror and brushing some color onto her cheeks, Kit had to grin at herself. She must be feeling better if she didn't want Monique to see her without makeup.

Yet something in the back of her mind was not so sure.

While they were not well-acquainted enough to actually dislike each other, they had nothing in common but Farley. Monique was younger than Kit and three inches taller with a neck like a ballerina, toned arms and shoulders that could elevate the clavicle to an art form. Technically, they had the same color hair, but Monique's beachy waves had nothing in common with the mass already coming loose from Kit's ponytail.

She tucked a strand behind her ear and remembered that the first thing her biological mother had told her when they were reunited was that Kit had her father's hair. That warmed her, even now. She had a family. And she had a friend she intended to find.

She focused on that as she drove to the radio station and tried to ignore the buzz of memories about the van that had followed her, the intruder in Farley's house and the smashed strawberry on her bedroom rug. As she pulled into the station parking lot – quiet, with only a few cars at midday – she glanced up at the hymn painted on the side of the church next door and reality set in. She and Farley had stood in this parking lot countless times through every season, laughing, talking and occasionally arguing. If he were all right, he'd find a way to let her know. One more time, she took out her phone and tried to connect with him on the app they shared. The map on her phone stared blankly back at her, its red dot frozen over the blue circle covering Farley's address.

As she put her phone in her bag and opened the car door, Monique came around the side of the building. One look at her and Kit's earlier thoughts disappeared. Monique's hair hung straight down over the blue sweater pulled over jeans. Unaware that anyone was watching, she shoved her hand through it and wiped away tears. Embarrassed to be witnessing her grief, Kit got out of her car. Monique spotted her and headed over.

'Have you heard anything?' Monique asked.

'I just tried calling again.'

'Me too.' She bit her lower lip. Without mascara and liner her eyes seemed larger, clearer than ever. 'Please tell me what you know.'

'No more than you do, Monique, and probably not as much. You were the last one to see him.'

'But I didn't see him. I took my own car because he wanted to check in with his friends first and make plans for the next day, and you know how Farley was about his surfing.' She took a breath and added, 'I mean, how Farley *is*.'

Kit decided against telling her just yet that Farley hadn't gone surfing. 'When was the last time you talked to him?' she asked.

'I didn't.' Her smile faded and she glanced away, toward the building. 'Unless you count some romantic texts. When was the last time *you* talked to him?'

'I only got texts as well,' Kit said, and had to keep herself from adding, *not romantic*. 'All he said was how glad he was to get away and that he'd call me later.'

'He wouldn't lie to either of us,' Monique said.

'I know.'

'He wouldn't ask me to meet him in Malibu and then just disappear. Do you know how many hours I waited in that room?' She wiped her eyes again. 'I thought maybe he was just late, maybe he was charging his phone. And by the time I figured out something was wrong it was almost five o'clock.'

'What time was he supposed to meet you?' Kit asked.

'You don't know?' Monique snapped out the question as if she had caught her in a lie.

'My last text was around three,' Kit said. 'He didn't mention when he'd arrive.'

'Something happened to him.' Monique's lip trembled. 'He had an accident or something worse.'

'Let's keep trying his phone,' Kit told her. 'Did he mention anywhere else he might stop on the way there? That might be a starting place.'

'Just one.' Monique nodded and pushed back the hair from her face as if it and everything else about this day were too heavy for her. 'He said he might stop and see you before he left.'

Standing there in the familiar parking lot, with the sun warming her face, Kit trembled. 'When did he tell you that?'

'In one of his texts.' Monique took her phone out of her bag. 'I still have it here.'

'I didn't see him, Monique, I swear.'

'I'm not accusing you,' she said. 'I just want to know what happened. I want him to be all right.'

'Do you have a key to his house?' Kit asked.

She shook her head. 'Don't you?' Monique glanced down and Kit realized she was clenching her own hands, twisting the wedding ring Richard had given her and that she wore on her right finger now.

'No, I don't.' She tried to decide how much to tell her and ended it there. Monique had enough to deal with. Sharing with her that Farley hadn't really gone surfing would only make her more guarded and suspicious. 'If you think of anything he said before or during his drive there, please let me know.'

'You too.' Tears welled in her eyes.

Kit squeezed her arm. 'It will be all right,' she said. 'Call me if you hear anything.'

Then she turned, fighting tears herself, and headed for her car.

'Kit, wait.' Monique caught up with her and said, 'I have an idea. You find people, right? I want to hire you to find Farley. You know everything about him. If anyone can figure out what happened to him, you can.'

Kit took a breath and wondered whether or not to be insulted. But no. Monique's wide-eyed expression made it clear that this was the only option she could comprehend. She was the daughter of the station owner, after all, and in that world of radio, the ones on top were happy to pay the creative talents below them to achieve their desired ends.

'He's my friend,' Kit said. 'If I can find him, I will.'

'My dad's on board for this.' Monique followed her to the car. 'He loves Farley like a son.'

Kit got the implication. 'I love him too,' she said and opened the car door.

'Wait.' Monique planted herself in front of the door. 'Just tell me how much your fee is. We'll pay you anything.'

'There's no need for that.' She got in, slammed the door shut and started the car.

As Monique's sapphire-blue Lexus pulled out of the parking lot, Kit tried to connect with Farley again. This time she got a glimmer. The red dot on her friend-finders app began to blink. Kit fought to keep her hands steady as she touched the screen and spread out the map. Somewhere outside Willits, California, between Willits and Fort Bragg, maybe Mendocino. As she called his number, her movements felt jerky, wooden. *Please let him answer.*

The phone rang this time. Good. It was working. Voicemail didn't automatically come on. Nothing came on, just one electronic ring after another. But the map was still there. She did a quick search and saw that Willits was an isolated community located on the Redwood Highway, close to Mendocino. If Farley had planned to go there instead of surfing, that would explain the vest, the hiking boots and even the allergy medicine. But why would he lie? Kit took one more look at the map.

Fill up the tank. Don't bother returning home for more than a lock-up. She issued orders to herself, trying to plan the fastest way to get to Willits. Should she let John Paul know that she'd be working on a lead? Kit pulled onto the freeway and knew that letting him know was the right thing to do, and she would – as soon as she got nearer to her destination.

The cars on the freeway seemed closer, more dangerous. She looked to her right. Every vehicle entering it seemed ready to push her off the road. Then her breathing changed again. The cars seemed aimed at her and she wanted to dodge them, to slow down. It was happening again, only on the road this time. *Breathe.* She knew how to do that in a structured environment, but the lessons she'd been taught made no sense now with the sweeping ramps and the speeding traffic.

'I can't.'

She pulled to the edge of the freeway, barely safe, even now.

'I can't.'

The sun seemed to blaze down on her car. The other vehicles raced past her at such a frantic pace the car shook.

All right, maybe she was losing her mind. Maybe the anxiety had finally pushed her over the top of the emotional mountain she had thought she could climb and conquer. Then Kit realized some-thing else, something more important than anything.

No one could know this.

No one could ever be aware that on the brightest spring day in Sacramento, she could not struggle to make even one move in the direction of finding her best friend, even though she now had an idea of where he might be. If she told this to anyone they would think she was crazy, and maybe she was. Maybe anxiety was the craziest response she had experienced in any trauma in the last two years.

A semi-truck shot past, blasting its horn.

I could die here.

No. She would pull off, calm down, and then she would drive to Northern California. She'd do it tonight.

Maybe just call the automobile club. Another truck tried to honk her off the road. Wrong idea, anyway. The auto club would need something to fix and nothing about the car was wrong. Just her.

Virgie. She scrambled in her purse for her phone.

'You OK?' Virgie asked by way of greeting.

'I'm fine,' Kit lied. 'Except my car broke down on the freeway. Any chance you can help me out?'

'Shelter van just got back. Hang on. I'll find you on my phone,' she said. 'Yeah, you're fifteen minutes from here, twenty maybe. I'm on my way.'

As the cars streamed past, Kit tried again to locate Farley. The swoosh of the cars unnerved her. She needed to move, pull farther off the freeway. Yet every time she thought about reaching for the ignition, her hands broke into a sweat. She stared into her outside rear-view mirror and watched the oncoming traffic until the shelter's familiar white Mazda van finally pulled in behind her.

Virgie jumped out, ran around the side and jumped into the passenger seat. 'What happened? You out of gas? You call the auto club?'

Kit shook her head. 'I don't know what was wrong but it's all right now.'

Virgie nodded slowly and narrowed her eyes. 'And what would you like me to do?'

'Just drive me to the shelter, and then we can have someone come back with you to get the van.'

'All right.' Virgie reached for the door. 'You look kind of pale.'

'I'm fine. I was able to locate Farley's phone. He's in Northern California. The Willits area, close to the Eel River.'

'So maybe he's all right.' For the first time, Virgie smiled. 'When you leaving? You are going there, aren't you?'

'Of course.' She needed a little rest, that's all. Just relax, and then she'd get back on the road.

Virgie got out of the car, came around to the driver's side and got in, moving back the seat to accommodate her legs. She turned the ignition and Kit's body stiffened.

'Do you think the van's safe there?'

'Sure.'

'Nothing will hit it.'

'It'll be fine, Kit.'

They drove in silence and Kit forced herself to unclench her fists. At least they were pulling off the freeway onto the side street. She would be fine once they just reached the street.

She exhaled as the light turned green and they turned onto Browning Drive.

'My brother,' Virgie said. 'He was in Afghanistan. I know a little about this.'

'I didn't know you had a brother.'

Virgie pulled the car in front of the shelter. With the motor still running, she said, 'This ain't about him.'

'I'm all right.' Kit rewound the band around her ponytail, as if this were any conversation on any day. 'I just got a little dizzy back there.'

'What if you get dizzy on the way north?'

That question had already nudged its way into Kit's brain. Yet, until recently, she had driven the Grapevine south every couple of months to visit her dad in San Diego. She drove Farley's little convertible to Malibu with the top down.

'I won't.'

'How'd you know?'

'Because this is the first time it's ever happened, and if I get dizzy again I'll just pull over until it passes.'

'Some of the drops in those parts are pretty steep. Two lanes most of the way.'

She remembered the mountains, the twisting roads, and felt lightheaded. 'I know that.'

'Roads are narrow.' Virgie crossed her arms and waited. Kit felt as if they were playing some kind of game, yet Virgie was one of the most direct people she knew.

'What are you trying to tell me?' she asked.

'That you've been losing sleep, good sense and everything else worrying about Farley.' She took the keys from the ignition and shoved them toward Kit on the palm of her hand. 'You really want to do this on your own?'

Kit stared at the dull gleam of the keys and knew Virgie was right.

'Virgie, I can't take you away from your job.'

'For what? A day or two? You got me the job in the first place. You sure can get me a few days off.' Kit started to protest but Virgie interrupted her. 'Where you're heading, you need someone else for back-up, no matter who's driving.'

She was right.

'I was planning on leaving right away,' Kit said.

'Then I would suggest you go in there right now and get me some time off.'

Kit reached for the door and her legs turned to water again. She touched the side of the car to balance herself. 'Be right back,' she said, aware that Virgie was following her every move. Kit stopped. No way could she take another step. 'I have a better idea.' She leaned back inside the car and placed the keys into Virgie's open hand. 'I can call back once we're on the road.'

'That's more like it.' Virgie wrapped her fingers around the keys. Kit's head cleared and she found her footing as if she had just crossed a narrow bridge and stepped onto solid ground. For the first time since the van had followed her, and John Paul had told her that Farley was missing, she could breathe without concentrating on it.

She sank into the passenger seat and, as Virgie pulled away, Kit glanced back at the shelter. It seemed to blur like the clouds beyond.

'My brother,' Virgie said as they headed for the freeway. 'He couldn't even ride in a car when he first got back. Now he's racing motorcycles.'

'Your brother?' Kit asked.

She grinned. 'Like I said before, this ain't about him.'

Virgie knew.

Kit could deny. She could lie. It wouldn't make any difference. 'You're a smart woman, Virgie.'

The grin vanished and Virgie stared straight ahead. 'This ain't about me either,' she said.

EIGHT

After that initial exchange, they didn't talk much. From the beginning, she and Virgie had given each other plenty of space and plenty of silence. But Virgie knowing her secret – that Kit was too damaged to drive north on her own – embarrassed her so much that she didn't know what she could say to change the equation of shame. All she wanted to do was appear as normal as possible and to stop Virgie from fawning over her.

After calling the shelter and making up one more lie so that the van could be retrieved, and after stopping only to pack a small bag, Kit sat beside Virgie as she drove Kit's car up the freeway toward San Francisco. After that, they would go farther north, all the way to Willits.

Every so often, Kit would try to connect with Farley's phone again, but she could not get anything except that virtual map with the red dot over the blue expanse of digital destinations.

In the meantime, Virgie asked if she needed more heat in the car, if she wanted the window cracked open. Although Kit knew she meant well, each solicitous question made her even more aware of how damaged she must appear.

As the car crept into the forest, Virgie said, 'You want me to turn on some music?'

'You asked me that twenty minutes ago.'

'Sorry.' She glanced over at Kit. 'But you ain't saying much. I thought you might just want to chill.'

'I'm OK.'

'Good. We probably ought to be figuring out where we're going.'

'Willits is a small town,' Kit said. 'Everyone knows everybody.'

'You been there with him?'

'No, but I remember something about it. I think Farley might have come here before.'

'You sure? With no surfing in these parts?'

'Farley's way more than a surfboard,' Kit said. 'A lot of that's for effect.'

'Not trying to be judgmental.' Virgie lowered her voice to a hum. 'Just thought it would be easier to look for him if you remembered anything. By the way, you OK if we pull over for some gas?'

'Of course.' Kit looked down and realized she was gripping the side of her seat. It was bad enough that she couldn't drive anymore. Now she couldn't even be a decent passenger. Virgie acted as if she hadn't noticed and pulled over in front of a general store with two pumps outside. 'Let's get something to eat while we can,' she said in that same too-calm tone.

'Water's fine.'

'Hunger just makes it worse.' Virgie parked the car beside one of the pumps and nodded at Kit the way she would a child. 'You need to eat something, even if it's just an apple or a protein bar.'

They walked inside the smudged glass door and headed toward the back of the store.

'You do need water too.' Virgie opened a cooler that contained beer, wine and sodas.

In the tight space, she swung around to hand Kit a bottle of AquaHydrate and almost knocked it into the display on the shelf behind her.

'Take it easy,' Kit said.

'No problem.' She frowned at the shelf. 'Be glad we ain't drinking this cheap wine,' she said.

The words resonated. 'Wait.' Kit couldn't move.

'What's wrong?'

'Say it again.'

'What?' she said. 'That we ain't drinking any of this cheap wine?' She pointed at the row of bottles in the case across from them, too cheap to warrant refrigeration. Tokay. White Zinfandel. Port. 'Hey, you drink wine?'

'Very seldom and not this stuff,' Kit said.

Yet something was wrong. She couldn't leave the store.

Virgie stood next to her, clutching her soda can. 'What then?'

'Port.' Kit picked up a bottle, trying to figure out the confused messages attempting to combine and connect in her brain.

'Well, if it makes the trip easier on you, I'm not going to judge.' Virgie squinted at the bottle. 'Still, you're going to have the biggest headache in the world.

'I'm not thinking about drinking it.'

Kit walked over and picked up one of the bottles. 'Remember that receipt Farley left behind?' she asked.

Virgie sucked in her breath. 'You're talking about the expensive liquor store receipt, but we don't know what Farley bought there, do we?'

'I do.' Kit put the bottle back on the shelf as chills shot up and down her arms. 'I know exactly what he bought, Virgie. Let's check out the receipt.'

'I'm on it.' Virgie slammed some bills on the counter and ran outside.

Once Kit joined her, Virgie leaned against the car, holding a receipt in one hand and the bag they had taken from Farley's in the other.

'Taylor's Port,' she said. 'Right? I just checked the price on my phone. It's an expensive port. So what do you know that I don't?'

Kit felt the panic crowding in again, and she was grateful for the fresh air and the solid pressing of the car against her back. 'That his mentor loves expensive port.'

'How do you know that? What mentor?'

'Jonas Case, his music teacher from high school. Farley always bought it for him when he visited. I never thought much about it, but Jonas is like an older brother to him.'

Virgie cupped her chin in her hands and gave Kit a hint of a smile. 'And just where might this Jonas Case live?'

'Northern California.' Kit reached for the car door. 'Now I remember why Willits seems so familiar to me. Jonas lives near there. He runs some kind of school.'

NINE

The pub smells like smoke. Either someone burned the steaks or Mickey has been setting Cheetos on fire again. But Mickey is behind the bar pulling a mug of beer. His scalp shines through his gray strands of hair and Willie Nelson braids hang over the front of his Loggers Jamboree sweatshirt.

A guy getting ready to leave stands up, waves at them and then stops as if he expects them to do the same.

'It's just Rudy,' Will tells Megan. 'Keep walking.'

Rudy. She should stop and talk to him, say something. She can't though. All she can do is keep her face set in this neutral smile that won't offend anyone. Not Rudy, and not this man they have come to meet.

Her spine stiffens as Will nudges her toward the back. No one pays attention to them, not even with her dressed like that, although one guy at the end of the bar turns to watch as they move past. Must be a newcomer. No one around here pays much attention to anyone except strangers, and that's the way it should be. Megan pulls the jean jacket closer and looks up at Will.

'I'll introduce you two and get a round of beer,' he says. 'It would be better if you took off your jacket.'

'I'm cold.'

'First impressions matter. Why don't you just take it off? Tie it around your waist if you like. It will hide your hips.'

'What's wrong with my hips?' She doesn't want to argue with him, especially since this is the last time. As Megan stands there, though, with the noise of too many conversations like fractured music in her ears, she knows that somehow something is different.

In the last of the three booths at the end of the pub, she spots a denim-covered leg sticking out from the table, and she knows that leg in the tan boot is her destination.

She turns to Will. 'If I'm going to go through with this I'm going to need a beer. Maybe more than one.'

His cheeks look burnished by something beyond the weather, and his blue eyes are so intense that they seem unnatural. He shoves a strand of hair behind his ear. 'What's wrong with you tonight?' he demands.

'Not a thing,' she tells him. But something is. She feels the itch of it under her skin.

'Can you at least take off your jacket?' He glances from her to the leg extending from the booth. 'Can you at least do that?'

'I'll try.' She lifts the heavy fabric from her shoulders and lets the jacket slide partway down her back. 'Will you get me that beer now?' she asks.

'Just let me introduce you first.'

'No need to,' she says. 'I'm perfectly capable of introducing myself.' If she has to do this, even though it is the last time, Megan needs some rules. She needs to be able to introduce herself to this stranger, to sit with him before they walk outside.

'Just remember, I love you.' Will pulled her into a rough embrace. 'I really do.' His kiss on her lips is light, sweet.

Megan glances at the booth, at the toe that is now keeping time with the music on the jukebox, Lyle Lovett singing about a boat.

'Love you too,' she tells Will. Then, as he walks away, she marches up to the booth, to the man she hasn't yet set eyes on and says, 'Hi. I'm Megan. You mind if I join you?'

TEN

Although Virgie had what Kit's mom would call a lead foot, she was a careful driver who navigated through the forest as if she had driven it many times before. Virgie's skill combined with their mutual exhaustion had settled Kit. Besides, they had a destination. Not just the general area of Willits, California, but Jonas Case.

'You got any clues how to find his place?' Virgie asked as she steered them around a curve that forced Kit to close her eyes.

When she opened them she saw a wooden sign that read, *Fresh berries ahead. Flowers. Herbs. Jam. Jelly.* 'I've never been there,' she said, 'but Farley's talked to me about it. Let's pull over and look at the map. Our best shot is to find the school.'

'Ain't no pulling over here.' Virgie's voice was rhythmic and calming, yet Kit heard something else beneath it.

'What's wrong?' she asked.

'Nothing.'

'You can tell me,' Kit said.

'Just my eyes playing tricks on me. For a minute back there, I thought someone was following us.'

Kit jerked around in her seat. 'Where? What did you see?'

'Not sure,' Virgie said. 'Maybe a van. No worries, though. I got this.' With a sharp turn, they left the main road onto a narrow one marked with more primitive wooden signs pointing toward the woods.

Kit caught her breath. 'I thought you just said we couldn't pull off back there.'

'We can't.' Virgie put down the windows and let the chilled air fill the car. 'I saw this road last minute. Thought it might be best for now.'

'You should have kept going,' Kit said. 'We might have been able to see who was in that van.'

'Not in this light. Besides, you don't want to go confronting people out in these parts.'

'I'm not saying we should confront anyone.'

'Not saying you are.' Virgie drove slowly and the mountain air chilled Kit, even through her sweater. 'Let's go a little farther, turn around and get back to the main road,' Virgie said.

Kit glanced behind them again and admitted to herself that Virgie had done the right thing. Out here they would have no protection, not even anyone to notify if they were in danger.

The blast of fresh air was probably another one of Virgie's anxiety cures, Kit suspected, and couldn't be angry. Virgie was only trying to help. She was just trying to help too much.

'Do you mind putting up the windows?'

Slowly Virgie pressed the switch, leaving a crack at the top. Perhaps it was Kit's imagination but the breeze, heavy with the scent of pine and redwood, seemed to have a soothing effect.

'You might want to re-think your career choice,' she told Virgie.

'Don't get smart.' She glanced over at Kit. 'You ought to be thanking me instead of making fun.'

Kit started to explain that she wasn't making fun, but then she just said, 'Thank you, Virgie.'

Virgie shrugged. 'No big deal.'

Kit spotted a stand on the other side of the road. Beside it stood another sign. *Berries. Jam.* 'Look,' she said. 'Maybe someone out here has seen Farley.'

'Or knows Jonas.' Virgie paused and slowed the car. 'Guess it won't hurt. But we should hurry. I don't want to head any deeper into these woods and I don't want to be here much later.'

Kit peered ahead into the quiet darkness and the narrowing path bordered in green. 'Neither do I. But Farley loves fresh berries. I promise you, if he found this place he would have stopped.'

Virgie turned the car around and they returned down the road.

Kit couldn't help glancing around. If that same van were still tailing her, it would show up again, and if it had anything to do with Farley's disappearance she almost hoped it would return.

At first, she thought the stand was one of the Little Free Libraries that people put up in their front yards. But, although the structure was similar, this was no micro-library.

'Looks like some kind of store.' As Virgie parked the car beside what appeared to be a freshly painted white stand, Kit spotted bunches of lavender and jars of purple jelly. A large vase in front was marked for donations.

'Nobody here,' Virgie said. 'Might as well head back.'

Just then, a slender brunette about Kit's age wearing a prairie-style skirt and sunglasses rimmed in white plastic appeared from behind the booth. She smiled at them and walked behind the counter.

'Come on,' Kit told Virgie and opened the car door.

As they approached the woman, another one, a little older and with hair down to her waist, joined them from behind the booth. Her hair was a variegated blonde that would ease into silver and then white as she aged. Before her pregnancy she must have been slender.

'Welcome,' she said. 'We have fresh blueberry jam today. Would you like a sample?'

Kit hesitated but the brunette joined them carrying a small tray with crackers smeared a chunky purple. The scent hit Kit's nostrils and she took a bite of fruit so pure and sweet that she could taste the sunlight in it.

'It's wonderful,' she said. 'Actually, we're looking for a man named Jonas Case. He has a school out here.'

The two women glanced at each other, their smiles frozen in place.

'There are many schools out here.' The pregnant woman gestured at the shadows of the trees surrounding them. 'It's getting dark, though. I wouldn't go looking for it tonight.'

'Good idea,' Kit said. 'But there can't be that many of them, can there? I'm Kit, by the way, and this is Virgie.'

'Pleased to meet you.' The woman put out her hand.

'And you are . . .?'

'Priscilla.' She nodded toward the younger woman, who was pulling her dark hair back into a ponytail. 'And this is Megan. We are a small community here, but we have a fair number of schools and I couldn't begin to tell you how to find most of them.'

'That's kind of hard to believe,' Kit said, a little more confrontationally than she had intended.

'Not really. My daughters are too young, especially this one.' She patted her stomach. 'I don't mean to be rude, but Megan and I need to close up now. Driving at night out here can be treacherous.'

'We better go,' Virgie muttered.

'First, I'd like to buy some of your jam,' Kit said.

Megan turned from where she was trying to balance a large cardboard box on a middle shelf. 'I need to get home, Priscilla.'

'Tell you what.' Priscilla walked over, picked up the jar she had used for the sample and handed it to Kit. Her thick hair blew around her face as if she were standing in front of a fan. 'My gift to you. I hope you enjoy it as you continue your trip.'

'We can pay for it.' Virgie headed toward the jar on the other side of the booth just as Priscilla handed it to Megan.

'We're not about materialism out here. Safe travels tonight, you two.'

Virgie glanced at Kit as if to ask how far they should push it. Kit had no idea what else to say. Darkness moved in by the moment, and these women, pleasant enough on the surface, had no intention of telling them where Jonas Case's school was, assuming they knew. Kit clutched the jar of jam and started to leave. Then she realized she couldn't just do that. This might be their only hope. She placed the jam on the counter.

'A friend of mine from Sacramento visited the school recently.' She dug into her purse. 'I have his photo right here. His name's Farley Black.'

'Never saw him.' Priscilla rested her hand on Megan's shoulder.

'What about you?' Kit asked and showed the photo to Megan.

'Never.' Although she shrugged, her voice came out faint.

'We all know each other around here,' Priscilla said. 'We don't mix much and that's the way we like it. If your friend came this way, he probably drove on through.'

'He wouldn't have done that,' Kit said. 'Jonas was his teacher. Farley would have been on his way to the school.' Then she remembered. 'Ananda Free School. That's the name of it. Are you sure he didn't stop here to pick up something?'

Megan took in a sharp breath. Virgie moved beside Kit. Priscilla's placid expression crumbled.

'I told you, I don't remember seeing your friend,' she said. 'That doesn't mean he didn't stop here, of course. Many people arrive when we aren't even around. That might have been the case with him.'

'He drives a fancy Corvette. Black.' Virgie cleared her throat the way she did when she disagreed with someone. 'Would have been hard to miss.'

'Well, apparently we did miss him.' Priscilla lowered her voice. 'I wish I could say it is safe out here at night. I can't do that, though. Especially not on a weekend with all the tourists passing through.'

'We *are* staying,' Kit said.

'Your choice.' She turned her back and joined Megan. 'I think that's enough for tonight,' she said to her. 'Let's leave the rest here in case anyone comes by early.'

Even though Kit could still see her, it was as if Priscilla had shut a door behind her. She and Megan were real, but at the moment they were shadows under the darkening sky.

Kit and Virgie nodded to each other and headed back to the car.

Once inside, Virgie shuddered. 'Well, that was creepy. They sure wanted to get rid of us, didn't they?'

'Priscilla did.' In spite of the façade of calmness outside, Kit realized how tense the exchange in this isolated little spot had felt. 'Let's head for the campground where Farley keeps his car when he's here.'

Virgie started the car and drove it toward the dim lights of the main road. 'You know where we're headed then?' she asked, and Kit tried to rub the stiffness out of her neck.

'Not really.'

ELEVEN

All Kit could remember Farley saying about the campground where he left his car when he visited Jonas was that it was located north of Willits off of the 101.

'Why don't he just take the car to his friend's place?' Virgie asked. Then added, 'Never mind. I forgot. Farley's particular about it, ain't he?'

'He'd say he's caring for his investment.' Kit felt a pang as the reality of Farley's absence hit home once more. He vacuumed the top of the Corvette, removed stains with an old toothbrush, cleaned the engine with furniture polish and buffed his exhaust pipes until they sparkled. Even at the mall, he protected it with a gray silk cover lined in fleece. 'Yes, I guess you could say he's particular,' she told Virgie. 'Maybe Jonas Case doesn't have a garage.'

About five miles north of Willits, they spotted the sign and Virgie turned right over an unsteady wooden bridge. Before them, in a thick woods surrounded by tall, thin redwoods, several simple cabins were scattered among forty or fifty RV and tent sites.

'This has to be the campground,' Kit said. 'I know the one he's talked about is close to town and we didn't pass any others.'

Virgie surveyed the old vans and other vehicles. 'Looks like a lot of people living here fulltime.'

'Over there.' Kit pointed at a covered wooden structure large enough for at least four cars. 'This is the place.'

The structure was vacant, and Virgie backed inside one of the parking spaces.

At the first cabin, they spotted a pristine wooden sign with the word *Manager* neatly painted onto it. They went inside but encountered only an immaculate table holding a bowl of beads and an overstuffed chair with a footstool holding a partially beaded strip of fabric and a folded newspaper.

'You ladies need any help with your bags?'

They both jerked around. From behind them, a long-haired man, who might be fifty, maybe sixty, entered the cabin, ducking under the low door and then smiling over at them as if apologizing for the intrusion.

'We're fine.' Kit pointed at the bag over her shoulder.

'You just here for the night?' His accent was southern, his appearance vintage California hippie, right down to the coral- and gold-beaded headband.

Kit squinted in the dim light and realized that his silver hair still held onto some auburn strands. 'One or two nights,' she said.

'You can pay by the day.' He nodded at Virgie and put out his hand. She kept her arms glued to her sides. 'They call me Nickel,' he said. 'Like the coin.'

'Pleased to meet you.' Virgie stretched out an arm and shook his hand. Kit did the same.

He walked in front of them and leaned against the edge of the table. Kit inhaled the sharp scent of liquor, whiskey maybe, or gin. He took the cash Kit handed him, studied her and then Virgie, and said, 'This is a peaceful place with peaceful people. If you need anything, just knock. I'm up most nights.'

'We'll be fine.' Kit backed away from him, toward the door.

'Where you ladies headed?' he asked.

Kit started to ask him if he knew Farley but Virgie nudged her as if she could read Kit's mind.

'Just sightseeing,' Virgie said. Kit followed her gaze to the bowl of variegated blue stones. 'Pretty beads.'

'Blue crazy lace agate. I'm almost finished with a new headband.' He nodded toward the footstool and then at Virgie. 'It would look great on you.'

'I'll think about it,' she told him as they stepped outside.

'I'll give you a fair price,' he called behind them.

The fragrant air now seemed out of place.

'Why didn't you want me to ask him anything?' Kit said.

'I don't know.' Virgie stared into the slender trees. In the darkness they seemed to spread into the sky. 'It was just a gut reaction, and I always go with my gut.'

They entered their cabin, rustic but clean – two large rooms and a bathroom. This wouldn't be so bad.

'I'll go with your gut too,' Kit said. 'But I'm going to ask him tomorrow.'

'Ladies, wait.' As he headed closer to the open front door of the cabin, Kit and Virgie stepped outside.

'What is it?' Kit asked.

'You overpaid me.' The bills he held out to her fluttered in the breeze. 'You said one night but you gave me money for two.'

'I paid for two nights,' she said. 'We're looking for a school and I don't know how long it's going to take us to find it.'

'Lots of schools around here.'

'This one's run by Jonas Case,' Kit said.

Nickel's eyes widened slightly.

'Do you know him?'

'Might've run into him.' He rubbed his chin. 'Everyone around here pretty much knows everybody else.'

'What's the name of his school?' Kit could almost feel him hesitate.

'You ladies wouldn't be law, would you?'

Virgie snorted. 'First time anyone accused me of that.'

'It's just that you're asking a lot of questions,' he said, 'and most people around here know where they're heading.'

'Jonas Case is a friend of a friend,' Kit told him. 'I need to talk to him.'

'Well, good luck.' He turned and started back toward his cabin.

'Wait.' Kit followed him. 'You seem like a decent person and I really need your help. The sooner I find Jonas, the sooner I can locate our friend. We're not trying to cause trouble for you or anybody else. We're just . . .' Her lip trembled and she couldn't continue.

'The school's not far from here,' he muttered. 'Just remembered.'

'Thank you.' Kit sighed. 'We'll drive over there right now.'

'It's getting late,' he said. 'Besides, I think they might be closed for spring break.' His voice softened. 'But from what I recall, Jonas lives on the property.'

TWELVE

When the women arrived that evening, Jonas was ready for them. While waiting, he had urged his mind to let go of everything but the music. It was like a body of water to him. Sometimes he dove into it headfirst. Other times, on late afternoons like this one, he floated on its surface. Chopin supplied the ripples and Jonas imagined Isadora Duncan, her scarf soaring upward like a wing. As he went to the front of his cabin to get a better look at the two who had just driven in, it occurred to him that music was his only true addiction. Something about that pleased him and eased him into what might be an uncomfortable situation.

The women parked under the trees, clearly unaware of what the redwood sap would do to the paint on their car. Inexperienced travelers, for sure. Jonas went outside, going for a pleasant but bewildered look as if perhaps these were visitors who had lost their way.

The driver got out of the car and didn't return his visual greeting. Jonas assumed she would be larger but her power lay in her stoic expression and her tight, muscular body, hidden in a down vest. Kit Doyle got out moments after, paler and more fragile than in her photographs, curly hair pulled back from her face. Even in the dim light, it gleamed.

'Hello there,' he said, making eye contact first with the driver and then with the Doyle woman. 'I'm Jonas. Are you here about the school?'

'I'm Kit Doyle and this is my friend, Virgie Logan.' Kit marched across the stone path and stopped in front of him. 'We're here about Farley.'

'Of course,' he said and stepped back as if really seeing her for the first time. 'Kit Doyle! How good to finally meet you. Come in.'

A gust of wind blew through and she rubbed the arms of her jacket. His front door jerked open.

'I need to get that fixed,' he said. 'Come on. I don't have a great deal of time, though. I wish I had known you were coming.'

They went in ahead of him and stood in front of the woodstove of the cabin, glancing at each other and around the room. He joined them and rubbed his hands together over the stove.

Kit looked into his eyes. 'Where's Farley?'

'I have no idea. On his way, I hope.'

'When was the last time you heard from him?'

'A text,' he said. 'On Thursday, maybe Friday. I believe he had another stop first.'

'He's missing. You know that, don't you?'

'No way.' Jonas motioned them to the spotless round oak table with its clean smell of lemon oil and thought about his response. Once they sat in the chairs, Kit Doyle next to him and Virgie across from her, he said, 'As you're probably aware, I've known Farley since he was in high school, and I can tell you punctuality is not his strong suit.'

'There's a missing person's report.' Kit's voice was scratchy and strong, a radio voice, but Jonas could detect the emotion she was trying to hide. 'He didn't show up where he was supposed to be. He hasn't called into work and none of his friends can reach him.'

'That explains it.' Jonas spread his open hands before him on the table. 'I haven't been able to get in touch with him either, not since that last text.'

'And you haven't seen him?' Kit's eyes were as probing and expressive as Virgie's were blank, but they both sat up straight in their chairs as if taking in his every word.

'I just told you that. Not a text. Not a phone call.' He shrugged. 'Nothing.'

'We have reason to believe he was on his way here,' she said.

'He was.' Best to keep it as close to the truth as possible. 'We try to get together a couple of times a year.'

'And this was one of those?'

'Not really.'

She waited for him to say more. Jonas tried to change the subject.

'When we met, he was very young, very gifted.'

'And very troubled,' she finished for him. 'Farley told me about the cello scholarship you got for him right before he got into the fistfight that broke his left hand.'

'All true.' This chuckle came easily. He didn't have to force it. 'I'm sure Farley's fine but I want to do whatever I can to help. Can I have your number?'

She reached for her phone and Jonas got a glimpse of her calf. Nice. 'Where does he stay when he comes here?' she asked.

'With me, of course. I have plenty of room.'

'But he keeps his car somewhere else.' Her eyes were steady, her expression almost mocking. 'Doesn't he?'

'You're right.' If he lied now, she'd know it. Surely Farley had shared details with her in the past. 'He babies that car and would never leave it under those trees out there, with the sap and all.'

'So where does he keep it?' she asked.

'A campground not far from here.'

'Can you tell me where to find it?' This was a test. She thought she had him now.

'Sure,' he told her. 'Better than that, I can give you directions.'

Carefully he outlined a makeshift map to the campground on

the back of an envelope. 'Give me a call if you get lost,' he told her. 'I've picked him up there many times. And let me know as soon as you hear from him.'

The weather cooperated with his need to get them out of there, kicking up rain, wind and dust, rattling the windows.

The two women glanced at each other again and Jonas truly wished he could tell them the truth. He took a sip from his glass and then realized that he should have offered them a drink.

'You must think I'm rude,' he said. 'Once you told me Farley is missing I didn't think about anything else. Would you like a glass of wine or some tea before you head for the campground?'

'No, thanks.' Kit's lips pressed into a line, and Jonas followed her gaze toward the counter.

'Keep in touch then.' He opened the front door and bolted it behind them.

As he watched them standing outside, the sun began to set. He picked up his glass, went to the sink to refill it and glanced at the bottle. Just like that, Jonas realized what Kit Doyle had been staring at and why her tight lips had turned up into a smile of recognition. Now he couldn't just sit back. He had to do something.

They walked outside, away from the loud classical music and Jonas Case, and Kit tried to make sense out of what she had just seen.

'He's watching us out the window,' Virgie said as they sat in the car.

'Let him.'

'I never did trust a guy who tried to match his clothes to his eyes.'

'He seems to be pulling it off.'

'Seems way too into himself to be Farley's friend.'

'Friends don't have to be clones,' Kit said, and Virgie responded with a huffing noise.

'He's lying, ain't he?'

Kit nodded, still trying to figure out why a man who had been so important to Farley didn't want her to find him now. 'You're right,' she said. 'He's lying. Did you see that bottle on the counter?'

'I knew he was drinking something before we got there. There was a glass on the table next to him.'

'It was port,' Kit said. 'Expensive port. I'll bet that's the bottle Farley bought him.'

They sat like that for a moment as Kit realized that Jonas probably knew what she had figured out.

'We should go,' she told Virgie.

'Yeah.' She turned to see her friend's steady gaze, as if hypnotized by the rain striking their windshield.

'What's wrong?' Kit asked.

'That.' Virgie jabbed her finger at the barn beside the house. 'Looks pretty secure to me. Why do you suppose Farley can't park his car in there?'

'You're right.'

Before Kit could decide what to do next, the front door opened and Jonas stepped outside. He walked toward the passenger door of the car as if unaware of the raindrops pasting his thick brown hair to his scalp.

'Having problems finding your way?' he asked. 'It can get a little weird out here at night.'

'Not at all,' Kit said. 'No problem.'

Before he could say anything else, Virgie pulled out of the drive. Kit turned in her seat to watch him, still standing in his driveway and still apparently unaware of the rain, or at least not caring about it.

THIRTEEN

The rain let up about eight-thirty. Kit had heated two bowls of chili they had picked up on the trip, and she and Virgie sat at the large window with mugs of tea, watching the downpour. Nickel shuffled past the window with a lantern, carrying a glass of his own.

'Just me,' he said and lifted it like a man accustomed to making toasts.

'At least he seems to look after the place,' Kit said.

'Maybe when he's sober.' Virgie pushed her bowl away. 'Looks pretty shabby around here if you ask me. Can't imagine Farley wanting to keep his car here.'

'It *is* close to the school,' Kit said, 'and the parking area is clean. Besides, Farley always covers it.'

'But . . .' Virgie rested her feet on the stepstool and pushed back in her chair. 'What do you make of that barn Jonas Case has on his property?'

'I don't know.' Kit had wondered the same thing. 'I can't imagine what he would have in there that would keep him from offering it to Farley.'

'So,' Virgie said, 'either Farley don't want to park it there or Jonas don't want him to.'

'Maybe Jonas has something in there,' Kit said. 'Something valuable.'

'Maybe.'

They sat for a moment, disconnected thoughts flying through Kit's head. Finally she sighed and leaned back in her own chair. 'You think Farley's car is in that barn, don't you?'

'It has occurred to me.'

'You think we ought to go back there tomorrow?'

'Tomorrow?' Virgie rolled her eyes.

'You're not thinking about going back tonight?'

'It's the best way,' she said. 'Trust me, that Jonas guy won't be expecting us back so soon. Once we left he probably just finished his glass of port and turned in early.'

'But what if he didn't?' Kit said.

'If there's a light on we'll see it from far down the road and we can just turn around.'

'It might rain again. Have you thought about that? The road out there is already mud.'

'It's clear you never committed any crime,' Virgie said. 'If it rains there won't be anyone there to witness what we're doing, and he won't be expecting us either. You get that, right? We *want* the rain.'

Kit gripped the edge of the table and tried to squeeze the thoughts of what had happened to her before out of her head. 'What are the odds that Farley's car is even there?'

'What are the odds it ain't?' Virgie glanced down at the table, at Kit's hands, and paused. 'I have a better idea,' she said. 'Why don't I just drive back there and you stay here?'

'No.' Kit shot to her feet.

'I've dealt with danger before – more than even you know about.' Virgie stood up as well. 'I won't take chances. Besides, he's Farley's friend.'

'Farley's friend who has already lied to us.'

'You stay here.' Virgie took her jacket from the back of the chair and slipped into it. 'We need someone to watch our stuff. I can take care of this in no time.'

'We have this.' Kit lifted the key of the cabin off the table, her hand steady now. 'And we have Nickel, for whatever he's worth. Besides, if we lost everything in this place, how big a tragedy would that be?'

'I don't know.' The look Virgie gave her wasn't about their possessions or this room.

Kit hated the way it made her feel. 'That settles it,' she said. 'We're going.'

Virgie started to object but Kit shook her head. 'I was trying to pretend that you were wrong about heading back there tonight,' she said. 'But you're right. Jonas is not going to expect us back so soon, and if we wait another hour or two you know he'll be asleep.'

A grin spread across Virgie's face and she nodded. 'Then we might as well sit back down and wait until it gets really dark.'

Two hours later, they pulled out of Nickel's camp and drove to the muddy path that led to Jonas.

'Not a light on anywhere,' Virgie said as they drew closer. 'I'm going to park down the road.'

'Good idea.' Kit no longer feared what would happen next. She just wanted to find out what was in that garage.

She opened the car door and Virgie touched her arm. 'I know how to do this stuff,' she said.

Kit met her eyes. 'You think I don't?'

'All right then. I hear you.' Virgie's expression went blank and so did her voice. 'But let me go first and don't say a word to me. Don't even think until we get there.'

Kit nodded and they moved through muddy grass. Once they got closer, Kit could see a single light on the property, and that was a bulb above the barn. But the glow it cast was thin and watery. Kit and Virgie glanced at each other and moved closer. If Farley's car were in this garage, all of this would be worth it.

Virgie nudged her and pointed to the right of the barn. Kit followed her and they crept around toward the back. Two windows faced the far side of Jonas's land. Kit wanted to rush up and try to see inside but she turned back to Virgie, who shook her head.

No, she mouthed.

The windows were covered with fog from the rain. That meant the place must be heated. Virgie motioned toward the window and made a gesture suggesting she was going to break in.

'And what the hell are you doing?'

Jonas Case stood behind them, wearing the same shorts and denim jacket he'd had on earlier. A rifle dangled from his right hand.

Kit stifled a scream. 'Put that down,' she said.

'I might when you tell me what you're doing back on my property.' The rain started again – just a few drops at first. He shoved his hair back from his face.

'Put down the gun and I'll tell you,' Kit said.

'I need something to convince you women to leave me alone. If it takes a gun, that's what it has to be. I don't like it any more than you do.'

'What about the Taylor Port?' Kit asked.

'So I like good port. Everyone's allowed a vice or two.'

As he spoke, his fingers relaxed on the rifle and Kit knew that she and Virgie would be safe for now, at least.

'I understand if you're trying to protect Farley,' Kit told him. 'But you don't have to protect him from me. I'm one of his best friends.'

'I'm sure you are.'

'Don't trivialize what I'm trying to tell you,' she said. 'If you speak to him, tell him Kit Doyle is here. He will tell you how close we are if he hasn't already.'

'Indeed, he's mentioned you. But I'm going to have to ask you not to come back. I don't appreciate being stalked.'

'It's not you we're trying to find,' Kit shot back.

'Then you need to go.' He looked down at the rifle again and Virgie nudged Kit.

'Come on,' she whispered and turned toward the road.

Kit glared at Jonas, both of them standing there in what was soon to be a drizzle. 'Farley loves you,' she said. 'You've been like a big brother to him.'

Without changing his expression or his grip on the gun, he replied, 'I feel the same way.'

'I know he brought you that bottle of port and I think you know where he is.' Her throat tightened and she realized she was close to tears.

'Kit,' Virgie said.

'I'm coming.' She turned back to Jonas. 'I'm going to stay here as long as it takes, and I'm not going back home without Farley.'

Their gazes locked. Finally Jonas shrugged. 'It's late. This stunt of yours got me out of bed.'

'We're leaving,' Virgie said. 'Soon as we know you're inside and not pointing that thing at our backs.'

'Fine. But I will be watching from in there.' He turned without another word and marched toward the front door.

'Ready?' Kit asked.

'Not until he and that rifle are out of sight.'

Jonas walked into the cabin and closed the door behind him.

Kit glanced back toward the barn. There was something in there – something that might be the reason the place was heated. It couldn't be Farley, though. If he were here he'd be inside the cabin, not outside.

Virgie stared at the barn as well. 'Don't even think about it,' she told Kit under her breath. 'Not tonight, at least.'

Kit nodded, and together they hurried back down the muddy path to the car, trying to outrun the rain.

Jonas snapped off the piano concerto and picked up his phone. Although they weren't supposed to have phones out there, as was the case with everything else in life, some people lied.

Kit Doyle didn't lie, though. She had more courage than Jonas had guessed upon their first meeting and, he conceded, she had a kind of restrained sex appeal. It wasn't all about her features either, or those taut, muscular legs which he could see clearly defined through her jeans. Kit Doyle wasn't beautiful the way Megan was but, like Megan, she was both vulnerable and brave. Off limits, of course, both of them, and he had learned about off limits years ago, the hard way.

Finally his call got through.

'What's happening, friend?'

Jonas felt a sudden chill and crouched in front of the woodstove in hopes of driving it away.

'She came back,' he said. 'She and the other woman tried to break into my barn.'

'What did you do to her? Do you need assistance?'

'She's gone,' he said, soaking up the heat of the stove. 'But she's not leaving the area. Staying as long as it takes, according to her, and says she isn't going back without Farley.'

'Oh, really?' Jonas wasn't sure but thought he heard a chuckle. 'We'll see about that, won't we? Call if you have important news.'

'Of course,' Jonas said, but realized the call had already ended and he was talking to himself.

FOURTEEN

'He knows where Farley is.' Kit stared straight ahead as they drove back to their cabin.

Virgie shook her head. 'Next time I'm going back alone, and I'll find out what he has in that barn of his.'

'Next time we'll go back together,' Kit said. 'Seriously, though, I'm exhausted. Let's get some sleep.'

The sleeping bag over the wood bedframe was surprisingly comfortable. Early the next morning, the sun woke her and Kit realized the rain had stopped sometime in the night.

When she got up, she looked out the front window and saw Virgie already outside with her tea mug and a small bakery box. For a moment, Kit watched her and wondered how wise she had been to involve Virgie in this search. The very habits that had gotten Virgie in trouble in the first place were the ones they were depending on to get the information they needed now. Yet, other than her brother who had been in the war, Virgie never discussed her family or her past.

'What are *you* looking at?' She jerked around and stared into Kit's eyes.

'Just trying to guess what the weather will be like today. Looks sunny for a change.' Kit stepped outside and joined her at one of the four wicker chairs around a redwood table topped with navy-and-white glazed Catalina tile.

'You were standing at that window for about five minutes.'

'As my mom would say, you must have eyes in the back of your head.'

'I'm always watching even when it don't look like I am.' Although she said it pleasantly enough, Kit felt as if she were being warned not to get too close. Virgie motioned toward the box on the table. 'I got us some pastries down at the Safeway. They open at five. I couldn't sleep.'

Kit picked up a scone flecked with dried cranberries and knew at once that Virgie was holding back something.

'What aren't you telling me?' she asked.

Virgie glared at her over the mug of tea, and then put it down on the table. 'You're pretty good at this mind-reading stuff yourself,' she said.

'Meaning?' Kit asked.

'I had to try it one more time.'

Kit paused with her hand on the scone. 'You went by Jonas's again, didn't you?'

Virgie stared to squirm in her seat and then went motionless. 'Kind of.'

'Kind of what?'

'I kind of went by there but I didn't get very far. Was going to tell you anyway.'

'Why didn't you get very far?' Kit asked.

'Cars,' she said. 'Two in the driveway. And lights. He was playing that Chopin again. I could hear it from three houses away.'

'How do you know music?' Kit asked.

'My daddy raised us on everything from Beethoven to BB King, or maybe it was the other way around.'

Kit wanted to know more but knew what happened when she pressed Virgie for personal details. 'So that's all that happened?'

'Honest.'

Kit could tell by the sharp tone and clear-eyed, challenging expression that Virgie was telling the truth. She wrapped her hands around the mug of tea. 'You can't do this,' she said. 'If this is going to work, we have to be a team.'

'I know. But when you come up the way I did, you learn when to trust your gut when it says you ain't safe, and that's what it's saying right now.'

'Then we'll stay somewhere else,' Kit said. 'You just need to promise me that you'll never do something on your own again without telling me first.'

'Deal. Now, do you want to hear about what I saw in the driveway?'

Kit felt a flash of hope. 'Not Farley's car?'

'No. Sorry.' Virgie leaned across the table. 'There was some old kind of pickup parked out there.'

'Anything else?' Kit asked.

'That was the weird part. Jonas was leaning in the window of the pickup, talking to some woman.' Virgie sighed and shoved the mug of tea across from her.

'A woman? What did she look like?'

'I don't know,' Virgie said. 'Couldn't risk getting any closer. We have to go back to his place. He's the only hope we've got. But first we got to get out of here.'

Nickel headed toward them in a neatly pressed flannel shirt and jeans, carrying a bottle of strawberry soda.

'Not until we find out what this one knows about Farley,' Kit said under her breath.

'Glad to see you ladies enjoying the morning.' He glanced over at the bakery box.

'Join us,' Kit said. 'Would you like some pastry?'

He paused and then walked over. 'Don't mind if I do.'

He pulled out a chair next to Kit, took out one frosted in lemon and pinched off a piece. 'How was your evening?' he asked.

'Peaceful,' Kit said. She looked into his dark brown, bloodshot eyes. 'We're trying to find a friend of ours and we believe he stayed here recently.'

'Most here are long-termers.' He chuckled, and the scent of stale liquor wafted off of him.

'A white guy,' Virgie said. 'Driving a black Corvette.'

He chewed on the pastry as if thinking about it. 'There was a guy in a Vette here last week. Don't remember what he looked like, though. I only double-check the troublemakers, and I guess he wasn't one.'

'Here's his photo.' Kit took it out of her bag and placed it on the table.

'Oh, that guy.' Nickel wiped his fingers on a paper napkin. 'Now I remember him. A funny first name, right?'

This was too easy, Kit thought. It was almost as if he had wanted her to ask about him. 'Farley,' she said.

'That's the dude!' He squinted at the photo again. 'Well, you're a little late. He left Friday night and never came back. I don't remember where he was heading but I did direct him to the highway.'

'How did he seem when he left?'

'Just eager to get on the road.' Nickel played with some crumbs on the paper napkin and then took a long swallow of his soda. 'I got the impression he was going north. Oregon, maybe.'

'And this was the first time you met or talked to Farley?'

'I think so.' He shrugged and held up an unsteady hand. 'Sometimes my memory's not as good as it used to be, though. Sometimes I'm lucky if I recognize *myself* in the morning.'

He tried to laugh but it came out like a cough.

'Well, I guess we'll be checking out.' She glanced over at Virgie, who nodded as if they actually believed Nickel.

'Sorry to hear that.' He rose from the table. 'I'll get your refund, and I'm sorry it was less-than-ideal circumstances for you.'

Kit and Virgie stood as well. 'It was fine,' Kit said. 'You're welcome to the rest of the scones, if you'd like them. Please keep my phone number. If you remember anything about where he was going, text or call.'

'Sure thing.' He picked up the bakery box.

'One thing.' Kit asked, 'Which highway did you direct him to? That's the way we'll go as well.'

'The 101. I can show you ladies the best way to get there too.'

'That's OK,' Kit told him. 'We already know.'

And so did Farley.

Nickel squinted in the bright light. 'Hope you'll stop here on the way back.'

'No doubt we will.'

'What a liar,' Virgie muttered as he walked away. 'From what you've said, Farley knows that road like I know the streets.'

'Nickel just wants us out of here,' Kit said, 'but why?'

Virgie reached for the door of the cabin and paused with her hand on the knob. 'Because we're getting too close to something.'

'Let's get closer then.'

'You sure?'

'Of course I'm sure. Whatever this guy and Jonas are hiding has something to do with Farley. They want us out of here. Let's let them think we are.'

'We got to stay someplace,' Virgie said.

'We'll find something.'

'OK.' Virgie stepped into the room, leaned against the doorframe and exhaled heavily. 'Before we go far, though, let's check out Jonas again.'

Kit couldn't argue. That barn was the only lead they had. They parked down the road from the school that morning, determined to wait there with their leftover tea as long as it took for Jonas to appear again.

'Are you sure there was a woman in that truck?' Kit asked.

'Oh, yes. Unless Jonas has a wife we don't know about, she'll be leaving sooner or later.'

'No wife.' Kit remembered something Farley had told her. 'Jonas was right out of college when he taught Farley – young. He got involved with one of his students a few years later.' She couldn't remember more.

'Woo,' Virgie said. 'Did he get fired?'

'Maybe. I'm not sure. I just know the woman he was engaged to left him.'

'So who do you think is the woman in the truck?' Virgie asked. 'A student?'

'The sign in front of the school says spring break.'

'A girlfriend then? No wonder he was in such a hurry to get rid of us last night.'

The sun had moved behind them and its heat filled the car.

Virgie cracked the windows. 'You sleepy?' she asked Kit.

'No, because I didn't get up at dawn to stalk this guy. Close your eyes. I'll wake you when he comes out of the house.'

'Can't do that.' Virgie's eyes closed as she spoke. Soon she was breathing evenly. 'I'm fine,' she muttered. 'Fine.'

Kit watched her and wondered how they had ever gotten here

together. Virgie had been homeless with a history Kit knew only
by inference. Now she was the only reason Kit might find Farley.

As Virgie dozed and Kit finished her tea, she felt her phone
vibrate and saw a text from Monique. At first she thought there
might be news, but Monique was only asking if she had heard
anything. A second text followed saying that they had announced
Farley's disappearance on the air and given photos of him to the
media. As grateful as Kit was, she had no desire to communicate
with Farley's girlfriend just then. Besides, any movement or noise
would probably wake Virgie, who clearly needed a few minutes
of rest.

Jonas's front door opened and he stepped outside in what looked
like the same shorts, this time with a gray sweater. He had pulled
his long hair back into a knot and put on canvas shoes.

'Wake up,' she whispered to Virgie, who jerked awake, her fists
clenched. 'He's out there,' Kit said.

Just then, a woman stepped outside beside him. Her dark hair
was hidden under a knit cap but Kit recognized the white-rimmed
sunglasses and the long, prairie-style skirt.

'It's Megan,' she said, 'that woman from the roadside stand.'

Virgie squinted through the glass as Jonas and Megan stood
before his car. He put an arm around her, patted her shoulder, and
then opened the door.

'Gentleman, ain't he?' Virgie snorted. 'And she pretended she
didn't know him. Both of those women did.'

FIFTEEN

As Jonas and Megan drove off, Virgie started the car and
Kit's stomach lurched. *Not now. Just try to stay calm.* 'And
both of the women were lying.' She tried to keep her voice
steady but Virgie glanced at her anyway.

'You all right?'

'I'm fine.'

'OK then.' Virgie gripped the wheel and the car spun around
the steep curve.

Kit put on her dark glasses so that Virgie couldn't see the fear in her eyes. 'He's heading east, isn't he?'

'Seems to be.' The road widened ahead of them.

'Can you get any closer?'

'Afraid to. After being followed myself, I know how easy it is to get noticed, and I don't want to risk that.'

'No wonder Megan wanted to get rid of us in such a hurry. She knows where Farley is too.'

Kit realized she was hyperventilating and tried to slow her breathing. *Slowly, slowly. In through the nose, and out through the lips.*

Virgie glanced over at her again. At the same moment the car Jonas was driving disappeared.

'They're gone.' Virgie slowed down and they both scanned the side of the road, which had no direct access. Slowly, she took the next curve, and the edge of the road seemed to creep closer to them.

Kit didn't dare look to her right and the steep drop. 'They didn't get this far.'

'I know. Just looking for a little more room. There might be a lumber truck or something out here and I don't want to get caught trying to turn around in such a small space.'

Kit understood. A large vehicle coming down the steep grade toward them wouldn't be able to stop in time. She remained silent, letting Virgie focus her attention on the road. Instead of widening, it narrowed as they climbed upward.

'You've got to go for it,' Kit told her. 'It's not going to get any better.'

An old truck sped down the other lane. 'You see what I mean?' Virgie said in a tight voice. 'It would have hit us.'

'Well, it came from somewhere. We just have to keep going.'

Another mile and a turnout lined with a short fence on the cliff side appeared on their right.

'Do it.' Virgie could not hesitate because of her. Kit forced herself to watch the drop move closer as their car entered the turnout. It was like looking into a montage of green and blue. Her hands dripped sweat.

'Hang on,' Virgie said. 'You're doing great. You're doing fine.'

Then she went silent. The car felt like a vacuum, sucked free of any noise. It inched into a turn and entered the downward lane. It was as if someone had turned on the volume again. The sound of the wind exploded through the trees. Kit could hear Virgie's hard breathing. She could hear her own.

'You did it.' Kit bit her lip to keep from crying.

'I think I did.' Virgie exhaled and rubbed first one hand and then the other against her shirt. 'Lord, I don't ever want to do that again.'

Then for some reason she laughed, and Kit found herself laughing too, emptying out all of that bottled-up tension.

They passed the area where Jonas and Megan had disappeared. 'There must be a dozen roads along here,' Kit said.

'You sure you want to stay up here and keep looking?' Virgie stared straight ahead, speaking as casually as if asking Kit if she'd like more tea.

'If you'd asked me back there before we found the turnout, I don't know what I would have said.'

'And now?'

'We can't leave Farley.'

'Maybe he don't want to be found.'

'Maybe. But I don't believe that and neither do you. And even if you're right, I need him to tell me so before I even think about leaving here.'

'What about John Paul?' she asked. 'We know enough to help him out now.'

The distance had softened the anger Kit had felt just days before. 'Maybe I'll text him. Offer to work together.'

Virgie pulled back onto the 101. 'I hope Farley knows what a good friend you are to him.'

'Thanks.' Kit tried to think of a way to apologize for panicking on the road, but she knew that anything she said would be untrue. She couldn't talk about the rest. Her body ached and all she wanted to do was collapse into bed and close her eyes. But she couldn't do that, not yet. 'We probably don't have much time,' she said.

Virgie started to speak and then nodded. They both knew where they were going. 'Probably not,' she said. 'We don't know how long he'll be gone.'

Kit noticed that Virgie was speeding but didn't say anything. After what they had just been through, this was easy. Soon they

would be back at the barn, and they needed to get there as soon
as possible. Jonas had actually used a gun to scare them away. If
he found them in his barn, they could be in danger.

Virgie parked down the road again. Although it was still thick
with mud, the trees smelled clean and fresh and the muted sunlight
in the cloudy sky warmed Kit's face.

'How are we getting in?' she asked.

'Same way we did at Farley's.' Virgie picked up the pace as
they approached the barn and Kit followed.

If Farley's car were in there, it would all be worth it. Then she
would call John Paul. Together, they would make Jonas tell them
the truth.

'At least the sun's out.' Virgie lifted her face to it. 'I can still
feel that cold in my bones, though.'

So could Kit, only the chill running through her was fear.

'You watch the road,' Virgie said.

Kit shook her head. 'I'll watch it from inside. Jonas could have
booby traps and cameras in there for all we know.'

'We still need one of us outside.' Virgie trudged ahead. 'I mean
it. We've got to be smart and one of us needs to be out here. I'll
let you in as soon as I figure out what kind of alarms he has in
the place.'

'Just don't take any chances.'

'Every minute we waste is a chance we're taking.' She stopped,
took Kit's arm and steered her toward the drive. 'You hide here,
behind the gate to the garage. Door's right there.'

'I don't like it,' she said.

'I won't be a minute. Promise. Remember, this is what I do.'

Virgie disappeared in the back and Kit fought her impulse to
follow. This *was* what Virgie did – part of it anyway. And she
was right that if something went wrong, or if Jonas came back,
Kit needed to be outside the garage. Right now, though, all she
wanted was to be inside that garage with Virgie. Farley's car had
to be there.

'Come on.' A door lock clicked. 'Down this way.'

She rushed to the side entrance, past the windows the heat had
fogged before. They were clear now, covered by a shade.

Virgie stood at the open side door. A burst of warm air came
from the room.

'What?' Kit asked.

Virgie shook her head and motioned her inside.

Kit knew instantly that Farley's car couldn't be in there. In the dim light she saw the shapes. On two tables, mounted to the walls, everywhere, even on the ground, were the small and large curving objects, still yet somehow alive. Like dolls.

She moved closer to the first table and realized what she saw. Not dolls. Guitars. Maybe fifteen, twenty.

'So that's why he controls the temperature in this place.'

'Yeah. That's why.' Virgie motioned to a long table holding tools, plywood molds and threaded dowels. 'Jonas ain't hiding Farley's car out here. He's just storing guitars – hand-made, at that. Why would he care if we saw this?'

'I don't know.' The fresh wood smell and the warmth of the room made no sense. 'He was a music teacher. Why hide that he's making musical instruments?'

'Maybe there's something in them.' Virgie turned the one she was holding upside down and gave it a shake. 'Drugs or something. Money. We've got to leave now, though. He could be right behind us.'

Kit walked through the barn looking at them, smelling them, trying to make sense out of what she was seeing. 'These things are works of art.'

'Works of art or not,' Virgie headed back toward the window and lifted it, 'we've got to get out of here. You go first.'

Kit hurried to join her and then turned around one last time. On the table beside her lay a perfect guitar still exuding the sharp, oily smell of varnish. She felt the pull of recognition and reached out for it.

'Not now,' Virgie said. 'Come on. You want to get caught again?'

Then Kit spotted the guitar strap – the bold, beaded red-and-black Navajo pattern. She reached for the strap and traced the letters with her fingers. *Farley B.* This was his strap, his guitar.

'I said come on!' Virgie motioned toward the window but then slammed it shut. 'Someone just drove in. Hide.'

Kit heard the sound of tires crunching over the driveway as she and Virgie crouched beneath the table.

Kit reached up and pulled down the thin cloth as low as she could. At least it might hide them. If Jonas actually came in.

From outside, his deep voice drifted in with a fresh, stinging breeze.

Then came the muted tones of a woman speaking. Good. Maybe he and Megan would head inside his cabin and she and Virgie could get out of here.

Instead, the door opened and a shaft of light fell across the floor.

'So how are they coming?' Even if Kit hadn't recognized the low-pitched voice, she would have recognized Megan by her long, flax-colored skirt.

'I've found some excellent wood. Red spruce and cedar. Look at this.'

Her tan suede books moved nearer to their hiding place and Kit could smell her soft vanilla fragrance. Virgie gripped Kit's arm and gave her a look that, even in the dark, said they couldn't give up. Kit nodded and stared at Megan's skirt, so close now that she could reach out and touch it.

'Beautiful, Jonas,' she said. 'These are simply perfect.'

'And this strap is for your guitar.' He moved closer to her, closer to them.

Don't let them look down.

'It's stunning,' she whispered. 'The beads look almost alive.'

He must have touched her because Megan jerked back from him and pressed her fingers against the table.

Kit stared at the faded purple bruise on the back of Megan's hand and tried to pull farther back against the cold wall.

'I wasn't trying to . . . I mean, when you are ready, we can talk. I'm not going to rush you.'

In the silence that followed, Kit didn't dare look at Virgie. Instead, she stared at Jonas's canvas shoes, one of which inched closer to Megan.

'I can't,' she finally said.

'Because you love Will?'

'If he knew we were here together I don't know what he'd do. I need to get back there. If he checks, he'll find out that I didn't go with Priscilla today.'

'Priscilla would never share anything with him.'

'But they need him right now. *We* do. And he has ways of getting what he wants.' Megan leaned against the table, and as she pressed her weight it inched across the floor against the wall.

'From you maybe.' His voice dropped. 'I know you're in a bad place right now. We all are. But once it's over, just remember you can trust me.'

'I know that.' She stepped on her toes and hugged him, and his hand moved to the small of her back.

'I've got to get back now,' she said.

'One kiss.'

'I'm serious, Jonas. I can't.'

The hands hesitated, and then moved up her arms. 'Have a glass of wine with me before you go.'

'He'd know. He knows everything.'

'He just makes you think he does,' Jonas said. 'Come on. Let's have some tea, and then I'll drive you back to your truck.'

She paused. 'OK. One cup, but it will have to be fast.'

'You can drink it in the car.' He moved closer to her again and started toward the door.

Finally, Kit thought. Maybe they would actually get out of here.

'Where's my guitar strap?' Megan's steps paused. 'I didn't drop it, did I?' She lifted her skirt and crouched in front of them only a few feet away.

Kit shoved herself harder into the wall.

'It's right here,' Jonas said and she stood again, her hand dangling so close to Kit that she could almost touch her.

'Thank you. Now I really do have to run. I can't be gone this long again, not until . . . you know.'

Their voices dimmed and disappeared. Kit and Virgie got out from their hiding place. Virgie placed a finger to her lips and Kit nodded. Then she looked back at the guitar, its Navajo strap dangling over the edge of the table. This was proof that Farley had been here. She reached out for it.

'No,' Virgie whispered. 'He'll know it's gone. Come on, jump.'

Kit closed her mind to what could be on the other side and climbed up and out the window into the hard-packed mud. Virgie followed and gently closed the open window. All Kit could think about was that beaded strap with Farley's name on it. She and Virgie had found a bizarre factory of handmade guitars. They were hidden for a reason. If she could figure out why, she might find out what had happened to Farley.

SIXTEEN

The motel they found – the first one they spotted after leaving the barn – consisted of four units on each side in a field of pine trees and beer cans. From at least two of the other units the noise of the television blasted out news broadcasts and *American Idol*-type music.

'I felt almost safer at Nickel's.' Virgie walked over to the only window and pulled down the blinds. They looked yellow in the dirty light of the room.

'Most people who stay in this area are probably campers,' Kit said. 'It should be all right until we figure out what to do next.'

'You got any ideas about that?' Virgie sat on the ottoman across from her.

'We have to find out about those guitars.'

'Jonas ain't exactly friendly. And it's not as if he's breaking the law.' She paced the room, as if trying to find her way out of a cell with no doors.

Kit felt the same way. None of this made any sense.

'Why are there so many of them in his barn?' she said. 'Jonas must be selling them, but there's nothing illegal about that.'

'And what's Farley doing with a guitar anyhow? I thought he broke his hand in a fistfight.'

'That was a long time ago,' Kit said. 'He's never stopped playing.'

'Should have known.' Virgie turned her back to the shaded window and crossed her arms over her chest. The hard expression in her eyes softened. 'A musician makes music, no matter what. No matter how much it hurts him or anyone else.'

Her words were both angry and something else – sad, maybe. 'Are you speaking from experience?' Kit asked.

'Maybe.' She shrugged and her mask of indifference returned. 'So where'd he play around here?'

'There *was* a place.' Kit felt a chill. 'A pub of some kind. I don't think he ever mentioned the name.'

Virgie pulled her vest from the back of a chair. 'There can't be that many.'

Kit stood up from the sofa bed and then forced herself to stop. She was doing it again – possibly putting both of them in danger. 'I do remember that Farley said the place could get pretty rough,' she said.

'It can't be any worse than this.' Virgie flashed a bitter grin and glanced around the room. 'Let's go.'

Kit stopped her at the door. 'You've already gone out of your way for me.'

'You helped me out before.' She opened the door and the scent of pine crept into the room.

'Not like this.' Kit didn't move.

'Helped me out plenty.'

'That was just money,' she said. 'Driving me here was a huge favor but I never expected you to put yourself in danger for a guy you barely know.'

'It's not about him.' Virgie stepped out into the darkness. 'You told me not to head off on my own again so you can come along if you like. Either way, I'm going to find that pub.'

'All right,' Kit said and got into the car beside her. 'But this is the last time.'

'Hold on.' Virgie turned to her in her seat. 'That night last year when you and John Paul was leaving the shelter and you put that money in my hand, you changed what I was planning.'

They had never discussed what happened and Kit wouldn't have mentioned it if she didn't have to. Now, she did.

'I didn't expect anything back. You must know that.'

'I'm going to say it just one time.' Virgie sighed and leveled her gaze on Kit. 'Worse things than you know were coming down that night. I thought I was hitting up a stranger for change and then I saw it was you, and you took those bills out of your purse and shoved them in my hand. Something in me shifted then. That's all.'

Just like that, Kit was back there, on that broken sidewalk, trying to fix this woman's life with what she had planned to donate to the shelter, knowing that money couldn't fix anything for long even as she did so. She could feel the cold of that night, the uncertainty.

'Virgie, I . . .'

'I said that's all.'

They drove in silence while Kit tried to block her own emotions the way Virgie always did. Right now, they just needed to figure out where Farley was, and in order to do that, she couldn't think about anything other than how to find the pub where he had played.

Ten minutes from their motel they spotted a beer bar. Kit asked the female bartender where they could find some music and she replied, 'The Gas Lamp. It's the only place around with live entertainment.'

Had she not given them exact instructions they would have needed a map to find the Gas Lamp. Once they did, Kit knew they were in the right place.

'Look at that,' Virgie said and pointed at a flickering light in front of the narrow, fog-shrouded structure.

For the first time since they had started this trip, Kit felt in control of herself once more. She and Virgie headed inside and sat at the bar. In spite of the uncertain weather, the back door of the place, at the end of a short row of booths, stood open.

The bartender, a balding man with long gray braids, waved and called out, 'Just a sec.' Then he handed two tall Bloody Marys to a couple across from him and made his way down to where Kit and Virgie sat.

'Five-dollar cover charge, ladies.'

'We're not here for the entertainment,' Kit said.

'Five bucks just the same. Once the place fills up there's no way for me to tell who paid and who didn't.'

They handed him the money and he reached down beside the cash register and picked up a rubber stamp from a pad. 'This way you can come and go, if you like,' he told them. 'Music starts in a few minutes.'

Kit lifted her hand and he pressed the stamp into it. As he turned his attention to Virgie, Kit stared down at the mark on her hand with a shiver. Odd-shaped and purple, it looked like a bruise. Megan had also been in this place.

'What will it be, ladies?'

'Beer's fine,' Kit said and forced herself to look away from the stamp mark.

'And what about you?' He smiled at Virgie in a slow way, as if trying to guess her age.

'Water,' she said, her tone indifferent.

'Don't worry about that.' He pointed at Kit's hand and she knew he had caught her staring at it. 'It fades fast.'

'How fast?'

'A day or two at most. Soap and water should do the trick.'

He turned to the cooler and Kit whispered, 'Megan's been here, and recently. Her hand was stamped like this too.'

The bartender brought back a draft beer and a tumbler of water with a straw in it. 'I'm Mickey.' He leaned against the bar and his skinny braids fell over his shoulder. 'We have a new singer tonight. You ladies enjoy.'

'What about Farley Black?' Kit said.

'Farley?' He looked down at his pale, puffy hand and his immaculate fingernails and then back at her. 'He was supposed to play tonight, Saturday too. But he canceled on me.'

'Canceled how?' Kit asked.

'Didn't show up.' His eyes narrowed. 'Why does it matter?'

'Because he's disappeared.'

'What are you talking about? I just saw him.'

'When?' Kit said.

'A couple of nights ago when he played here.'

'Friday?'

A woman carrying a guitar entered through the rear, waved at Mickey and began setting up by the Bloody Mary-drinking couple.

He returned her wave. 'I've got to get back to work,' he told Kit. 'You might check with the guy who runs that Ananda school close by. His name's Case.'

'Jonas hasn't seen him either.' Kit didn't add that he had denied Farley had been in the area at all.

'Now, that's weird.' He leaned farther across the bar so close that Kit could see the clear blue of his eyes, younger than his wrinkled skin. 'What's he done?'

'Nothing that I know of,' Kit said. 'He was traveling and, all of a sudden, we lost touch.'

'You ever think he might not want to be found?'

'Farley's not like that.'

'I never thought so either.' He shook his head and squinted at her again. 'I didn't think too much about the first guy. But now, with you asking the same question, I don't know.'

'What first guy?' Kit asked.

He studied her, then Virgie. 'Someone else asking about Farley. Yesterday, I think.'

'A man?' Kit asked.

He nodded. 'Black guy,' he said. 'Tall. Walks kind of funny, like he's got a limp or something.'

SEVENTEEN

'John Paul!' Virgie said after they were outside again. 'Have you heard anything from him?'

'Not a word,' Kit told her. 'But he's going to hear from me.'

Still outside the car, she phoned him. When he answered, she said, 'I know you're here.'

'It's good to hear from you too.' He chuckled. 'Seriously, I was going to call you.'

'Right.'

'Where are you?' His tone went straight to cop voice. 'I want you to help me find something.'

His silver pickup pulled into the parking lot several minutes later. Only then did Virgie agree to return to their room. Before he could get out of the truck, Kit opened the door and climbed in beside him.

'Good to see you,' he said.

In spite of the new-looking gray sweater, which with its zipper at the neck was too dressy for the area, his usually perfect boots were scruffy, which probably meant he had been here a while. The citrus scent of the truck felt warm and familiar. They were a good team, and together they could find out what happened to Farley faster than either of them could alone.

'Why didn't you tell me you were here?' she said.

'I intended to.'

'When? How long have you been in town?'

'Hey.' He let the truck continue idling as they sat there over-looking the creek. 'I told you how I felt about you getting involved in anything so soon.'

The soothing sound of the water failed to ease her mood.

'And I told you I'm good at finding missing people.'

'So am I,' he said, 'and I guess we both proved it. We ended up in the same place.'

He wanted something – probably to know what she'd found out. 'I told you before,' she said, 'I'm willing to work with you.'

He stretched his arm across the seat and began to pull out of the parking place. 'Farley played in that pub Friday night.'

'I know that.' He was just placating her. 'What else have you found out?' she asked.

'That his buddy Jonas isn't all that cooperative.'

She wasn't about to share any information about Jonas until she knew John Paul was willing to share what he had found out.

'How'd you get this far?' she asked.

He glanced over at her as if trying to make up his mind. 'His phone. It's dead now, but we were able to locate the general area.'

'Where is it?' she asked. 'Have you found Farley's phone?'

'Not yet, but we're close. I thought you might want to come along and help me look.'

'Why?' she asked.

'Because you're safer with me than on your own.'

'So you knew I was here?'

'I only just found out. An old guy named Nickel at the place Farley always stored his car said there had been two women there asking a lot of questions.' He flashed her a straight-lipped smile. 'He gave a pretty vivid description.'

She felt herself flush. 'Meaning?'

'Basically that an attractive woman with curly hair was looking for the guy with the Corvette. That's not exactly how he put it, but I knew he was talking about you.'

'Well, I hope you got more out of him than I did.' She refused to let him distract her.

'Just that Farley left here on Friday night, heading north.'

'Do you believe him?'

'Not sure.' He pulled the truck onto the freeway. 'His response seemed a little pat. Besides, if Farley were leaving, why wouldn't he take his phone with him?'

'And why wouldn't he be in touch with one of us?' So that's where this was heading. John Paul was asking without asking. 'I haven't heard from him,' she said. 'I wouldn't lie to you about that.'

'What *would* you lie to me about?'

'Nothing that important,' she shot back. 'What about you?'

'Hey,' he said again, and this time his voice was soft. 'We both want the same thing. Let's not argue.'

They wouldn't have to if she could trust him, but there was no point getting into that right now. 'I agree,' she said. 'And John Paul, I'm glad you're here.'

They drove without speaking for a moment. He glanced down at the paper on the seat beside him and took a right off the highway. At the stop sign, he looked at her, and the thin moonlight coming into the car made his light brown eyes seem to shine. 'I'm glad I'm here too. And I'm glad you're with me.'

In the darkness, the winding road seemed endless and steep. Kit turned to him, so that she wouldn't have to look the other direction.

'Do you know where we're going?' she asked.

'Not exactly. We probably ought to come back tomorrow. I just wanted to get a look at the general area.'

'I don't think there's much out here,' she said.

'The school's a few miles from here. I thought the phone might be there but I couldn't find anything on the grounds.'

'Jonas isn't about to let you look around,' she said. His voice and the scent of the truck calmed her in spite of the blinding headlights coming down the hill. 'I've heard this isn't the safest at night.'

'Who told you that?'

Then Kit remembered. 'There's a berry stand somewhere over there. One of those little library structures, only they sell jam, jelly and herbs.'

'I think we passed something like that,' he said. 'I saw it earlier today when I was looking around.'

So he had already been here once today.

Kit's heart hammered and not because of the narrow road or the other car lights. Megan's hand had been stamped at the Gas Lamp. Megan was close to Jonas. Farley's phone was somewhere in this area.

'Let's search the stand,' she said.

'It's closed.'

'It never closes. They leave a jar there for donations.'

John Paul shook his head. Kit dug her fingers into her palms. He turned around and the primitive wood sign appeared again. 'It's right ahead,' she said.

He pulled the truck in front of the stand and turned the lights off. 'You stay here,' he told her.

'John Paul!' She grabbed the door handle. 'I thought you didn't want to argue.'

'OK,' he said. 'Got it.'

Together they approached the darkened stand. The air had calmed, quieted down and felt warmer.

Leaves rustled and John Paul drew closer to her.

On the counter, a large, clear mason jar like one that might be used for lemonade held coins and several dollar bills.

'I'll be,' he said. 'The honor system is alive and well.'

Lights approached and a vehicle slowed. Too late to hide, Kit thought.

The passenger window went down and a man called out, 'Need any help?'

'No, thanks,' John Paul said. 'We're just leaving.'

'OK,' the man replied, and the car took off down the hill.

'We'd better hurry,' Kit told him and squinted into the darkness. 'Do you have a flashlight?'

'Don't move.' John Paul ran back to the truck and returned with one. 'I'm going to look in the bushes outside.'

'I'll go through the jars and supplies.' Kit lifted the stack of dried herbs and breathed in the scent of lavender, basil and something sharper . . . fennel, maybe.

As she shoved her fingers under jars and boxes, she remembered the mark on Megan's hand once more – the stamp from the pub. She stopped and tried to visualize Megan when they had met the day before, her long skirt and those little boots with the buttons on the side. Priscilla, the pregnant woman, gave her the jam, while Megan, her long, dark hair in a ponytail, shoved a large cardboard box onto a middle shelf. Kit walked around and stared at the shelf. The box was there where Megan had put it, but she must have been on a stepstool in order to do so. The shelf was too high to reach. Kit climbed onto a bottom shelf, reached up and tugged at the box.

Headlights flashed and a car seemed to slow as it passed. She tugged harder. The box inched toward her. She yanked and it fell into her arms, against her chest. Kit gasped and held on tightly as she tried to keep from falling off the bottom shelf.

'What the hell?' John Paul grabbed her by the waist and steadied her against him. The flashlight lay on the ground where he had dropped it. 'Why didn't you ask me to help you?'

'A car.' Kit pointed into the night. 'I was trying to hurry.'

Together, they set the box on the counter. The smell of shredded newspapers stung Kit's nostrils.

'Jars,' John Paul said. 'Empty jars.'

'Right. Two layers of them.' Kit slid her hands down the side of the box, remembering how Megan's movements had seemed odd to her at the time. 'Why would they need to keep the empty jars here when this isn't where they make the jam?'

Glass pressed against her fingers and she turned the box upside down. The bottom had been covered with masking tape. John Paul reached for his pocketknife and cut through it. Together, they pulled open the cardboard flaps. On the inside of one of them, covered in tape, was a rectangular object.

'We've found it,' Kit said, her voice shaking.

John Paul expertly cut through the tape. With the tip of the knife, he nudged the phone out. 'We sure have.' He grinned at her in the moonlight. 'Now we just have to get it charged.'

EIGHTEEN

Chopin was playing again, and to Jonas the music sounded like a warning.

If Megan were as free as he was, he wouldn't even be here with this woman. But Megan was with Will and would be until she had the courage to leave, if she ever did.

He lifted his glass. It had been a fine evening so far but he was getting tired of her questions. When she had knocked at his door he should have directed her back to town. But he was a sucker for blondes. Megan was the only brunette he had fallen for in a very long time.

Now, he knew this woman had set him up. She was some kind of crime writer like Kit Doyle, maybe even working with her. He liked that she sat across from him wearing nothing at all but that soft knit cap on her head. There was a freedom in her attitude that he admired. Still, he knew that he couldn't give her what she had come here for and he had better think about showing her to the door.

'More port before you go?' he asked.

'Maybe later.' She crossed her legs and Jonas nearly fell out of his chair. 'You wouldn't have a beer, would you?'

'I don't think so, although there might be a pilsner in the refrigerator.' He forced himself to get up and walk over there.

Perhaps he should just go with it, reporter or not. He wouldn't have to tell her anything he didn't want to. All of her questions had been general, about the school, about why he had stopped teaching so early in a brilliant career. He opened the refrigerator door and a stream of cold air hit him on the bare chest.

'No pilsner,' he said, 'but there is a local craft beer in here. Would that do?'

'I don't see why not.'

He poured it into a mug he found in the freezer, handed it to her and went back to his chair. 'Like it?' he asked as she took the first swallow.

'Not bad.' She put it on the table beside her chair and grimaced.

Jonas looked at the inch of port remaining in his glass.

'Could I ask you something?' she said.

'You've been asking me all night, so, if you don't mind, let's just keep it easy between us. I'll pretend you really lost your way and you can pretend you didn't come here looking for me.'

'Very good.' She got up, walked behind him and placed her hands on his shoulders while the leaping, almost human images created by the flames from the woodstove painted the walls orange. 'You saw right through me, didn't you?'

'Well, I wouldn't put it quite that way.'

'You can at least tell me you know where Farley Black is, even if that is all you can say.'

So that's what this was all about.

'I don't know where he is,' Jonas said.

'What if I don't believe you?' Her hands slid down the sides of his body, tickling his ribs and arousing him again.

'Hey,' he said and grabbed both of her hands in his. 'I'd better send you away before you become a very bad habit.'

He didn't bother to close the curtains, didn't bother to herd her into the bedroom. On the rug in front of the woodstove, he didn't think about anything until later. Then he realized the window was not only open but blowing cold air into the room.

'What's the matter?' she asked. 'I thought you said you like the window open.'

'It's too cold.' That was a lie. The air was as invigorating as ever. But they were naked and exposed. He was.

Jonas got up, pulled on his shorts and shirt and, still buttoning it, went to the window. As he stared outside and reached for the curtains he saw a figure – a person – rush from his view into the trees.

'Now what?' She sat up from the pile of tangled covers on the floor.

'Nothing.' He snapped the curtains shut.

Someone had been out there, watching them. If he needed to use the gun, he would.

'Are you sure? You look worried.'

'Not at all,' he said and sat down beside her.

The heat of the fire warmed his back. When she finally said, 'I need to get going,' relief flooded through him as strongly as passion had earlier.

'Of course.'

Jonas put on his jacket and walked her outside. Never again, he told himself. He should have learned his lesson by now.

He thought of Megan again, felt guilty and reminded himself once more that Megan and he were only trusted friends so far. How trusted was still up to Megan.

'You can stay here if you need to,' he said, not because he wanted her to but because he didn't need any more guilt in his life.

'I'll be fine.' She brushed her lips over his. 'And now I really do need to go.'

'Before you do, would you tell me why you really came here today?'

'I'm a crime blogger.' The gleaming smile that had stunned him earlier now looked almost predatory. 'And as you may have

guessed, I'm trying to find out what happened to Farley Black. I
know he disappeared out here somewhere.'

'I wish I could have helped you.' He took both of her hands in
his. 'I'd like to keep in touch, though.'

'Let's leave the lies right here.' She squeezed his fingers. 'You
know that can't happen.'

'At least tell me your name,' he said. 'You certainly know a
great deal about me.'

Her smile relaxed and she looked into his eyes. 'Was I that
obvious?'

'Not really. I'd just like to know the name of the woman I spent
such an amazing evening with. It will make it more real when I
think about you.'

'My name is Kit,' she said. 'Kit Doyle. Farley's my friend.'

'I hope you find him.' He could barely find his voice.

Jonas watched her van pull out of the driveway and kept watching
until it disappeared into the night.

So he had two Kit Doyles looking for Farley. And the woman
he had just spent the evening with was not the real one.

As they waited for Farley's phone to charge, Kit and John Paul sat
in the parking lot of the motel so as not to disturb Virgie, who was
probably sleeping inside. As they talked, John Paul seemed to relax
the by-the-book approach he used as a wall between him and
anything he felt threatened by – including her at times. After the
nightmare she had barely survived, they had grown close. But it
was too soon after her best friend's death, too soon after her divorce,
and she had stepped back. In spite of everything she loved about
John Paul, she hadn't regained enough of herself to give anything
to anyone else. He hadn't pressed, and that allowed them to remain
friends.

'Why would Megan hide Farley's phone?' she asked him.

'Some kind of guilt. Could be anything. Once it's charged I
need to take it to the local police.'

'Once we go through it,' she said.

'Which we can do right away. After that you need to head back
home. I promise you I'll keep looking for Farley.'

'You're talking like a cop again,' she told him.

'I am a cop, regardless of my official status.' He lowered his window and let the cool air come inside. 'That's the major problem you and I have.'

'How's that?'

'You've got to know what I'm talking about.' He glanced down at the phone between them while stretching his right arm over her seat. 'Before you think I'm a total jerk for asking you to go home, remember that I was law enforcement before I was anything. Remember that you and I didn't start off as friends.'

'And now?' Kit looked into his eyes.

'I'm no more certain about that than you are.'

As they sat there in his truck, moving closer to each other, the charging light on the phone dinged and turned green. John Paul reached for it but Kit grabbed it first.

'Please,' she said. 'I found it.'

'Fine.' His voice held no emotion, but all Kit cared about at that moment was seeing the last messages Farley sent before his phone died.

'Texts,' she said, as she scrolled through them. 'Just as we thought – to Monique and me, pretty much, and a couple of texts to you. But there's something else here.'

'What?' He moved closer, and a photograph of the bottle of port Kit had seen in Jonas Case's house appeared on the screen. *Soon, Jonas,* Farley had written. *This for you, man. Beer for me. Can't wait.*

She could tell John Paul wanted to take the phone from her but that wasn't going to happen. She clicked rapidly on photos. The first one that popped up was the last thing she expected. Taken in the pub, it was a selfie of Farley and Mickey, the bartender. Both of them grinned into the camera, Mickey in a green shirt printed with a falling tree and the words, *Loggers Jamboree.* Farley's free arm was around Mickey's skinny shoulders.

'Friday night,' Kit said. She held up the phone to John Paul and he moved closer. 'He had the phone then. He was OK.'

Wearing a heavy gray vest Kit had not seen before and an open-collar, navy-blue shirt, Farley looked as intense as he always did when he was playing music. Yet he had lied to her about where he was going. He had lied to everyone.

Something behind Farley caught her eye. A dark-haired woman with a stunned expression stared into the camera. Megan. A short man beside her, his face blurred, held onto Megan's arm.

'You know them?' John Paul asked.

'Her,' Kit said. 'She works at the stand where we found the phone.'

'You think she hid it there?'

Kit nodded. 'I know she did. She was trying to cover it up the night that Virgie and I stopped at the stand.'

'And when was that?' His voice turned official.

'This isn't a police investigation,' she reminded him.

'It was a simple question, Kit. Don't get defensive.'

He was right, yet she couldn't give into him entirely or he'd do what he always did and leave her out.

'You're right,' she said. 'We saw her the night we arrived.'

Just then the door to their room opened and Virgie stepped out, blinking under the overhead light. 'Kit? You out here?'

Then she saw the truck and rushed to Kit's open window.

'Thought I heard your voice,' she said.

'What's wrong?' Kit asked.

'The van,' Virgie said. 'It followed me again tonight. I couldn't dodge it this time. Whoever is driving it probably knows where we are.'

John Paul jerked around. 'What van? Not the same one from Sacramento?'

'I don't know since I never saw that one.' Virgie pointed toward the road. 'This one followed me all the way up here.'

Kit opened the door and climbed down from the truck. 'We'd better leave here tonight,' she said.

'It's too late to leave,' John Paul said. 'I won't be far away. And tomorrow we need to talk more about that photo.'

Kit leaned back into the window. 'We will,' she said.

Once they were back in the room, Virgie was full of questions. 'Was he bristly or what? And what photo does he want to talk about?'

'I'll tell you in a minute.' Kit sank down into a hard kitchen chair. 'First, though, tell me about the van.'

Virgie pulled up another chair across from hers. 'I think it was the same one we saw on the road. It has kind of a flat front, not like your basic one. It followed me right up to the driveway, Kit.'

'Then let's go to bed early tonight,' she said. 'Because tomorrow we're going back to Megan's stand.'

'You think it's her van?'

'Probably not. Whoever was driving that followed us before we met her. I just want to find out what Megan knows about what happened to Farley.' She opened the door to the cabin. 'Come on. I want to show you what's on his phone.'

NINETEEN

This place feels wrong to Megan. She's still nervous about the photo Mickey took with the guitar player and she doesn't like the way Will is trying to take over. It's as if he is attempting to prove something to her, or maybe to himself. As she glances down at the mark on the back of her hand, Megan feels like a piece of beef being stamped prime. That world of cattle and grading was once as familiar as this bar is now. She has forgotten most of it, except that pretty girls don't finish first for long, not unless they have something else going for them.

As the man in the booth stands up to greet her, Megan is glad she sent Will back to the bar. There's a sweetness about this guy who rises to greet a woman, even a woman like her.

'Nice to meet you.' He puts out his hand and, in his grasp, Megan feels the leathery warmth of many summers. 'My name's Charles but they call me Chuck.'

'Megan.' She lets go of him and settles onto the hard wood of the booth. 'My friend is getting drinks for us.'

'I already did.' He motions to the frosty glass in front of her. 'Wasn't sure what you'd like so I ordered a margarita. Everyone likes them, right?'

'Right.' She can't help smiling at him and at the ridiculous first-date glass of ice and alcohol. 'That's very thoughtful of you.'

He sits down across from her and she looks at him – really looks – for the first time.

His black hair lightens to a rusty color in front where it falls over his forehead. The effect of the sun. Even here, winery workers run the same risks as field hands like her dad did back home.

'So where would you like to go?'

He says it awkwardly, and Megan hates herself for knowing that she must wait for Will.

'Let's just sit here a minute.' She picks at the salt crystals on the rim of the glass, picks it up and swallows enough of it that an icy headache explodes between her eyes. 'Let's just sit, all right?'

'That's fine.' His body is muscular and his eyes too dark, too careful in his appraisal of her to reveal much. But she likes what she sees. This won't be so bad.

'So tell me about yourself, Chuck.'

'Not much to tell.' He starts to reach for his draft beer and then presses the fingers of both hands onto the table. 'Actually, I guess I could say I've never . . . I mean, this is the first time I've done anything like this.'

'I understand.' She leans back in the booth and repeats the words Will has taught her. 'It's not really any different than meeting someone online.'

'I tried that.' A smile spreads across his face. 'Believe me, after that, this makes way more sense. And you're right. It's not really any different. When do you have to get back?'

Heat spreads across her cheeks and she takes a sip of water. 'I'm not sure.'

'I'm just asking because I have to pick up my daughter tomorrow in town. I hope that's all right.'

'Absolutely.'

Apparently Will hasn't discussed the time allotment with him, leaving the dirty work up to her again. But this one won't be a problem. He's not what she expected, not like the others Will has lined her up with. *Only* three, Will always says, but Megan has hated every one until now.

At least the last one is the nicest. Although alcohol is one of her least favorite things, she picks up the glass and takes a large swallow.

'Hey.' Will appears at their booth with a tray of glasses and slides in next to Chuck as he always does when they meet a man. 'Rudy said you like microbrew, Chuck.' He passes out beers all around.

'I wasn't sure what the lady would like.'

Will seems to grimace. 'The *lady* is fine with beer.' He glances at their glasses. 'I see you already have drinks but the place is packed and it's better to have too much than too little. Right?'

Chuck nods and smiles at Megan across the table. The guitar music drifts in and he clears his throat, reaches for his beer and takes a swallow. 'Would you like to dance?'

Will glares at her, but leans back in the booth as if anything is all right with him.

'I'd like that,' Megan says.

TWENTY

Kit set her phone alarm for five-thirty and woke up thirty minutes early. Even before she opened her eyes, she knew something was wrong. No snores or rustling came from the other sofa bed. It was empty, the thin blanket neatly folded back, like the bedspreads on the cots at the shelter.

She got up and looked out the window. A soft sunrise blended pastel colors into the morning. Virgie's vest hung over one of the deck chairs. Kit rushed outside.

Virgie sat on the steps to the room, her sleeves rolled up.

'Beautiful morning,' she said. 'Coffee's on the stove. I had to boil it. There's no pot.'

'Where have you been?' Kit gulped the fresh air, realizing she was both relieved and angry.

'Nowhere.'

'You didn't go back by Jonas's.'

'I told you I wouldn't.' Virgie stood so they were eye to eye. 'I don't break my word.'

'Sorry.' Kit looked down at the crushed pine cone at her feet and then back at Virgie, who nodded slowly. 'After everything that's happened, I jumped to conclusions.'

'No need to explain.' Virgie settled on top of a weathered log. 'Just like you have a problem driving a car on a freeway full of people, I have a problem sleeping very long in one place, even my own.'

'I understand.' Kit looked around at the clear sky and the iridescent rain puddles that only magnified the fragrance of the air. Even this early, the weather felt like spring, as if the storm had never taken place. From a nearby cabin the smoky scent of bacon floated out and Virgie rubbed her stomach, as if unaware of what she was doing.

'Megan's not coming to the stand this early,' she said. 'Let's walk down to that café we passed coming in and get some real breakfast.'

'I'm not hungry,' Kit said. 'I'll keep you company, though.'

'You might change your mind once we get there.' The path was steep and Virgie went ahead of her as they shuffled down it.

That was where the bacon smell was coming from. 'At least no van can follow us there.'

The café was set off from the hill a short gravel path from the road. 'Doesn't that smell good?' Virgie said. 'We deserve some decent food, right?'

'Sure.'

She stopped on the path and glared at Kit. 'He got to you again, didn't he?'

'Kind of.' She didn't bother pretending to misunderstand. 'He'll back us, though. Whatever we find.'

'Except?'

'Except we're a good team. I just wish he'd treat me as an equal.'

'Good luck on that one.'

'I know. Let's have some breakfast and get to the stand about the time they open up. The sign says seven o'clock.'

The sooner they got to the fruit stand the sooner she would know the truth.

As they stepped inside the café, Virgie said, 'You know John Paul will try to talk to Megan too.'

'Another reason for us to get there early. We have a photo that says she was in that pub with Farley. Let's see how she can explain that.'

The minute Kit sat at the table and picked up the plastic-covered menu with its snapshots of food, she realized that she was hungry after all.

'Look at the combination plate for two,' she said. 'Do you think we can eat all that?'

'That's more like it.' Virgie grinned.

'What?' Kit asked.

'Nothing.' She put down her menu and folded her hands over it. 'The stand won't open for another hour. We have plenty of time.'

As their car whipped around the narrow roads, Kit's anxiety was tempered by the smell of pine and the possibility of finally confronting the woman who might lead them to Farley. When they met that night, Megan had seemed distant – frightened, even – but not evil. If she really had hidden Farley's phone – and Kit was certain that she had – it might be because Megan didn't want any harm to come to him. Kit hoped that Megan was still protecting his phone because Farley was still alive.

With enough caffeine, bacon, eggs, grits and biscuits to fuel their day, Kit and Virgie parked in the woods just outside the fruit stand.

Shortly after eight, a battered pickup with peeling paint drove in and Megan got out. Instead of her usual maxi skirt she wore jeans and an off-white, long-sleeved T-shirt. Frantically she ran to the stand, pulled out a stepstool and yanked down the box she had tried to hide earlier. Although Kit and John Paul had replaced it in their rush to get out of there, they hadn't taped the bottom. When Megan reached for it, glass jars crashed around her and she screamed.

'Now,' Kit said.

'No, let's give her a minute.' Virgie scowled. 'See what she does next.'

Kit nodded.

Megan reached under another pile of boxes and took out a phone. 'I need you,' she shouted into it. 'Someone's been here. Stuff's missing. No, not jam. Please get here as soon as you can. I'm scared.'

'Now,' Kit said.

They got out of the car and approached Megan.

'You!' Megan shouted at Kit. 'You did this.'

'Where's Farley?'

'I told you before, I can't help you.'

'You lied before.' She pointed at the fading stamp on Megan's hand and then the one on her own. 'I know you were at the pub that night.'

'You can't prove anything.'

'Actually, I can,' Kit said. 'That stamp pretty much tells it all. Besides, Farley took a selfie on his phone when you walked into the place on Friday.'

Megan seemed to freeze. 'If you have a photograph of me, I'd like to see it.'

'Don't even think about trying to destroy it,' Kit told her. 'I emailed it to myself and my friend Virgie here has it on her phone too.'

'I have to see it. You could be lying.'

'No, you're the one who's lying,' Kit said. 'But you're welcome to look at it.'

Virgie pulled the phone out of her vest and opened the photo. Megan sucked in her breath as if someone had stuck her.

'Now,' Kit said. 'Where's Farley?'

She straightened her shoulders. 'I don't know what you're talking about. I was at the pub, OK? Somehow I got in that photo, but I don't know your friend and I didn't stick around for the music that night.'

'Who's the guy with you?' Kit asked.

'I have no idea. Never saw him before.'

'He has his arm around you.'

'People do that to each other in crowded places.' Megan leaned down and began placing chunks of broken glass into a paper bag. 'I don't know him, and if you don't mind I need to get to work now before the tourists arrive.'

'You called someone a minute ago,' Kit said. 'You asked them to get out here as soon as possible.'

'Then you know someone is coming to help me and you'd better get out of here while you can.'

Kit glanced at Virgie, who nodded. 'We're not leaving until you tell us about Farley.'

'No, we're not,' Virgie said. 'Lady, you hid that phone for some reason. You don't want Farley hurt, do you? We can help you make sure he's all right.'

'You don't understand.' Her lips trembled. 'If he finds you here I don't know what will happen. You need to get out.'

'But you called him to get rid of us,' Kit said.

'I called him because I was afraid of what you took. Now I'm more afraid for you. Please leave.'

She was trying to protect them as she had tried to protect Farley by hiding his phone.

'Just one question,' Kit said. 'Is Farley alive?'

Their eyes met. The sound of a motorcycle became louder. 'Go, now.' Megan stumbled back through the broken glass. 'He's going to be furious about the phone.'

'Tell me!' Kit shouted.

Megan's words were lost in the noise.

'Is he alive?'

'Yes.'

Tears sprang to Kit's eyes. 'Where?'

'Not here. Far away. But he's all right. Now, you've got to go.'

'We'll talk later,' Kit said, and she and Virgie ran for the car.

TWENTY-ONE

K it could still hear the roar of the motorcycle in her ears. Virgie didn't speak until they were on the highway again. 'What is it?' Kit asked.

'More people packing out here than in my old neighborhood. You think she's telling the truth about Farley or just trying to keep us from being shot?'

'I believe her.' Kit glanced out the window and realized that something about these uncertain hills and dependable fresh air felt somehow stable, even healing. 'I think she knows where he is.'

They went around the curve leading to the turnoff and Virgie tapped Kit's hand.

'What?' she asked.

'The van.'

Kit turned slowly in the seat. It was the same van, the same flat front, the same dark color. 'That's the one.'

'I'll lose it.'

'No,' Kit said. 'Let's make it follow us until we can see who's behind the wheel.'

'We'll have to do some mountain climbing.'

'That's fine.'

Again, they turned off the road.

The van followed.

She glanced down into the pointed tops of trees like dark green brushes against the sky.

'Go higher,' Kit said.

'You sure?'

'Absolutely. We need to go all the way up, the way we did before.' She knew it wouldn't be easy, but at least the person driving the van didn't know how the road would narrow. 'Our old turnout's up ahead,' Virgie said as the road narrowed and the drops grew steeper. 'You OK if I pull over there?'

'I'm fine.'

Virgie braked to the right, into the lane overlooking the tallest pine trees. Kit watched as the van slowed and then passed.

The driver glared at Kit's car, face frozen into a mask of shock that contrasted with the blonde hair that flowed in waves around her shoulders.

'It's a woman,' Virgie whispered.

'Monique.' Kit tried to find her voice. 'And it's the same van I saw before.'

'Monique? From the station?'

Kit nodded, her stomach in knots. 'I'm sure of it. Follow her.'

'We don't know what's up there.'

'But we know *she* is.'

'OK then, if you're sure, but once we get there it might be a rough trip down.'

No cars were coming and Virgie started up the hill again. 'Why would Monique be following you?'

'She's trying to find Farley.'

'So are we, but we ain't stalking each other.' Virgie paused and then added, 'Maybe she don't trust you.'

'She has to. She knows how close Farley and I are.'

'Exactly!' Virgie jabbed a finger at Kit. 'And that's the problem. She just don't know *how* close you are.'

'That's ridiculous. He and I decided a long time ago that we make much better friends.'

Virgie shrugged and stared straight ahead. 'I still say she's following you because she thinks you know where he is. He lied to her about going surfing, after all. For all she knows, he didn't lie to you.'

'Let's have her explain it.' She grabbed the phone out of her purse.

'You really want her to know you recognized her?'

'She knows.' Kit tried to call but couldn't get a signal. 'Nothing works up here,' she said. 'Let's just take this road as far as we can.'

'What happens if you get dizzy again?'

'I'll close my eyes.'

Kit's shock seemed to have driven away her anxiety. None of this made sense. Monique cared about Farley – probably loved him – and Kit was sure he cared about her too.

'Why would he tell her to meet him in Malibu?'

'They're working together and, from what you said, practically living together.' Virgie slowed the car as the curving road became narrower. 'Why don't they just drive down to Malibu in the same car?'

Her words started to make sense. 'OK,' Kit said. 'He lied to all of us and said he was going surfing. Instead he came up here.'

'With a vest, some allergy medicine and that bottle of expensive port. I'm telling you, she thinks you know where he is. Kit, the woman has been following you since before we even knew Farley was missing.'

Kit began to put the pieces together. This wasn't Monique the spoiled station owner's daughter with the flawless face and the excellent taste in interior design. If this woman really had been following her the entire time, she wasn't just looking for Farley. She was stalking him.

'She's probably the one who broke into my place.'

'And his after we broke in that day.'

'She said she didn't have a key.' Kit shook her head at her own vulnerability. 'But of course she would say that.'

Virgie flashed her a tight smile. 'Don't necessarily need a key to break into that place.'

At the top of the hill the road slanted down one side and, without asking, Virgie headed down it.

'I think that van's long gone,' she said. 'I hate to say this, Kit, but you've got to call John Paul.'

'If I do that he'll take charge again, the way he always does.'

'At this point, who cares?'

They drove a few more miles of road, and Kit said, 'I care. I'm willing to work with him but he's not willing to work with me and, frankly, I think we're closer to finding Farley than he is.'

'He still needs to know about Monique. She might be watching him too for all we know.'

Virgie was right. What they had just found out mattered more than her problems with John Paul. Monique was stalking her. She was probably going everywhere they had been – the roadside stand, Jonas Case's school. That was it!

'I have another idea.'

'Let me guess,' Virgie said. 'One that will keep you from talking to John Paul.'

Kit couldn't help smiling. 'You know me too well.'

'I know that man is one of the few people you let get to you.'

Her cheeks burned and she didn't try to deny it. Instead, she turned to Virgie. 'What if we talked to Jonas again?'

She made a face. 'Like he'd talk to us?'

'He might,' Kit said, 'if we tell him about Monique. You know she's probably tried to talk to him too.'

'What if he brings out that gun again? These people out here are like the old West.'

'He won't,' Kit said. 'He didn't like doing it the first night we broke into his garage. By now he's got to know we aren't dangerous.'

'Don't you remember any of those lectures they gave us at the shelter?' she asked. 'Like the definition of insanity, for instance?'

'Doing the same thing and expecting different results?' Kit said. 'Attributed to everyone from Benjamin Franklin to Einstein. This isn't the same thing. It's sharing news Jonas needs to be aware of.'

Virgie gripped the wheel as the curves of the road became wider and slower. Finally she said, 'I have a bad feeling about him.'

'You mean because he doesn't dress, look or act like your typical professor?'

'He talks the talk,' Virgie said, 'but he was checking you out.'

Kit squirmed in her seat. 'I don't think so.' Yet Jonas had pulled his chair so close to hers that she could smell the wine on his breath. Something about him did make her self-conscious.

'Checking out your legs. You still want to go back there?'

'No, I don't.' Kit watched the trees settle down to eye level again. 'But I'm going to.'

'And after that?' Virgie asked in that flat, noncommittal voice.

'I'll tell John Paul about Monique.'

TWENTY-TWO

Megan had done it again. As usual, she had stayed too long for tea with Jonas. Each time they met, being there – across the table from him or watching him work on the guitars in the barn – seemed natural and right. Tonight, she could barely keep herself from telling him the truth about hiding Farley's phone and about Kit Doyle finding it. She had lied to Will once he had arrived at the stand right after Kit and her friend left. But Will was getting quieter, more secretive, and Megan had no idea what he really knew or suspected.

After parking the truck, she started toward the back way, the night quiet except for the cooing of the mourning doves. The air was as clean as she could remember. It smelled of hope. The gnarled path toward their shelter would take only a few minutes.

Megan stopped and took a deep breath. Then she touched her lips where Jonas had kissed her. Only once. Only softly. Without a word. Yet, without speaking, they said it all. Finally, she trusted someone enough to share the truth. Now that Kit Doyle had Farley's phone, Jonas needed to know. But then he would ask how it got to the fruit stand and she would have to tell him that she disobeyed Will when he told her to destroy it.

'You can tell me anything. I won't let anyone hurt you.' She could still hear his voice, the way it sounded the moment before he kissed her.

Maybe it was time to trust someone.

'There you are.'

Branches snapped behind her and she jumped.

Will stepped out from behind a tree, his teeth white even in the twilight. She didn't trust the smile any more than she trusted his unexpected presence here.

'What's wrong?' she asked.

'No worries.' He took her arm and led her toward the camp. 'I know how easily you lose your way after dark.'

'My night vision is fine.'

'I'm not talking about your vision, Megs. I'm talking about losing your way.' He held on tighter and she decided not to fight it.

A screech from the trees sent chills along her arms. 'What was that?'

'Just an owl. They do that to scare the rodents into moving. If they stay still, the owls can't see them.' He traced a finger down her neck and she shivered again. 'You're awfully jumpy.'

'I'm fine.'

'So where have you been?'

'Nowhere.'

'As long as you're breathing, you're somewhere.' He pulled her closer and Megan stumbled on the path.

'Well, last I checked, I was breathing. Would you slow down?'

'No. You speed up. There's another storm coming.'

She tried, although her skirt caught in her shoes. At least the camp was close now. 'I can't go any faster,' she said. 'Besides, the sky looks clear enough.'

He seemed to slow reluctantly, and Megan thought of the boys she had gone to elementary school with who shoved their heavy shoes on the back of the heels of anyone they could bully.

'Where were you anyway?' Will asked in his doctor voice, the voice that said she owed him an answer.

She recited what she had mentally rehearsed. 'Helping Priscilla clean up the stand.'

'Interesting.' He studied her as if he were seeing her for the first time. She started to feel frightened but remembered what Jonas had told her. *You are worthy.*

'Seems to be taking you longer and longer, these sessions with Priscilla.'

'She's pregnant, Will. And I'm grateful to her and Michael.'

'Don't forget that I'm helping them too – and in a major way, I'd say. Without me, do you know where this camp would be right now?'

'Of course. I'm glad you're doing the right thing.'

'I'm sorry I couldn't get there any sooner today. You never saw who broke in?'

She shook her head. 'Probably just vandals. They got away before I got a good look at them.'

He gazed down at her face, right at her lips. 'Who would vandalize a roadside stand?'

'Beats me.'

As they crossed the tiny creek that led to the camp, she wiggled out of his grasp and picked up her skirt.

He pressed his lips into her hair and inhaled.

'You smell different,' he said.

'Like blueberries?' She giggled to distract him, but he leaned in again anyway.

'Gritty or something.'

'Gritty?'

He stopped on the other side of the creek. 'Like sawdust. Look. You've got some on your shoulder.'

She forced herself to chuckle. Soon they would be back with Priscilla, Michael and the others. Soon, none of his veiled accusations would matter.

'I don't see anything. How would you know sawdust anyway?'

He scrunched up his nose and his eyes narrowed. 'My dad was a contractor. That's how he put me through medical school.'

He had changed it from pre-med, had changed it from dropping out of college, but she didn't dare go there in this or any conversation. If she did, he would remind her that she was raised in an apartment above the movie theater in Corcoran, California, where her dad was serving time. He'd mention her mom, who left Megan and her brother and her alone so she could work at the beer bar on Whitley Avenue. This was the dance they did, Will and her. He was almost a doctor, and she was almost like Priscilla and the others here.

'What are you thinking that makes you look so sad?'

'Oh, I'm not sad,' she told him. 'Just glad to be back home.'

She moved toward the flickering lights and felt almost physical warmth pulling her in to where the others waited. If she screamed now, someone would hear her. Someone would come.

Will touched her arm again, lightly, almost playfully this time. 'If you like it here why are you gone so much?'

She gazed up and realized she was looking into the eyes of a stranger. 'I want to do my part, just like you.'

'As if we're equals?'

'That's not what I mean.'

'What do you mean?' He rested his hands on her shoulders and squeezed until she had to catch her breath. 'And why do you stay away so often at night now? If I found out you lied to me, I don't know what I'd do.'

'Will, I don't lie to you. I wouldn't.'

A light snaked toward them on the ground. Priscilla's flashlight. She always waited nearby until Megan was back. Michael wouldn't be far behind.

'A very good answer.' Will's voice was short and clipped. He glanced down at the light. 'We seem to have company. Keep your voice low.'

'It's probably just Priscilla,' she whispered.

'Maybe.' He pulled her back into the shadows. 'Let's not take any chances, though.'

TWENTY-THREE

Even after Kit's phone was able to receive a signal again, Monique would not answer her calls. Neither would Jonas. She and Virgie stopped by his cabin anyway, but his car was gone and he didn't answer the door.

On the way back, they passed a stack of stones that had not been on the side of the road before.

'What's that?' she asked Virgie. 'Some kind of memorial?'

Virgie parked the car and they got out and walked over for a closer look.

'I don't think so.' Virgie reached out and touched one of the rocks. 'It's probably a message for hikers that they're going in the right direction. There's some fancy Gaelic word for it but I just think of it as mountain road signs.'

'Beats the graffiti at home,' Kit said.

They got back in the car. 'Remember that day we broke into

Farley's?' Virgie asked. 'You was so upset about that graffiti outside
the shelter that I thought you might fall apart right there.'

I wish you missed me. That's what had been written on the wall
in the alley.

'It seems like years ago now. I just thought it was incredibly
sad that someone could write that.'

'We've all been there.' Virgie took the final turn that led to their
motel. After she parked, they got out of the car and walked through
the light mist toward their room. 'You know,' Virgie said, 'it's kind
of like Monique and Farley.'

'Except she does miss him,' Kit said.

'But he don't miss her.' Virgie kicked a pine cone out of the
path and studied Kit. 'That's it, you know. She hasn't done
everything she has, including stalk you, because Farley loves her.'

'But because he doesn't,' Kit finished.

'And now?' Virgie grinned. 'Are you ready to tell John Paul
she's here?'

'I guess I have no choice.'

It wasn't going to be easy. As always, part of her hoped they
could share information but that wasn't going to happen. He'd
already proven that, and as she and Virgie had discussed, expecting
anything different was the definition of insanity. But John Paul
picked up and she told him that Megan had said Farley was still
alive. She'd save the rest for when they met.

The sun was just starting to set when he arrived at the motel.
When he got out of his truck, she tried to read his thoughts, but
as he walked toward her and the sun glinted on his skin, she saw
him only as a tall, handsome man whose scowl disappeared when
their eyes met. Then the moment was gone and her only hope was
that they could help each other.

'I had an idea,' he said. 'There's a brewery about thirty minutes
from here. Why don't we have dinner there?'

'Maybe we should go somewhere closer.' She climbed into the
truck. 'I really need to talk to you.'

'Down the hill then,' he said. 'There's a breakfast place that
stays open until ten o'clock. It has an outside patio.'

'I know the place.' She sighed and told herself she just needed
to get through this. John Paul was the professional and he needed
to know.

'What's wrong?'

'Monique. She's the one in the van, John Paul.'

He turned off the ignition. 'Are you sure?'

'I recognized the van before I saw her. It has a weird flat front.' He nodded as if to encourage her to keep talking. 'Then Virgie pulled off the road to let her pass and I got a glimpse of her face.'

'Did she see you?'

'I know she did, and she isn't taking my calls now.' Kit knew she needed to slow down but his questions seemed to come too fast.

'Where were you?'

'I'd have to show you. Up a hill with very few turnouts. That's how we managed to see her.' She needed to vary the exchange of questions and answers. 'What about you? I know you've found out more than you've shared with me.'

'I'd like to know where that hill is.'

'I'll show you in the daytime once you tell me what you know.' She turned and faced him in the seat. 'You realize what this means? Monique has no idea where Farley is and she thinks I do.'

He nodded. 'She's not the only one.'

'What?'

'It's natural to assume he'd tell his best friend where he was heading.'

'But you're one of his best friends.'

'I'm a buddy,' he said. 'A work buddy and sometimes a drinking buddy. Not like you two.'

'John Paul.' She reached out for his arm and then hesitated. 'Did you ever think, for one minute, that I had any idea where Farley is?'

'No, never. I watched your face the night I told you. No way could you fake that kind of fear.'

Watched her face, not *saw* her face, as if waiting for the truth to reveal itself.

She pulled her hand away. 'Watched me how?'

'From the moment you called me that night and said you were being followed, I thought that the van had something to do with Farley.' He leaned back in the seat and crossed his arms.

'But you suspected that I knew something about what happened.'

'Monique said he told you everything and that you'd protect him, no matter what.'

'You think she'd figure out that if I knew I'd have gone straight to him.'

'Exactly.' In spite of his casual tone, he seemed to wait for a reaction. 'You wouldn't have wasted your time with that broken-down camp or Jonas Case.'

Kit fought the impulse to lash out at him. 'So you know I spoke to Jonas.'

'It wasn't that difficult. Besides, I don't want to keep anything from you now.'

She felt herself exhale. If only he meant it. 'I feel the same way. What else do you know?'

'That Monique was lying from the start. That's why I didn't want you to go to the station that Sunday. I wanted to keep talking to her, trying to get her to mess up the way liars do if you keep asking sequential questions.'

'But how did you know?'

'Because I can spot a liar.' He turned so that they faced each other in the seat, and for a moment, in the hazy light, his features seemed magnified, almost fierce. 'I guessed that Farley hadn't invited her to go with him. He was trying to get away from the woman.'

'Why didn't you just tell me that?' she said.

'That's not how I operate. Besides, I didn't have any proof, just my gut.'

'And what did your gut tell you about Farley's trip?' she asked.

'Same thing. I knew he was lying but I figured it was a personal issue and didn't give it a second thought.'

'It never occurred to me that Farley wouldn't be anything but honest about whatever he was doing,' Kit said. 'You realize that if you had told me what you suspected, maybe we would have figured out sooner that she was the one in the van?'

'It's occurred to me.'

'Would you do it differently the next time?'

His tight lips broke into a smile. 'I would now. Back then, I thought I was doing the right thing.'

She sighed to keep herself from saying something she'd regret, and he added, 'It wasn't the best judgment on my part, OK? I wasn't sure how'd you react if I said I thought Monique was lying.'

'There's more I'd like to tell you,' she said. 'If you're willing to really work together now.'

He reached down, took her hand in his and lifted it. 'What are we going to do about this?'

In spite of the warmth that spread through her, she didn't hesitate. 'What we've been doing all along, I guess. Only one thing matters right now.'

'Ah,' he said and let go of her. 'Finally we agree on something. Let's go have dinner.'

They drove slowly through the hills and Kit leaned back in the seat, wondering what else he hadn't shared with her. Even with the windows up, she could smell the scent of the trees and the wind in his truck. John Paul had been as honest as he could with her tonight. He had accepted what she said about putting whatever else they were thinking about on hold.

Headlights from a vehicle behind washed over them and she jumped.

He shook his head, as if he knew what she was thinking. 'Monique's too smart for that. My guess is that she's revisiting old leads, trying to find someone vulnerable.'

'Vulnerable how?'

'Character flaws. Weaknesses. Someone who will buy whatever she pretends to be selling.'

Kit pictured Jonas in her mind but said nothing.

TWENTY-FOUR

If Farley didn't improve in the next twenty-four hours, Jonas was going to contact Kit Doyle – the real one. He should have done it sooner but too much was at stake. Lying in bed, he tried to sleep, tried to stop worrying. If he had to come forward about what had happened to Farley, they would figure out a way to get Megan out of there first. This wasn't like before, not this time. He cared about her. Priscilla, Michael and the others were good people. They could start fresh again somewhere else. They had committed no crimes.

Trying to drift off to Debussy, he kept thinking about Megan – the way she looked at him with trust, the way her lips had hesitated when he kissed her. She was smart, both forceful and gentle. If it worked out for them, he'd help her with her education, her goals. And if it didn't work out for them?

I'll help her anyway.

He woke to silence and something else, an itching in his nostrils. Smoke. Jonas stumbled out of bed, threw on his clothes and ran outside. A gray stream drifted from the open barn door. Jonas rushed inside and ran into a wall that hit him in the chest.

Just like that, Jonas was on the ground, looking up into the blurred sky. His nostrils burned and he remembered why he was out here. Slowly, he climbed to his feet. Whoever had attacked him had disappeared. The barn door stood open. Still shaky, Jonas rushed back to his cabin, yanked the extinguisher from the closet and ran back to the barn. The wall and the counters flickered and spread their fire. As his vision cleared, he saw it all – not one blaze but many. His guitars – only the guitars – were on fire, on the work tables and on the walls.

Choking, Jonas shot the extinguishers at each crumbling instrument, knowing he could stop the fire but not the destruction. His guitars – all that work and love – were gone. Sweat ran down his face and he felt as if the fire had spread to him. As the flames died and soot filled his lungs, he heard a moan from the back of the barn. He headed in the direction of the sound and spotted someone trying to crawl toward the door. As she stretched her arm toward him he realized it was Virgie, Kit Doyle's friend.

'Help,' she whispered, and then collapsed to the floor.

Jonas dropped the extinguisher, ran to her and half-dragged her outside. Still moaning, she coughed and gasped for breath.

'What are you doing here?' He realized his voice was shaking. 'Why have you done this? Why?'

'I didn't.' On her knees, somewhat revived, the woman managed to get to her feet, still fighting for breath. 'But I saw who did.'

TWENTY-FIVE

Kit and John Paul had eaten dinner in the brewery and taken their time over coffee. Megan's assertion that Farley was alive was comforting but it didn't bring them any closer to finding him. Tomorrow they'd confront Jonas together and convince him to tell them the truth.

'Anything else?' He glanced at Kit's empty cup. 'More coffee? Another beer?'

'We probably ought to get back.'

He nodded but seemed to be watching her from across the table. 'What's bothering you?'

'Nothing but the obvious.'

As they neared his truck, he said, 'What is it? I've told you everything I know. I wouldn't lie to you.'

'Do you think we'll find him?' She could hear the tremor in her voice and knew John Paul heard it too.

'I don't know,' he said.

She felt both close to him and far away. Part of it was this place, the sound of the ocean and the breeze with what felt almost like a human touch on her shoulders. 'What do you think happened?'

'Don't know that either.' He opened the door of the truck for her. 'Other than the fact that Monique is some kind of stalker girl and that Farley lied to her and everyone else about going surfing.'

As they began to drive back, Kit realized that, in this truck, the sharp turns and deep drops didn't shove her into panic.

'Jonas is our best shot,' she said.

'You're right.' He turned off the main road and headed toward the motel. 'We all care about Farley. Surely we can make him see that we want to help. I'll pick you up, OK?'

'Just tell me when.'

He parked the truck and they hesitated. Then he reached over and hugged her. 'Deal,' he said. Then he stared, as she did, at the empty parking place. 'Where's your car?'

'I don't know.'

She got out, ran to the motel room door and, with shaking fingers, managed to unlock it. They both went inside.

The two beds were the same as Kit had left them – only Virgie's vest was missing from the foot of hers. John Paul threw open the bathroom door.

'She's gone,' he said.

Kit's cell rang. She grabbed it out of her purse. 'It's Virgie,' she told him. 'Where are you?' she demanded into the phone. 'Are you all right?'

'This is Jonas.' The voice on the other end sounded unemotional, almost robotic. 'I think she'll be OK but you need to get over here. Someone set my barn on fire.'

By the time Kit and John Paul arrived only a thin spiral of smoke drifted in the air. Virgie stood outside, holding onto the open door. She spotted them and broke into a smile.

Kit jumped out of the truck and ran to her. 'What happened?'

'Not a hundred percent sure.' Virgie allowed Kit to hug her for a moment and then shrugged her away. 'But I saw who did it. As soon as I came through the window, I realized someone was standing next to it. I tried to get back out but he hit me from behind.'

'He?' John Paul stepped closer to Virgie, studying her as intently as he had the barn.

'I think so.' She rubbed her head. 'It was dark and he was wearing a cap.'

'What were you doing here?' His tone was polite yet impersonal.

Virgie marched past him and headed inside. 'Come on,' she said. 'This wasn't no ordinary fire.'

Jonas stood in the middle of the room, arms at his side. Wearing flip-flops and a wrinkled shirt, open at the neck, over his shorts, he looked at Kit with a stunned expression. 'Why?' he asked. 'Who would do this?'

The remaining smoke stung Kit's eyes and she rubbed them as she took in the damage in the barn. The once-elegant guitars on the walls were shriveled now. The ones on the counter collapsed into rubbles of ashes.

'Why would anyone burn only the guitars?' she asked him.

'I don't know.' His voice was a rasp.

John Paul wandered around the room and then joined Virgie, Jonas and her. 'What did you intend to do with these anyway?' he asked.

'Only good.'

'Were you selling them?'

'Donating.' Jonas squinted at Virgie, who leaned against the counter. 'Are you all right? Are you sure you don't need medical attention?'

'I'll be fine. I'm more in shock than anything else.'

'I can't even imagine how anyone could do this.' Jonas motioned to the destruction around them. 'I asked you before to stay away from here. Now I hope you'll respect my wishes.' He walked toward the door.

John Paul didn't budge. 'You've got to report this,' he said.

'I don't have to do anything.' Jonas turned around and gazed at each wall. Then he started toward the door again. 'Stay here as long as you like. There's nothing you can do that's any worse than what's already happened to me.'

'Wait.' Kit caught up with him at the door. 'If you have any idea who did this, you have to tell us.'

'I told you two to stay out of here.' He turned and pointed at Virgie. 'Yet you didn't respect that and now I have a barn full of worthless works of art. Do you really think I'd talk to you about anything?'

'Not if you're trying to cover up what happened to Farley,' Kit said.

For a moment, he didn't move, didn't speak. Then he leaned down, lifted a guitar from the floor and brushed the ashes from it. 'I don't know what you're talking about.'

'I know he's alive.'

'I've never doubted that.' He picked up a small brush from a side table and whisked it gently across the surface of the instrument. 'You people need to go back where you came from. Or don't. Just leave me alone.'

He put the guitar over his shoulder and the variegated blue stones caught the overhead light.

Kit's chest tightened. 'Beautiful strap,' she told him. 'Blue crazy lace agate, right?'

'So you know beads,' Jonas said. 'Impressive, but it won't help me recover what was taken from me in here. I'm going inside now. If I see any of you here again, I will shoot you.'

He stomped out of the barn, clutching the guitar.

'I believe him,' Virgie said.

'I can't imagine why anyone would do this.' Kit breathed in the smoke and stepped outside to keep from coughing. 'There's no doubt that destroying those instruments was the reason for the fire. It's not just the barn. It's every guitar except that last one that was under the table.'

'Pure hatred,' John Paul said. 'Do you remember anything else about the person who hit you, Virgie?'

'Nothing.'

'And you were here because . . .?'

'Come on, Kit.' Virgie nudged her with an elbow. 'I don't feel like explaining myself right now.' In spite of her harsh voice, her eyes were weary.

'She needs rest,' Kit told John Paul.

'I'm sure there's an urgent care facility somewhere around here.' He crossed his arms and leaned against the barn door. 'I'd be happy to drive you.'

'I can drive my own self if I need to,' Virgie said. 'Right now, I've got to sleep.'

'And you aren't going to tell me what you were doing out here tonight?'

'You and Kit were out. I figured I'd do some checking.' Before John Paul could ask more, she added, 'Checking for Monique, I mean. Since she's stalking Farley and his friends, I just figured she'd show up here. Guess I was wrong.'

'Guess you were.' John Paul lowered his voice and Kit realized that was exactly what he did when he wanted information from her. 'If you don't mind I'll stop by tomorrow, just to be sure you're all right.'

'Call first,' Virgie said. 'Come on, Kit.'

From the moment they got into the car, Virgie seemed to gain strength. 'Don't say nothing,' she whispered as she backed out onto the road in front of the barn. 'For all we know, John Paul can read lips.'

Kit laughed from relief as much as anything else. 'Welcome back,' she said.

Once they were on the road, Virgie turned to her and grinned. 'Blue crazy lace agate.' She sang the words in the stillness of the night. 'Want to see if Nickel is still awake?'

'Absolutely,' Kit said.

TWENTY-SIX

They pulled into the camp and encountered pure silence. No Nickel. Just a calm, gray evening sky with few stars disturbing its surface.

'You really want to wake this guy?' Virgie asked.

'Do we have a choice?'

Virgie rubbed her head again and Kit wondered how much of her own pain she was trying to hide. 'We know Nickel made at least one of those guitar straps. He needs to tell us what else he's doing.'

They parked and approached his cabin.

Kit knocked on the door and it moved. Not latched. She pushed it the rest of the way open.

The place smelled like Murphy's Oil Soap. In the flickering candlelight, Nickel sprawled, face-down, across his immaculate table, an open bottle of beer beside him and a partially beaded guitar strap over the chair across from him. Behind the chair, on the kitchen counter, sat the bowl of beads they'd seen before. One beefy arm was flung over his head and his body lay still.

'Is he dead?' Virgie whispered.

'Huh?' He mumbled indecipherable words and curses, and then grabbed hold of his chair as if trying to keep his balance. 'Who?'

'Guess he ain't dead, after all.' Virgie walked to the tiny hall. Kit knew she was checking to be sure they were alone.

Nickel jerked himself the rest of the way awake and glared at Kit. 'Too late for check-in.'

'We're not here to check in,' she said.

'Then please leave this park.' He breathed alcohol fumes at her and managed to lift his sturdy frame from the table.

'Nice guitar strap you made with the blue crazy lace agates,' she said.

'Shit.' He stood from the table with the grace of a sober man. 'Who are the straps for?'

'The kids.' He staggered to the cast-iron coffeepot on the still-glowing woodstove, lifted it and filled a white mug.

'What kids?' Kit asked.

'I don't know. You tell me.' Holding his cup, he roamed the small room as if trying to remember how he got there.

'You just told me the straps were for the kids.' She lifted the partially completed one from the back of the chair.

'I was half-asleep. Didn't know what I was saying.' He returned to the table and leaned over the back of one of the chairs. 'Lady, you got no right coming into my place uninvited.'

'We're not leaving until you tell us about these straps.' Kit reached into the bowl of blue beads, lifted her hand and let them slide through her fingers. 'I saw one that you made with these in Jonas's barn.'

'Oh, Lord.' He poured the coffee back in the pot, pulled out the chair, slid into it and reached for the beer. 'You act like it's a crime or something.'

'If it's not then why are you lying about it? And why did you lie about Farley leaving here and driving north?'

'I didn't.' His face turned a deeper red.

'Farley knew this part of the country and wouldn't need you to show him the way to the freeway.'

He rubbed his temples and sighed. 'You don't understand people out here. We chose this life and this place because we want to be left to ourselves.'

'Then why do you run a campground?' Virgie asked from the back door.

'I think I told you most the people here are long-time tenants. Besides, I'm different from some of the others.' He lifted the beer bottle, looked at it and shook his head. 'Bad habits make you unreliable, and clearly I am.'

Virgie opened the back door. 'Kit, he's got a marijuana plant back here.'

'It's legal,' he said. 'Yeah, I've got a few plants in the back. But I'm not breaking any laws.'

He got up, more alert now, and strode past Virgie into his tiny fenced backyard. Kit and Virgie followed. The resin smell of the plants was unmistakable. Blending with the scent of pine and the sound of water, it would have been peaceful under the right circumstances. Two wicker lawn chairs with off-white cushions sat on either side of a small fire pit. This must have been Nickel's refuge. At the moment, though, he looked as if he were caged.

'Why did you lie about knowing Jonas?' she asked.

'I didn't think it was any of your concern.' He took a swallow of the beer and sat down in one of the lawn chairs.

'You told him we were trying to find him that night, didn't you?'

'What if I did? As I said, we're wary of strangers up here. Jonas and those people are even more wary. Some of them keep to themselves full time and they don't want anything to do with outsiders.'

'Jonas and what people?' she asked.

'The people from his school. The others around here.'

'Like Megan and the pregnant lady from the fruit stand?'

This time the gulp of beer was more reflexive and desperate. Kit crossed her arms and waited.

'You're lucky I'm a peaceful person.' He wiped a knuckle across the corner of his mouth. 'Most of us are, but not everyone.'

'Like the person who set the guitars on fire in the barn?'

He shot out of the chair. 'What are you talking about?' He glared at her and then at Virgie.

'Someone burned up those guitars you were making straps for.' Virgie shrugged and walked up to him. 'Set fire to every one of them and knocked me out too. You wouldn't know anything about that, would you?'

'No way.' He backed toward the door. 'You women need to leave.'

'Jonas has had a rough night,' Kit said. 'You shouldn't bother him right now.'

'Don't tell me how to treat my friend.' With his hair tangled in the breeze and his angry stance, he no longer looked like a harmless drunk.

'Before he was a guy you might have seen around,' Kit said. 'Now he's your friend?'

'Don't.' He put up his hand. 'Just don't go there.'

'Tell us about the women from the fruit stand.' Kit followed him back inside. 'We know that Megan was at the pub the night Farley disappeared.'

'You don't know anything!' He pointed toward the front door.

'They know what happened to him and so do you.'

He jabbed his finger at the door again. 'If you don't leave right now, I will call for help.'

'Let's go, Kit.' Virgie moved toward the door.

'He can't do anything,' Kit said. 'Nickel, I'm ready to stay here all night until you tell me where Farley is.'

'Can't.' Virgie made hard eye contact with her and then softened her voice. 'I'm almost asleep on my feet.'

'I didn't appreciate your sending your cop friend over here,' Nickel said. 'I don't appreciate your invading my home tonight. We do have some enforcement out here and I will contact them.'

Virgie made eye contact with her again. 'I need to get out of here. My head's about to explode.'

Once they were in the car and Kit was backing out of the parking place, she met Virgie's wide-eyed grin and said, 'All right. Tell me what you did.'

'Stole something.' Virgie lifted her vest and reached into it. 'Thought I might be out of practice but I haven't lost my touch.'

Kit pulled off the road and stopped the car. 'What is it?'

Virgie lifted a binder covered in coarse blue fabric. 'Took it off that neatly organized little desk of his,' she said. 'It's full of information about the guitars and which kids got them. That's all I saw before I stole it.'

Kit took the book from her. In architect-perfect printing, Nickel had labeled the yellow, lined pages with the words: *Lavender Fields*.

'Not a school,' Kit told Virgie. 'It's some kind of camp or commune.'

It was all there. Each guitar was listed by a number, followed by the name of a child and that child's age.

Abigail, 9.

Jenny Marie, 7.

Brianna, 10.

Cameron, 13.

Anna, 5.

Megan.

No age was listed for her.

'He made a guitar strap for Megan too,' Kit told Virgie. 'Probably the one Jonas gave her. Nickel knows where they live.'

She nodded. 'He's also going to tell them we're getting too close.'

The truth of her words stopped Kit. 'You're right. We've got to be really careful from now on.'

'Like not going back to the motel?' Virgie made a face. 'Not that I'd miss those sofa beds from hell.'

'Maybe a different motel,' she suggested. 'Something closer to Mendocino.' She started to hand the book back to Virgie and stopped.

Farley Black.

No date. No anything.

'Virgie!' Kit shoved the book into her hands. 'Nickel made a guitar strap for him.'

'The one we saw in the barn,' Virgie said.

'Exactly.'

A soft breeze blew through Virgie's open window. 'So what do we do now?' she asked.

'Are you really as sleepy as you pretended to Nickel?'

'Me? Sleepy?' Virgie grinned. 'That was an act. Let's go find these people.'

TWENTY-SEVEN

Megan stood just inside the camp and walked slowly toward the small wooden house where Priscilla and Jonas waited. She still wasn't certain how any of this had happened or how everything got so ugly and secretive. Before they were just private people. Now she felt like a fugitive.

When Priscilla let her in at the front door, Megan could tell she'd been crying. Jonas stood in the kitchen in jeans and a navy blue sweater, looking as worried as Priscilla.

The piano where he had taught Megan to play sat beside the door to the hall. She breathed in a combination of fruit smells from the jars on the table and the underlying scent of something else – pizza, maybe, or spaghetti.

'Michael will be back in a moment,' Priscilla told her. 'He's checking on Farley.'

'Is there any improvement?' Megan could barely say the words and Priscilla shook her head almost before she could finish.

'If anything, he's worse. Will thinks we need more time and he's a doctor, after all.'

'No.' Megan's voice came easier than it had before. 'Will was pre-med but he dropped out. We need someone else to look at Farley.'

'What we really need is to get him out of here,' Jonas said. 'I told you that, Priscilla.'

'Is that so?' The front door opened and Will stood there, his eyebrows raised.

Megan automatically stepped back and nearly bumped into the piano bench. The others didn't move. Will wore a white jacket over his jeans. His hair was pulled back and, in spite of the smile on his face, Megan could feel his simmering anger. The heels of his boots clicked as he marched into the room and crossed his arms.

'So now you're doubting me? Meeting in secrecy?'

'We're worried.' In spite of Priscilla's soft voice her meaning was clear, and for the first time Megan thought they might avoid whatever Will was planning.

'Worried about what?' He crossed the room and stood between Megan and Priscilla. 'What's gone wrong?'

'Farley's not improving,' Priscilla said. 'If anything, he's declining. We need to get him out of here now. To a hospital.'

Will gave Megan a look that said they'd talk about this later. 'We've got a problem with that,' he told Priscilla in the voice that to him probably seemed casual but to Megan was a reminder of how his anger could build. 'The minute he's out of here everyone will know where we are. We'll have publicity, intruders – all the things we hate.'

'I understand that.' Priscilla rested her hands on her stomach. 'I dread the thought of that as much or more than you do, but we can't let someone die because we don't have the knowledge to save his life.'

'I have the knowledge.' Will started toward the back bedroom where Farley had been drifting in and out of consciousness.

'Wait, please.' Priscilla put out her hand. Her voice was low but full of power. 'When you and Megan joined us, I thought you said you were a doctor.'

'I am a doctor.' He put his arm around Megan and pinched her waist. 'Tell them, honey.'

'It's not Megan's place to tell us,' Priscilla said. 'It's yours.'

Will shot her that smile that won over everyone. It had won over Megan once, but not now. 'We dropped out of the system before all the paperwork was completed,' he said. 'That's why we're here, though. We don't want to be part of the system.'

'That's the reason we're here as well.' Priscilla crossed the room and stood in front of the hall that led to the room where Farley Black was. 'But when we can't do the work better than the system does – when someone's life is at stake – then we have to find the right resources.'

'So you're saying you distrust me.'

'I'm saying that Farley's not improving and now we have his friends coming up here, disturbing our lives.'

'Not to mention the fire in my barn.' Jonas moved closer to Megan but stopped short at the end of the sofa. Despite their distance, she had never felt closer to him. Maybe now, somehow, they could save Farley. She already knew Will either didn't know enough or didn't want to.

'You know one of those women set the fire.' Will glanced at Jonas and then at Megan. Then he gave Priscilla a tight smile. 'Kit Doyle will do anything to find Farley.'

'Because they're friends,' Jonas said. 'They're as close as any of us are, and in some respects probably closer.' He looked at Megan. 'Kit isn't going away and we need to get some care for Farley – some real care – right now.'

'You're saying my care hasn't been real?' Will let go of Megan and approached Jonas just a few feet away. 'I'm the reason he's still alive. What don't you understand about that?'

'I guess,' Jonas said, 'that I'm not sure what happened to threaten his life in the first place.'

'I told you that.'

'You said a guy in the bar.'

'His name was Chuck.' Will turned back to Megan. 'Do you remember his last name?'

'No.' She tried to recall and realized that Chuck had never given her anything but his first name. Yet he was a gentle man who wouldn't have started a fight. 'No, I don't.'

'Well, he's the one who attacked Farley.' Will faced Jonas now and Megan couldn't help comparing the two of them – Jonas with his easy-going manner but quiet strength. Will with his red face, fast speech and his posturing.

'You saw it?' Jonas asked.

'I came in at the end when Farley was on the ground.' Will's voice grew deeper, more certain, as he continued speaking. 'I saved his life, and if you give me just another day, two at the most, I can bring him out of this.'

'That's unacceptable,' Priscilla said. 'You've had four days. Do you know what it will do to this place and to all of our plans if he dies?'

'Do you know what it will do if anyone traces him to us?' He shook his head. 'Two more days. That's all I ask.'

'What about Kit Doyle?' Jonas demanded. 'She has a cop friend of theirs up here now. I'm not about to wait two more days. I'm not about to wait one more.'

'Neither am I,' Priscilla said.

Megan knew that was what needed to happen, even if it destroyed their camp. They could move somewhere else and start up again. Will wasn't really helping Farley with all that pain medication. She took the teapot off the stove, walked over to the table and began filling cups. It would be all right now. They would do the right thing, as she had when she hid Farley's phone.

The hall door opened and Michael stepped out. As always, his true emotions were hidden behind his long blond hair and beard.

'He tried to talk.' Michael put his arm around Priscilla. 'We need to get him out of here. Tomorrow, at the latest. Maybe tonight.'

'Not yet.' Will stalked past Jonas and Megan and confronted Michael. 'I can help him.'

'He's not a real doctor,' Priscilla said.

'Pre-med,' he added. 'I helped you, didn't I, when you nearly lost Callie? Are you really going to tell me you don't trust me to take care of a stranger?'

'He's not a stranger,' Jonas said. 'He's my friend. I say we take him into town tonight.'

'Which town?' Will asked. 'Willits? Mendocino? How much time on the road do you want to put him through? You could kill him, you know, just transporting him somewhere else.'

'Then we should have someone else come out here and look at him,' Priscilla said.

'And expose our entire community? You said you dread the thought of that.' He widened his eyes and put out his hands in the way he did that made him look genuine and concerned. 'Priscilla, I'm one of you. Two days. That's all I'm asking.'

Priscilla looked over at Michael, who shook his head. 'He's getting weaker.'

'Two days is too long then,' Priscilla said.

'One day.' Will moved closer to the hall. 'Twenty-four hours. Will you give me that much time?'

'I don't know.' Priscilla glanced at Michael again. 'We need to decide something tonight.'

'I delivered your daughter.' Will moved closer and spoke softly inches from Priscilla's face. Her eyes filled with tears. 'I saved Callie's life and maybe yours. Are you really going to deny me twenty-four hours to save Farley?'

Priscilla shook her head and stared at the floor, blonde hair scattered over her shoulders. Michael put his arm around her. As they walked out of the house, she turned back and met Will's eyes. 'Twenty-four hours,' she whispered.

Will nodded and headed down the hall.

'Megan,' he said, 'I'll need your help.'

She glanced at Jonas. He shook his head but there was nothing she could do. This was the first time Will had wanted her to help him. It couldn't be good. Nothing about handing Farley's care over to him had helped this poor guitar player.

'Megan,' he said again. 'Come on, will you?'

'Coming.' She took one last look at Jonas, put the teapot back down, and then turned and followed Will down the hall.

TWENTY-EIGHT

The smell of a campfire drifted into the car and, although the rain had stopped some time before, the trees were still dripping. Kit soon realized that Virgie hadn't been lying to

Nickel. This might be the one night she got some decent sleep. Her head tilted back in the seat, Virgie breathed evenly and looked ready to drift off.

'Maybe we ought to wait until tomorrow,' Kit said. 'We're not going to find anything out here tonight.'

'They aren't that far.' She sat up with a jerk. 'Remember when Megan called the guy on the motorcycle? He was there in a few minutes. They're all close by, and Jonas's place isn't that far away from them either.'

'Which will make it that much easier for us tomorrow,' Kit said.

'We've got to find them tonight.'

The roads connected to numerous paths that shot off without warning. After taking a few of them, Kit realized they were only going in circles.

'Tomorrow,' she said. 'We'll come back here then.'

'I don't want to go back to that motel.'

'Well, as I said, we can find another one farther north.'

'Better let me drive,' Virgie said.

'You rest. I'm fine.'

She was, too. Although she knew the panic could be waiting around the next curve of the road, the next steep drop, Kit felt more focused and less frightened. The serenity of the forest had played a part in that, but most of what calmed her was relief that had flooded through her from the moment Megan had told her Farley was alive.

'You sure?'

She relaxed her fingers on the wheel. 'Just being in this place has been healing in a way.'

'The Japanese have a name for it. Means forest bathing. Works on all kinds of stuff, even blood pressure, immune system, that kind of thing.' Before Kit could ask how Virgie knew that, she added, 'I think we ought to stay around here.'

'Why?'

'Because of Monique.' She spun around in the seat. 'Kit, you know she's here and she's not about to go back until she finds Farley. She stalked you. Now, why don't we stalk her?'

'First we have to find out where she is.'

'How many places could she be out here?'

'Not Nickel's,' Kit said. 'At least not tonight.' Then she slowed the car as she thought about Monique before Farley's disappearance. Monique the beautiful station owner's daughter, buying original, pricey art for the walls, throwing catered open houses the first Wednesday of every month. Monique, with her fountain of hair and closets of clothes, was spoiled, insistent and focused on finding Farley, as if somehow that would make him love her.

'Feel like a beer?' she asked Virgie.

She yawned and flashed Kit a grin. 'If it's at the Gas Lamp, I do.'

They pulled in close to ten o'clock.

From inside the open door, the place sounded like a church revival.

'Come on,' Kit said and got out of the car.

As they started toward the music, Virgie nudged her. A van that looked like the one that had been following Kit was parked right in front of the place. Not black, as she had thought, but dark green. It had the same strange front.

'She's in there,' Kit told Virgie.

They approached the front door as a guy with a trumpet playing 'When the Saints Go Marching In' paraded across the bar, jumped down and led a group of followers outside.

'Looks like a drunk night out,' Virgie said.

'Let's see what it looks like inside.'

They walked up to the bar, where Mickey grinned, said, 'Hello, ladies,' and motioned toward his stamp pad.

Kit placed some bills on the bar and put out her hand, even though the fading image on it was still there. Even before the stamp connected with her flesh, she spotted Monique at the first table in the back. She ran to her. Monique started toward the door but Kit blocked her path.

'So you're going to physically restrain me?' Monique looked down at Kit from platform boots.

'You won't go far in those,' Kit said.

'Depends.' Monique tugged at her hair again. 'I've gotten farther than you have dressed like that. Some men are more willing to talk to an attractive woman.'

So that was it. That was everything. This woman, regardless of her beauty, was intimidated by her.

'Why did you stalk me?' Kit asked.

'Oh, please.' Monique lifted the glass of water beside her untouched drink and sipped it. 'I followed you, OK? But only because I thought you might lead me to Farley. I would hardly consider that stalking.'

'What about climbing into my bedroom through the strawberry vines?'

Monique's fierce blush spread across her cheeks, even in the dim light of the bar.

She pointed at her table. 'Sit down.'

'Come on, Virgie,' Kit said.

'Not sure I want to sit across from a stalker.' Virgie moved closer to Monique. 'Why'd you do that? Following someone you pretend to be friends with is crazy. Breaking into someone's home is even crazier.'

'I asked you to sit down.' Monique slid into one side of the booth and motioned toward the other. 'He's my guy, all right? All of a sudden he lies to me, and I know only one person who might know where he is.'

'Except that he lied to me too.' Kit sat down on the other side of the booth. Virgie still stood as if trying to decide. 'You scared me, Monique. No wonder Farley ran from you.'

'You see!' She pounded the table. 'You knew he was running from me.'

'I didn't know anything. I told you that. But now I'm sure he did.'

Virgie made a noise of agreement and sat down beside Kit. 'How'd you break into Farley's place that day?' she asked.

'What day?' Monique folded her hands around her glass.

'You know,' Virgie said.

Monique looked down as if summoning more lies.

'Don't,' Kit said. 'You broke into his house and tried to break into his bedroom when we were in there.'

'You were in there?' Monique's voice rose and she pressed her fingers over her lips. 'He said no one had the new keys.'

Virgie sneaked a smile at Kit.

'So how did *you* get in?' Kit asked.

'I had the old keys and he hadn't changed the front door yet.' Monique wiped her eyes. 'Believe me, I know how pathetic I sound, but I know he loves me and I was desperate to find out where he was.'

'And now?' Kit asked.

She wiped her eyes again and expertly removed the black streaks beneath them. 'I just want him to be safe.'

'So do we,' Kit said.

From outside, the music turned bluesy and a saxophone played *Harlem Nocturne*.

'And you really don't know anything about where he is?' Monique asked.

'I really don't,' Kit said. 'If I did, I'd tell you. It can't be fun going all the way to Malibu to meet your boyfriend only to find he's not there.'

Monique stared into her drink.

'Wait,' Kit said. 'You told me you two exchanged romantic text messages. There weren't any on his phone.'

'You have his phone?' Monique stood. 'Give it to me.'

'I don't have it with me.'

'You're lying.'

Virgie got up and Kit slid out behind her. 'Let's get out of here,' Virgie said. 'It's been a long day.'

'I want his phone.' Monique attempted to block their way back to the bar.

'That's not a good idea.' Virgie's voice was flat. 'You go back to your drink, lady. We'll be leaving now.'

'Don't you tell me what to do. I love Farley and I will find him. We need to talk, work things out.'

The music outside stopped abruptly.

Monique turned toward it and Virgie and Kit walked past her just as Mickey moved from behind the bar into the collection of people now speaking and shouting outside.

'A body!' one of them yelled. 'I saw it right out there.'

Kit could barely breathe. She grabbed her phone and called John Paul. 'Get out here,' she said. 'Someone saw a body in the creek outside the Gas Lamp.'

TWENTY-NINE

On the dance floor, Megan and Chuck move closer, dancing to a song that makes her think that this one will be easy. All she has to do is pretend it is more than it is.

'You're beautiful,' he whispers in her ear. 'Guess everyone tells you that.'

She wraps her arms around his neck and looks up into his eyes, which in this light are not just as black as his hair but tinged with blue-green. 'You're pretty nice yourself,' she says. The motel is a short drive down the road. Three hours max and she and Will can laugh again about the easy money that Priscilla, Michael and the others know nothing about. But it's different now. For just this night, Megan wishes she had a forever man, someone like this guy.

Across from them, Will slumps against the wall, his glare like a weapon that's losing its power by the moment. Just then, Megan decides to let Will see what it's like on her end of their arrangement.

She pushes closer to Chuck and brushes her cheek against his.

'Megan.' He pulls her tighter and kisses her right there.

Nice lips. Decent man.

She opens her eyes to see Will stalking across the room as the guitar player begins another song.

'Want another drink?' Chuck asks.

'We need to get going.' Will nods toward the door.

'I was asking the lady,' Chuck says. 'Would you like another drink . . . a margarita?'

She can feel Will's gaze burning into her back. 'Thank you,' she says. 'I would. Let's have another round.'

'I told you no.' Will grabs her arm so hard that his grip feels like fire.

'Easy, buddy.' Chuck's smile is pleasant enough. Still, he puts his arm around her and brushes the pain from her skin. 'We're having another round and you're welcome to join us.'

They have another drink. They dance again. They defy every plan Will has dictated for this night. Although Megan doesn't know where they are heading, she feels free for the first time in a long time.

'Let's get out of here,' she tells Chuck. Even as Will approaches, Chuck takes her arm and they walk outside.

The cool air hits her and Megan grabs Chuck's hand.

'Maybe this wasn't such a great idea,' she says.

'The best idea I've had all year.' He squeezes her hand and she realizes he is just thoughtful and careful in a way that Will won't ever be.

His watch is unusual and old fashioned, made of a lovely rose gold with a curving face.

'Why are you smiling?' he asks.

'Your watch. No one wears them anymore.'

'It was my dad's Waltham. You ever hear of that company?'

She shakes her head. 'No.'

'My dad worked for them for a while. I'll tell you about it.' He glances at Will, who has stalked out behind them. 'Later.'

He motions toward his pickup, which is parked a few spaces down from Will's bike. 'I'll be right back,' he says. 'Wait here until he and I finish our business.' Then he heads down toward the creek where Will is standing.

'Wait.' She reaches out, kisses him one more time and then gets in the truck.

'Hey!' Will walks up to them. Something is wrong with his voice, with his eyes, which can't seem to focus.

You're supposed to wait. That's what Megan wants to say. *I'm not supposed to be around for this part.*

'I have one thing to say to you before I take your money.' Megan feels her face heat at the mention of it.

'What's that?' Chuck seems to rise up even taller. Will seems to shrink.

'Inside there, you told me how to touch my woman. Don't think you can do that.'

'You didn't touch her,' Chuck replies, his voice calm. 'You grabbed her.'

The anger that had been building in Will is getting close to the surface. 'Don't think you can tell me how to treat my woman. I tell her what to do and who to do it with. Give me the money and let's get this thing done.'

Chuck reaches for his wallet. 'I'll give you the money, all right. But I'm also going to show her how a woman should be treated.'

Megan shivers inside his truck. This isn't how it's supposed to go. As the two men stand off against each other, she realizes that Chuck has left his keys in the ignition and she wonders if she should just drive away. It would be the perfect solution, if she had anywhere to go.

'Keep your money,' Will tells Chuck. 'I'm calling this off.'

'Too late for that.' Chuck turns his back on him. Through the open passenger window he squeezes her bare arm, and the touch makes her feel safe in some crazy way. 'I'm going to get you out of here,' he tells her. 'You don't need to be with this little creep.'

'You're the creep.' Will reaches into his saddlebags, pulls out a wrench and swings it at Chuck.

'Stop it!' Megan shouts.

'Shut up.'

Chuck grabs his arm and they struggle, Will still gripping the wrench.

'Get in there,' Will tells her. 'Don't let anyone come out.'

She hesitates.

'Go,' Chuck says, and pins Will against the driver's side. 'You need to just chill for a bit, buddy,' he says as Will struggles against him. 'No one saw anything. We're going to be just fine.'

Megan gets out and runs back inside the bar.

The guitar player must be on a break. Mickey is talking to a couple at the end of the bar. No one seems to know what has gone on. Good. She heads back outside and sees Chuck and Will struggling down on the creek bank.

She runs out just as Will smashes the wrench into Chuck's head.

'Someone help!' she shouts. 'Help!'

'Shut up.' Will looks up at her, his face a river of sweat. 'Go back inside.'

'No.' She rushes down to them, crouches and grips Chuck's arm. But it is not Chuck. It's the guitar player, passed out on the bank, blood soaking through the tangle of hair covering his forehead.

'Where's Chuck?' she screams.

'Call the police,' the guitar player moans. 'Tell Mickey.'

She rushes back inside, where Mickey hurries over from the bandstand. 'Where's Farley?' he demands.

'Out there.' She keeps her voice low. What happens next could destroy Will and her, but if she doesn't tell Mickey the truth, Will could harm Chuck. 'They're fighting.' She doesn't add that the guitar player told her to call the police.

'You stay here.' Mickey rushes around the bar. 'Don't tell anybody anything.'

She nods.

With the guitar player gone, the couples on the dance floor seem lost. Several drift over to her with empty glasses.

'Where's Mickey?' one of them asks.

'He'll be back in a minute.'

The sound of a gun explodes outside. Everyone rushes for the door. Megan stands as they go, hand against her stomach as if she is the one who has been shot. Finally, she inches toward the door just as Mickey heads back in holding a pistol.

'It's OK,' he tells her. 'No worries. Just a little fight I had to break up.'

But Megan does worry. Megan wants to scream.

He leans down and whispers into her ear. 'Your friend needs you out there.'

THIRTY

Kit rushed outside with the others.

'Farley!' Monique shouted and burst into tears.

'Shut up,' Virgie told her and ran ahead, pausing at the front door. 'Come on, Kit. You OK?'

Her short, labored breaths seemed to come from the top of her chest. 'I'm fine,' she said.

The noise outside grew louder.

'Pull him in,' a deep male voice shouted. 'Someone jump in there.'

'Oh, God, no.' Monique sobbed and crowded next to them.

John Paul's truck pulled to a stop in front of the pub. Kit ran to him.

'What happened?'

'Someone saw a body in the creek. Monique's out there. She's screaming that it's Farley.'

'No one knows that.' He put his arm around her. 'Come on. Someone needs to contact law enforcement. Has the owner called anyone?'

'I don't know.' She couldn't get rid of the fear or of the tears almost out of her control.

Monique caught sight of them and ran to John Paul. 'So glad you're here,' she sobbed. 'I'm scared.'

She wrapped her arms around him and he expertly released himself. 'You need to get it together,' he told her in that law-enforcement voice he used when he wasn't pleased. 'There's no way of knowing what anyone saw out here tonight, if they saw anything at all.'

'A man.' She wiped her eyes and seemed to sober up on the spot, almost as she remembered that these people worked at the station her father owned. 'If it's Farley, I don't know what I'll do. We were going to get married. Even my dad was on board.'

'Right.' John Paul strode up to the crowd and then put his arm around Kit again. He leaned down and whispered, 'This could get ugly. Why don't you go inside?'

'Can't,' she said.

'OK, then, stay here. Where's Virgie?'

'Over there.' Kit pointed to the edge of the green cover of the creek where Virgie, along with a few others, was following the murky water that was already up to her waist.

'Got him!' Virgie's sharp scream shot up Kit's backbone. She started back, holding onto something, someone.

'God, no.' Monique ran to the water's edge.

Kit pressed her face into John Paul's shoulder, unable to stop the tears.

'I can't,' she sobbed.

'It's OK.' He patted her back. 'Might be nothing. Might be anything.'

'Not Farley. Please not Farley.' With her eyes squeezed shut, Kit saw him clearly – Farley laughing after they did a great segment. Farley risking his job to help her when she searched for her mom. He was her best friend. This could not be happening.

'I know you love him.' John Paul squeezed her arm. 'Just don't get carried away. We don't know anything yet.'

The crowd shouted and Kit pulled away from him. Virgie and Mickey stood on either side of a lifeless body they pulled onto the shore. The first thing Kit saw was the man's boots. The second was his dark hair.

'Law enforcement is on the way,' John Paul said. 'You wait right here.'

'Not Farley.' That was all she could say. This poor dead man they had pulled from the creek was not Farley. And that meant – it just might mean – that Farley was alive.

John Paul became the cop again, shouting instructions, making sure everyone knew not to touch the body, not to leave the premises.

Virgie walked up to Kit, thoroughly soaked, her eyes wide. 'Wasn't Farley,' she choked out. 'Some other guy but not him.'

'Thank you.' Kit hugged her so hard that they both laughed and cried.

'You're gonna stink like I do,' Virgie said and pushed her away. 'It's horrible, but you'll be OK now. Farley too.'

Kit looked up and saw John Paul watching them.

'Hey, JP.' Virgie waved him over and he approached with a stern, professional expression.

'They're going to want a statement from you,' he told her.

'That's fine.'

He looked at Kit in a way she couldn't define. Until then, he had either been in cop mode or had seemed to care for her.

Now he just looked tired. That and something else she couldn't find words for.

'You'll be out of here soon,' he said. 'Why don't you two go inside the bar for now?'

Kit stared at the body on the shore, the one Virgie had helped to drag in and said, 'We're fine here.'

'All right then.' Without another word, he headed back down toward the dead man, who was face-down on the ground.

Kit watched him and fought tears again.

'Come on.' Virgie nodded toward the bar. 'He's right about one thing. We need a drink and some time away from this mess.'

Kit looked from her to John Paul, who took charge of the situation on the creek bank with the impersonal, professional approach of someone who was focused on doing his job.

'What's wrong with him?' she said.

Virgie rubbed the back of her neck. 'Probably just the way he is. Let's not worry about him right now. Let's go in and wait. We don't need to watch any more of this.'

Together, they walked back inside. Mickey had beat them there. Clearly too busy to worry about stamping hands or collecting fees, he handed out beers and mixed drinks.

'I didn't know anything about this,' he said. 'We never have any trouble around here. You know that, right?'

No one paid any attention to him, yet, compared to the manic fear and uncertainty outside, the bar felt almost normal. Kit didn't. She had driven herself most of the way to panic because she feared the man they'd pulled out of the water was Farley. John Paul had held her, comforted her, and yet she had sobbed too hard and revealed too much of her pain to him. Now he had a reason to convince himself that she was too unstable to trust.

'Here you go,' Mickey said. He'd taken off the Loggers Jamboree sweatshirt. The black T-shirt underneath it was dark with sweat across the chest. He shoved two mugs toward them.

'I know you don't drink beer,' Kit told Virgie.

She shrugged. 'Tonight, I drink anything. John Paul will tell us what they find, won't he?'

'I think so.' But Kit no longer knew what John Paul would share with her.

They tried to return to the table in the back, which overflowed with people. Monique now shared it with three men Kit hadn't seen before.

She nudged one of them and got out when she saw Kit and Virgie. With her hair pushed back from her face, Kit spotted a shading of dark roots. So much for natural blonde. That should have made Kit happier than it did. Still, all she could feel was relief that it hadn't been Farley's body in that water.

'He's alive.' Monique wiped her swollen eyes.

'We don't know that,' Kit told her.

Virgie made a noise of disgust and returned to the bar.

'Well, that's kind of a negative attitude.'

'Not really.' She stepped back from the table. 'I know now why Farley scheduled this trip.'

'You'd love to have me be the problem, wouldn't you, Kit?'

She leaned against the narrow wall and held her drink in both hands. 'Have you ever considered that he might be worried that you were going nuts and unable to work on the air? That all you could do was volunteer at some homeless shelter?'

'Only one thing wrong with that,' Kit told her. 'He wasn't having a relationship with me. He was having one with you.'

'That depends on who's telling the story.' She tilted her head and flashed Kit a smirk. 'I know you had a relationship. He told me so.'

'We kissed,' Kit said, her words almost smothered by the noise. 'One time. Long before he knew you. OK?'

'Except that he kept referring to you as his best friend, even after you left the station.' She narrowed her eyes, and Kit could see that without the eyeliner and mascara she looked predatory. Or maybe she always looked that way and Kit was just seeing it.

At one time, Kit would have told Monique that there was nothing between Farley and her. She would have tried to convince her. Now she didn't care what Monique thought.

'There's a dead man out there,' she said.

'But not Farley.'

'A dead man,' Kit repeated. 'That doesn't mean Farley's all right.'

'You're still claiming you don't know where he is?'

'You know that,' Kit said, 'because if I did, I'd be there with him.'

Monique took her time processing that. She took more time taking another sip of her drink. Finally she said, 'I guess you just proved my point. Poor John Paul.'

'John Paul?'

'Don't pretend, Kit. You're no good at it.'

She started back toward the table and Kit had to fight the urge to grab her arm.

'I know why he wanted to get away from you,' Kit said. 'He always went to see his mentor when he was worried about something. He was worried about you, Monique. Think about that before you try stalking anyone else.'

'His mentor?' She looked up at the rickety ceiling fan and seemed to think about it. 'That would be Jonas, right?'

'Yes,' Kit said. 'That would be Jonas.'

'I'll bet you didn't get anywhere with him.'

'Are you saying you did?'

'All I'm saying is that I will find Farley, with or without your help.' She turned, placed her drink on the table, whispered something to the men there and headed toward the bar and out the door.

THIRTY-ONE

Earlier, John Paul had told them about a bed and breakfast that was nearby, cheap and comfortable. Located in a redwood forest, the farmhouse was surrounded by blackberry vines and gardens with blooming lacy-looking flowers.

'Wild rhododendrons,' Virgie had said as they crossed the path and the chickens scattered for the henhouse.

John Paul glanced at her and she shook her head. She had gotten so used to Virgie's diverse and assorted knowledge that nothing she said surprised Kit.

Now, after the shock of seeing the body pulled from the creek, they returned there.

Kit knew that all she would be able to see when she closed her eyes was the man.

The rooms were small with one overlooking a pond that gleamed in the moonlight.

'You take that one,' Virgie told her, but Kit didn't want to look at water.

'Do you mind taking it?' she asked. 'I think I'd rather be in the one with the fireplace and bookcase.'

When they were settled, exhausted from the discovery, Kit went to the kitchen to fill a bucket of ice for Virgie and her. John Paul stood on the other side of the ice tub, a tumbler of whiskey in his hand.

He glanced down at her with more warmth than he had since she had sobbed in his arms, terrified that Farley was dead. 'Want one of these?'

'Not tonight, thanks. I'm afraid to close my eyes and yet I know I need to sooner or later. This is a perfect place. Thanks for recommending it.'

'I'm glad you came. At least I can keep an eye on you.'

'Right.' She watched as he tossed another cube in his glass. 'Where are you going from here?'

'I don't know. Back to question Monique, I guess. I've also got to talk to local law enforcement. That guy they found – someone knows him. He has a family and friends.'

For the first time since they had been on the road, Kit felt more at ease in the strange yet comfortable bed. Knowing that John Paul slept next door to her might have been part of the reason.

The knock came on their cabin before the sun rose. Will was still asleep on the pallet bed and Megan had awakened for the fourth or fifth time. This time, she got up and headed for the front, wondering if she had imagined the knock or if it might be a bird or animal noise from outside.

Jonas stood there, his eyes wide and red-rimmed, wearing the same sweater and jeans he'd had on the night before. Megan wanted to hug him but she knew that Will might be watching.

'You're awfully early,' she said. 'Come in.'

'We need to meet away from here,' he said. 'Right now.'

Will came up behind Megan and moved in front of her. 'Why?' he asked.

'Priscilla's worried about anyone seeing us together.'

'Even our own people?' Will asked.

'Even them. That's why we need to leave before any of the families wake up. The lighthouse is in walking distance. Try to be there in twenty minutes.'

Will closed the door and leaned against it, facing Megan. He wore only his shorts, no shirt.

'These people get crazier by the day. They aren't like they were when we first came.'

'That's because of us, in a way.' She sat down on the hassock and began pulling on her boots over her thick socks.

'How is it our fault that Farley got rolled by some guy at the pub?'

She stopped, even though the boot was not all the way up her leg. Usually she would let it go. She'd just think of words like the wind and let them blow past. That's what she would have done before.

'We're the reason the guy was at the pub in the first place.'

'Rudy said he was good people. How were we supposed to know?'

She remembered that awful night. 'Rudy wouldn't know good people because he's not one.'

'Whatever.' Will nudged the side of the hassock with his foot. 'Come on. Hurry up.'

'I just hope Farley's OK,' she said.

'You don't even know this guy and now you're calling him by his first name?' Will shook his head. 'Really, Megan. I expected better of you.'

'Because I care about what happened to the singer? Because I'm calling him by his name?'

She pulled her boot the rest of the way up and tried to see past Will's superior expression. He had been nice to her once, tried to help her by getting her away from a life that was taking her nowhere.

'Because you don't care about what's going to happen to us if we don't get out of here right away.'

Will walked outside and waited. Megan followed because she no longer knew what else to do. They hiked the short distance to the lighthouse as the sun rose in fragmented sparks against the dark blue sky. At any other time, Megan would have found it beautiful. Now she just hurried to keep up with Will, who refused to speak to her.

Surrounded by brush, the lighthouse seemed to rise out of a red-roofed barn. It looked like a miniature version of the Space Needle in Seattle, where her dad had worked before he got into trouble with drugs. The glimmer of the light was blurred by a swirl of fog that grew thicker as they approached.

'I should be with my patient right now,' Will said. 'Besides, I'm tired of these games Priscilla is playing.'

Early on, he had told Megan that once he tired of the rules of the camp, they would take the money the others had stashed and he and Megan could move on.

Megan wouldn't steal from Priscilla and Michael though, and she certainly wouldn't steal from Jonas. He was her only hope. Each time he looked at her or brushed his arm against her, she felt their connection and knew that he did too. At least he would be at the lighthouse this morning. That alone would make the trip worthwhile.

'How are we going to get in?' she asked.

'It's always open. Just the gift shop is closed.' He nudged her with an elbow. 'Haven't you heard anything I'm saying? These people and their secretive antics are starting to wear on me.'

At one time, she would have reminded him that being off the grid was part of what attracted him to the group. Now she just nodded and said, 'I heard you.'

'Then don't be surprised when I tell you we're leaving.' He marched ahead of her to the door. 'Come on.'

Surrounded by antique equipment, they gathered on the bottom floor, just Michael, Priscilla, Jonas, Will and her. Megan had expected more people.

'It's a lovely morning, isn't it?' Priscilla smiled at the foggy light filtering in as if hosting a perfectly normal gathering. 'Michael and I started coming here right after we arrived. Except during visiting hours, it's like being alone in the world.'

A faint oily smell mixed with the scent of the sea.

'What's so important that we had to come all the way out here?' Will asked.

'I wanted to speak with you all first,' Priscilla said. She lifted her hair back from her face and leaned against Michael.

'You OK for this?' he asked her.

Megan felt the gentleness in his words and knew he hadn't faked the tone. This was the way a man spoke to the woman he loved.

'I don't have a choice.' Priscilla walked to the spiral staircase and said, 'We have trouble here, I'm afraid. We're going to have to find medical help for our friend back at the camp. And we're going to have to do it today.'

Megan could feel Will's body twitch beside her. He sighed and shifted position but said nothing.

'Is he worse?' Megan asked, and Will made a noise in his throat that let her know that he didn't approve of her speaking up here.

'The same.' Priscilla lowered her voice. 'There's something else, though. They found a body in the creek by the pub last night. A man.'

Megan forced herself to stifle a scream. 'A man?' she managed to say.

'A winery worker.'

Just like that, Megan knew. Her mind exploded with images. 'What does he look like?' she asked. 'What's his name?'

'Calm down.' Will pinched her arm. 'There's no way they can know that this soon.'

'They do know who he was.' Priscilla leaned against the railing. 'They know his name.'

'Not Chuck?'

Will pinched harder.

'Charles,' Priscilla said. 'Did you know him?'

'Yes. Yes, I did.'

'She met him for ten minutes in a bar.' Will's laugh was sharp but not convincing. 'That's all. Isn't that right, Megs?'

'I'm not sure.'

'Sorry he's dead.' Will gave her arm a shove. 'But he's the guy I told you about, the one who attacked Farley outside the pub.'

'Is that true?' Priscilla asked her. 'Did he attack Farley?'

Before she could reply, Will said, 'Megs didn't see it. She was inside the bar when that happened.'

Jonas frowned and moved around the staircase to Megan's other side.

'I think it's clear to all of us,' he said, 'that regardless of what it costs our community, we are finding medical care for Farley today.'

'Absolutely,' Priscilla said.

'Agreed,' Michael said. 'What about you, Megan?'

She looked away from Will at Jonas. 'I agree too,' she said. Although she felt Will glaring at her, she refused to look over at him. 'I agree,' she said again.

'Guess I'm the only one who disagrees.' Will walked to the front door of the circular room. 'Just for the record, I'm really sorry that you can't let me do the job I'm trained to do. Now it's in your hands. Good luck.'

As he strode out the door and the salty air blew in, Megan felt a flood of relief. Yet she didn't know how she could continue without him. If he meant what he seemed to be saying. If he really would be leaving the camp alone.

Jonas moved closer and touched her shoulder. 'It will be all right,' he said. 'I promise you.'

'It will.' Priscilla stepped into the place Will had been and put her arm around Megan. 'You are one of us now. I'm no longer sure about Will.'

'Neither am I,' Megan said.

'What do you mean?' Priscilla dropped her voice the way she did when she was frightened. 'He was the reason we invited you to join us.'

'I know.' She turned away from Priscilla and looked down at her scuffed boots. 'I'm sorry.'

THIRTY-TWO

K it awoke before sunrise that morning, and the first thing she thought about was the man who had drowned in the creek. He had to have something to do with Farley's disappearance. Someone tapped at her door. 'It's me,' Virgie whispered.

Kit let her in and Virgie said, 'At least I got some decent sleep for a change. What about you?'

'Same,' she lied.

'Guess you know where we're heading. You going to tell John Paul?'

'After we get back,' Kit said.

Virgie shook her head. 'Let's get going then before he wakes up.'

'Oh, he's already up, I'm sure. That's why I asked you to park at the back of the field.'

They pulled into Jonas's driveway at about eight-thirty. In spite of the chilly morning, he wore only a thin short-sleeved T-shirt as he hauled a bag of trash from his barn to the dumpster outside.

When he saw Kit and Virgie, he shook his head and waved them away.

Virgie parked the car and they got out.

'Don't,' he said as they approached.

'All I need is a few minutes.' Kit walked up to the dumpster, inhaled the scent of burning wood and realized that Jonas was getting rid of his guitars. 'I'm sorry about what happened here.'

'It all started when you arrived,' he said.

'It started when Farley disappeared.' She slammed her hand on the dumpster. 'It started when you didn't tell me the truth about what happened to him.'

'Because I didn't know,' he said.

'That's not true.'

Virgie ignored them, and before Kit realized it she had poked her head into the barn.

'Guess what?' she told Kit. 'Nickel's in there, cleaning up the place.'

Jonas leaned against the dumpster, took a deep breath and said, 'If you care about Farley, please leave. I'll tell you what I can when I can, but I can't say anything today.'

'When?'

'As soon as tomorrow.'

Nickel drifted out, dragging a trash bag behind him. When he spotted Kit and Virgie, he jerked back.

'It's too late to hide,' Kit said.

'All right, then.' He dragged the bag the rest of the way and then he stopped beside Jonas, who was shoving a bag into a large barrel. 'Sorry, man.'

'You don't need to apologize,' Kit said. 'You lied about not knowing him and you lied about Farley leaving here on Friday. Don't you think it's time you tell the truth?'

They glanced at each other. Jonas stared into Nickel's eyes and shook his head.

'I'll be leaving now,' Nickel said. 'This man just lost his music and a good part of his life. That's the only truth I know.'

As he stalked past Kit, she caught the smell of alcohol. She looked at Nickel, who walked as carefully as if he were sober.

He glanced back at Virgie and said, 'Stealing a man's property is about as low as you can go.'

'If you're talking about that little book of yours, I shouldn't have had to take it,' she shot back. 'How else would we know which kids at Lavender Fields you made them guitar straps for?'

'What's she talking about?' Jonas let go of the trash can lid and it slammed shut. 'What have you told her?'

'She stole my book, man.'

'Had to,' Virgie snapped. 'You wasn't about to tell us anything.

You've been lying since we met you. Said you didn't know Farley. Said you didn't know Jonas.' She counted them off on her fingers. 'We will find this Lavender Fields now, but it would be really nice if you would just tell the truth for once.'

'It would be really nice if you didn't steal for once,' he said.

'Wait a minute,' Jonas interrupted. 'Nickel is a friend but he isn't a colleague.'

'A friend of Lavender Fields?' Kit asked.

His nod was short and his expression sad. 'Give me until tomorrow,' he said, 'and then I'll take you there.'

'You really want to wait another day?' Virgie asked as they drove away.

'Absolutely not, and I'm going to tell John Paul.'

'Good.' She glanced over at Kit. 'You hungry?'

At the mention of food, she realized she was. 'I think they have breakfast back at the farmhouse. Let's pick up some supplies anyway. I saw a store on the way in.'

'The only thing we can do is try to find this Lavender Fields,' Kit said.

'Except we don't know where to start.'

Soon they stood outside the store which, with its wooden façade, seemed to blend into the surroundings.

'Look at that.' Kit pointed at it. 'I'll bet the place is like this store in a way. It'll blend in and we won't see it until we're almost inside.'

Virgie took the two steps to the weathered porch. 'Getting inside will be the easy part. Finding it might take some work.'

They walked past a table of warm cider and Kit grabbed one of a few remaining shopping carts. Just ahead, a round counter displayed cheeses, olives and various packaged salads. Kit pushed the cart slowly around it and realized that most of this food was intended for those passing through and not for those who lived here. No wonder it was open so early. Yet all of the items were for lunch, not breakfast. She lifted a package from a stack of sandwiches.

'What about hummus and pita bread?'

Virgie made a face. 'Rabbit food.'

'This pizza's really great,' said the man pushing the cart ahead of theirs. He held up a French bread-shaped package and placed it in his cart.

Kit looked up at him and, as she met his gaze, she had to smile at his enthusiasm.

'Really?'

'They make it fresh every day. I got the last two samples.' He handed his paper plate to Kit. 'I had some on my last trip through. You two can have mine.'

So earnest was his gesture that she took one of the pieces and handed Virgie the other. 'Thanks,' she said. The pizza was good but not outstanding. She spotted an assortment of granola and reached for it. The man continued to stand there. She glanced in his basket and saw three of the pizzas under the one he had just placed there, along with a bottle of wine and various cheeses.

'As you can see, I'm celebrating.' Although he was handsome, his appearance was secondary to the sense of wonder and fun he had managed to bring to a simple shopping trip. 'Actually, I just graduated from medical school.'

'Congratulations.'

He looked like a med student with his aloof yet friendly manner, his dark hair just long enough to highlight his angular jaw, and his voice that, although not all that deep, was firm, almost as if he had made up his mind before he spoke.

'I'm on the way to see my parents in Mendocino. Dad's a doctor too so I never stood a chance.'

So he was from the area. 'Have you ever heard of a place called Lavender Fields?' she asked.

'What kind of place?' He squinted and shook his head. 'A restaurant?'

'A camp. Kind of an off-the-grid community.'

'I don't think so.' His eyes widened. 'Sure I can't sell you on the pizza?'

'It's a little early. Granola will work, though. What do you think, Virgie?'

'It'll do.' She raised an eyebrow at Kit. 'I'm going to look for bottled water. Be right back.'

Virgie walked away. The man didn't move.

'Well, thanks for the tip,' Kit said.

'Glad I could help you out.' He reached for his cart but then stopped. 'Are you staying here or just passing through?'

'Passing through,' she said.

His eyes were so wide and so blue that he must be wearing contacts. 'The best coffee in the area is right next door.'

'Really?' She clutched the handle of her cart.

'Why don't you meet me there? I could use some caffeine before I deal with the graduation party preparations I'm sure my mom is making right now.'

'I don't have time.' She needed to end this grocery-store flirtation.

'Not even for coffee?'

'Afraid not,' she told him. 'We're getting ready to leave. Just looking for something to eat on the road. In fact, we're already late.'

'Enjoy your day then. And have a safe trip wherever you're heading.' He stopped and grinned back at her. 'I'm Will, by the way.'

'Kit.'

'Nice to meet you.'

She watched him walk away, a confident, successful-looking guy who would probably be fun to talk to and nothing else. Yet, as he left, the space she occupied seemed somehow less vibrant, less interesting.

Virgie walked up empty-handed.

'I thought you were going for water,' Kit said.

'Couldn't find it.' Then she smiled at a stack just behind Kit. 'Oh, there it is. Don't know how I missed it.'

'Right. Let's get out of here.'

'There's free local cider and hot chocolate up front,' Virgie said. 'I wouldn't mind some of that chocolate.'

'Warm cider sounds good to me. Let's get some after we check out and sit on one of those benches out there. Maybe we'll come up with a plan.'

They paid for their purchases, got a cup of cider for Kit and hot chocolate for Virgie and sat on two of the glider chairs on the porch of the store. The sun felt relaxing and calm, and Kit knew that they were closer than they had ever been to finding the camp. Once they did that, they would be that much closer to Farley.

'Looks like you aren't in such a hurry, after all.' Kit looked up into the blue eyes of the guy from the store.

He held two paper cups of coffee and handed one to her. 'I was hoping you'd still be here.'

Kit took the cup and put it on the table beside her. 'You didn't have to do this,' she said.

'I know. I just wanted you to see what I meant about it being the best in the area.'

'I'll save it for the road,' she said. 'Let's hope it wakes me up.'

'Oh, it will.' He grinned at her and headed for the steps. 'Glad we had a chance to talk.'

As he headed toward the parking lot, Virgie said, 'Guess you still got it.'

'Meaning?'

'Meaning he ain't bad.'

'As if I don't have enough problems?'

'Right.' Virgie reached over and took a sip of the coffee. Then she grimaced and spit it out.

'What's wrong?' Kit asked. 'Too strong?'

'I can handle strong but there's something wrong with this.' Virgie shuddered. 'It's bitter, Kit. It's gross.' She dumped the rest over the porch rail.

'Let's hope his taste in pizza is better than his taste in coffee,' Kit said.

'Yeah.' Virgie looked down at the now-empty cup in her hand. 'Now, as for his taste in women . . .'

'Stop it!' Kit shuffled down the stairs and headed for the car. 'Let's start looking for that camp.'

THIRTY-THREE

They could not find a doctor who would visit until the next day. Priscilla told them that she would sit by Farley's bedside all night. Michael said he wouldn't hear of it and Jonas insisted that both of them needed to get some rest. He was happy to sit with Farley. Megan realized that, without saying it, Priscilla, Michael and Jonas doubted Will. Part of that was her fault. She shouldn't have told them the truth about his education, maybe even how much he changed the truth around to suit his needs. Poor Chuck would not have tried to roll anyone, and she had only Will's word that Chuck had attacked Farley.

As she warmed the cast-iron teapot Priscilla had given her, she cut a Meyer lemon into small wedges on the wooden board beside it.

'What are you up to?' Will appeared from behind her in the secretive way he had been doing lately.

She drove the knife through the lemon onto the cutting board and refused to jump the way she knew he wanted her to. 'Making tea.'

'You know I hate tea.'

'I'm going to take some to Jonas. Priscilla is out of ginger and they want it for Farley.' She waited for the attack that would follow, the pinching of flesh, the yanking of her arm. Nothing happened. Will stood perfectly still behind her.

Finally he moved closer and she could feel his warm breath on her neck. 'You think that's a good idea when they're trying to keep us away from my patient?'

They're not trying to keep me away from him.

She couldn't say that, of course, but Will would know if he could see her face, so she just kept bending over the lemon as she sliced it.

'We don't have anything to say about that anymore. They're going to find a doctor and Farley will either improve or he won't.'

'Kit Doyle's the problem.' He moved around in front of her and leaned against the counter. 'Until she got here, our lives were good.'

'Farley's wasn't,' she said.

His hand shot out for her arm and then stopped in mid-air. 'It's not his fault that Chuck attacked him. I had to control Farley's pain and that's all I've been doing.'

'You've kept him alive.' She realized she was speaking in a sing-song voice, the way her mother spoke when she was talking about Megan's dad and why he was serving time in Corcoran.

'If these people get any weirder we're going to have to leave.' He shifted against the counter and the sleeve of his sweater slid up from his wrist. On it rested a curved watch with a rose-gold band.

Megan almost dropped the teapot.

'You don't like my watch?' He reached out and pulled her to him.

'I just didn't realize you had one. I mean, no one wears them but it's very pretty.'

'And you've never seen it before?'

'Never,' she told him, and hoped nothing in her expression reflected the fear she felt. 'Can I make anything for you before I take this down to Jonas? Coffee?'

'Thanks for thinking of that, Megs.' He patted her on the ass. 'I picked up some cider at the store today but I forgot and left it in the truck. Would you mind getting it for me?'

'Sure.' There was something wrong with his smile, something wrong with his everything. Megan stopped at the front door, reached down and pretended to tie a shoelace, and then parted the burgundy curtains in the front window. 'I'll be right back.'

She stepped outside, crouched and looked back inside.

Will moved deliberately toward the teapot, reached into his pocket and lifted out a handful of capsules. He lifted the lid of the pot and crushed them into it. Then he replaced the lid, leaned back against the counter and crossed his arms with a smile that carried more satisfaction than she had ever seen from him, not even in bed.

These were the same capsules he'd been giving Farley – pain meds, he said. Now he wanted to give them to Jonas – and to her – without their knowledge. She made her way down to where the truck was hidden. No sign of cider anywhere. Playing for time. That's what her mom would have called what Will was doing by asking her to go down there. Megan wasn't sure what she'd call it. She knew only that she was scared for her life and that she needed to get to Jonas as soon as she could, before Will did anything else.

When she walked back to the cabin the curtains were still open. She exhaled but couldn't get rid of the tightness in her chest. Will planned to drug her. Or worse. At least he didn't know she had watched him put the pills in the tea. With a smile on her face, she stepped inside.

'I couldn't find the cider, Will. I hope no one took it.'

'Might have left it on the counter.' He stretched his arms over his head. 'I'm going to take the truck back to the store and get it.'

'Kind of late for that,' she replied, trying to look at him the way she did when she was concerned.

He grinned as if she had passed the test. 'Thanks for caring, Megs. I'll be fine. See you in a couple of hours.' He nudged her with an elbow. 'Depending on how long you stay with Jonas, of course.'

'About ten minutes, more or less.' She walked up to the pot on the stove. 'Be careful in town.'

Megan brushed her hair in the broken mirror. She cried and then washed her face, forcing herself to accept what she had just witnessed. Will didn't love her. He never had. That should make the rest of this easier.

She walked to Priscilla's and Michael's cabin and knocked softly at the door.

Priscilla opened it and hugged her.

'You OK?' she asked.

'Not really. I need to speak to Jonas.'

'He's with Farley.'

'Would you mind watching Farley and letting Jonas come out and talk to me for a moment?'

'Is it about Will?' Priscilla asked.

Megan nodded and tears filled her eyes. 'I'll wait out here.'

The creek outside the cabin moved softly past. A piercing screech filled the air and she remembered what Will had said about the owl they had encountered earlier. Her skin crawled.

Then she heard the crunching of feet on the path and she turned to see Jonas, his face weary. She ran to him.

He wrapped his arms around her and she knew he didn't want to let go any more than she did.

'What's he done this time?' he asked.

That made her cry. With his arms still around her, she looked into his eyes. 'He asked me to get something out of the truck. Instead, I looked in the window. Jonas, he was putting pills in the ginger tea I was making for you.'

'Do you think he knows?' He stroked a finger under her chin. 'About this?'

'But there is no *this*, Jonas. We've been so decent. You have.'

'So have you.' He smiled at her. 'You're a good woman, maybe the best I've ever known.'

'I'm not. I've done things that are pretty bad and I'll tell you once I work up the courage. There is something I have to tell you now, though, and it's not easy.' She looked away from him, into the trees. 'I'm sorry I didn't say this sooner.'

'Now is just fine.'

In spite of his soothing voice, she could barely bring herself to speak.

'I'm afraid Will has been drugging Farley, maybe even trying to kill him.'

'And what makes you think that?'

She walked away from him, nearer the trees and their soft, still scent.

'Look at me, Megan.'

'I can't.'

'All right then.' He moved close behind her but didn't touch her. 'Why do you think Will's trying to harm Farley?'

'Because Farley saw something that Friday night,' she said. 'When I went back outside the pub that night, Farley and Will were fighting and that didn't make any sense to me. Will hit him with a wrench he took out of the saddlebags on his bike.'

'So that's what happened. It wasn't the guy whose body they found? He wasn't the one attacking Farley?'

'Chuck wouldn't have harmed anyone.' The sharp scent of the redwoods burned her nose like smoke. 'He was trying to protect me from Will.'

'Why didn't you tell me?' He squeezed her shoulders from behind and she turned around to face him. 'Were you afraid of Will?'

'Yes, but not just that.' She reached up and lifted his hands from her shoulders. 'I didn't want anyone to know how I met Chuck. Especially, I didn't want you to know that Will had set us up.'

He squinted as if trying to understand. 'What do you mean?'

'Through a guy we knew from the vineyard. I think you know.'

She expected disappointment in his expression. Maybe even disgust. But Jonas only shook his head and took both of her hands in his.

'I'm sorry you had to go through that.'

'I'm so embarrassed.' She could barely swallow through her tight throat. 'I wouldn't do it now but he controls everything I do. I hate having to tell you this.'

'I haven't been perfect either, you know.'

Megan felt the warmth in his fingers and hung on. She had taken a chance with the truth and he still cared about her. Even better, he was sharing his own truth.

'You mean how you lost your job?'

'I loved the girl,' he said. 'But she was underage, not to mention my student.'

'Will told me.'

'I lost everything. That's when I decided to drop out. I knew Priscilla and Michael because I had taught music to Priscilla. She and Farley were two years apart in school.'

'What happened to the girl?' She realized she was whispering. 'The one you loved.'

'She couldn't stay with me after what happened. Too much guilt.' He lifted her chin. 'And, since we're being honest here, she wasn't the first one.'

'Chuck wasn't the first one either.' The truth popped out, just like that.

'Did you love him?' The question sounded tender, innocent.

'I knew him less than an hour but he treated me like a lady,' she said. 'There were two others, a guy named Rudy and another one. Chuck was supposed to be the last.'

'Only three, and then no more?'

'That's what Will said but it was probably another lie. He said we needed the money but it wasn't that. He was just trying to control me, and he did.'

He nodded and squeezed her hand tighter. 'More than two for me, but I talked myself into thinking I cared for them, that somehow I could be their great protector.'

His honesty calmed Megan. It also stabbed her heart.

'Is that how you feel about me?' She knew he wouldn't lie and forced herself to take a breath.

'It was at first.'

'And now?' She picked at her skirt, unable to look at him.

'Don't you know?'

'I know my hopes,' she said. 'I'm really afraid, though, not just for us, but for Farley.'

'I'll stay with him tonight. Tomorrow we go to town and get help.'

'What about Kit Doyle?' she asked.

'I'm not sure. If she exposes the camp they'll all have to move, and they aren't hurting anyone here. It might be hard on the kids. But Kit knows it exists. I promised I'd bring her here tomorrow.'

'Do you think that's a good idea?'

'Once we get a doctor here she might as well come too. She deserves to see her friend.'

He was such a good man that she had to fight to keep the tears from coming. She hadn't known men could be like that. 'There's one more thing I haven't told you.' She made herself look into his eyes this time.

'What's that?'

'When I saw Farley on the ground that night, I told Will we had to bring him back here or I would report what happened. Will wanted to get out of there before any more people came outside the bar. He handed me Farley's cell phone and told me to get rid of it.'

'Then of course he planned on killing Farley, but why?'

'Because Farley witnessed whatever happened to Chuck. That's all I can figure.'

'You have to tell Priscilla and Michael,' Jonas said. 'They deserve to know.'

'Even though Will saved Callie?'

'Even though. If he did. The man's a liar and a latent sociopath. I wouldn't trust anything he says.'

Although she wasn't sure what all of that was, she already agreed with it and she knew she had to say the rest. 'I didn't get rid of the phone.'

'You didn't?' He grabbed her arm.

'I couldn't. Instead I hid it at the fruit stand and planned to come back for it. Before I could, Kit Doyle found it. She let me know and told me there was a selfie Farley took at the pub that Friday with me in the background.'

'Kit Doyle again.' Although he didn't move, he seemed to pull away from her. 'Then we are definitely going to bring her here tomorrow. For now, let's just stick close to Farley. I don't want you going back to Will. He's too dangerous.'

'I'm afraid to leave,' she said. 'He'll kill me if I try to.'

Jonas took her by both arms and moved closer to her. 'He already tried to kill you tonight. He tried to kill both of us.'

THIRTY-FOUR

Kit sat on the wooden step leading to the cabin where Jonas hadn't been all night. Virgie had insisted on sitting there with her but Kit finally talked her into going back to the farmhouse.

'You OK to drive?' She had tried to hide a yawn.

'Of course,' she said. 'It's an easy road. As soon as I talk to him I'll be back in my room.'

The cold, hard front step didn't lend itself to more than occasional moments of drifting off until a night sound – a bird screeching, a pine cone dropping – roused her. Yet Kit had to do that because Jonas could no longer keep avoiding and lying to her.

A light piercing her eyes roused her. Morning maybe. No. The sharpness of it made her squint. A flashlight. She waved it away.

'What are you doing here?'

Kit blinked into his eyes. Jonas glared back at her. 'Waiting for you.' She glanced around and realized from the pale light in the sky that it must be close to dawn.

He sat down beside her and Kit could almost feel his weariness seep into the step.

'What do you want now?'

'The truth,' she said. 'I'm sure you know about the selfie in the bar and Megan in the background.'

He glanced down. 'What makes you say that?'

'I'm tired of not sharing information with you.' She turned to face him. 'I know you care about Farley and I'm certain you know where he is. Can't we just level with each other?'

'We can try.' In the dawn light, his face looked angry and uncertain. 'You go first.'

'OK.' She took a breath. 'I was in the barn when you showed Megan the guitar strap.'

'How?' He seemed ready to bolt but stayed where he was.

'You wouldn't tell me the truth and you still haven't, by the way.'

'You were in the barn?' Color flooded his cheeks.

Kit looked away. She knew he was remembering trying to kiss Megan and figuring out that Kit might have witnessed that.

'And thanks to Nickel, I know about Lavender Fields. It's a beautiful name, by the way.'

He put his head in his hands, sighed and looked at her. 'It's a beautiful place. Do you know how many lives and futures you'll destroy if you bring attention to it?'

'All I care about is Farley's life right now. Farley's future.'

'Me too,' he said, and she was struck by how much older he looked than he had when she had first seen him on Sunday.

'Where is he, Jonas?'

'He's there. He's improving. That's all I can tell you now.'

Her throat tightened and she tried to hold herself back, just keep him talking. 'You said you'd tell me more today.'

He gestured around them. 'It's barely today,' he said. 'Check back with me later. I need to be sure he's all right. We've had some problems I'll explain later – not Farley, something else.'

'What's making you hold back?' she asked, and in the dim light caught the color in his cheeks. 'Are you worried about Megan?'

'Of course. I'm worried about all of them.'

'You don't have to be. We can keep her out of it. I'm pretty sure she didn't kill that guy at the bar. You've got to tell me where she is, though. Where the kids are.'

'Very soon.' Jonas rocked back and forth as if in the chair on the porch instead of the top step.

'Now,' she said. 'All I want is to find Farley. I don't care if you've broken laws. I don't care what you're growing in your backyard.'

'We're breaking no laws,' he told her, 'and the casual assumption that we are insults me.'

'I'm sorry,' she said, 'but you know what I do for a living. What I *did* for a living.' She crossed her arms over her chest and tried to buffer herself from the cold. 'If you're not breaking the law, not even selling pot or whatever, what are you trying to hide?'

'Ourselves.' His voice was soft. He rose and said, 'You're cold. Come on inside.'

The back door stood open and Jonas stepped back. Unlike Nickel's backyard, the place was a mess of folded lawn chairs, piled-up sprinklers and twisted and cracked hoses.

'Does it always look this way?' Kit asked.

'I find my sense of order with music, not this stuff.' Jonas walked back to the door and bent down. 'Someone managed to destroy the lock.' He lifted the mangled piece of steel to her. 'You wouldn't know anything about this, would you?'

'If I did, would I be sitting on your front step?'

'Good point.' He sighed. 'Farley always said you would be the first to understand our life out here.'

'And he does?'

'He definitely does.' Jonas pulled out a kitchen chair and sat backward on it. 'Do you know the term permacuturalist?'

'It's a way of producing food, right? So that you don't destroy the earth's resources. Is that what Lavender Fields is?'

'Not entirely. There are a lot of off-the-grid groups in places like this – people who believe technology is destroying the planet and the people on it.'

'But if they are not breaking the law,' she said, 'everyone is content to leave them alone.'

'Unless someone in their group does break the law,' he told her. 'About eight years ago, Priscilla and Michael were working at a Southern California community college when Priscilla was in a wreck that almost killed her and her oldest daughter, Abigail.'

'I thought Callie was her daughter.'

'She's younger, just a baby. Abigail was about the same age Callie is now when it happened. The air bags exploded and trapped them inside. No one stopped to help Priscilla. All they did was take photos with their phones until a Good Samaritan came along. Priscilla and Michael decided to move off the grid and give up every electronic crutch they had ever leaned on. That's it.'

'They aren't breaking the law?' she asked again.

'Absolutely not. They and the others there are raising their kids the way they could never do in mainstream society. They have strict rules for membership. That's why Nickel can't join, even though he's been extremely helpful.'

'He told you about Virgie and me!' She pulled a chair across from him. What looked like a hand-woven pillow covered its hard wood seat. 'When we came here that day, you were expecting us, weren't you?'

He glanced down at his hands and pushed an imaginary cuticle with a fingernail. 'You're right. And even then I wasn't smart enough to hide the port. That should give you an idea of what kind of hardened criminals we are.'

'But you don't live with them?' Before he could answer, she got it. 'Of course not. They can't send the kids to public school so you tutor them, don't you? And you teach them music.'

He nodded. 'It's one of the most rewarding aspects of my life. Each one of those kids is like Farley was when he came to me. *Tabula rasa*. A blank slate.'

'How did Farley get there?' She held her breath.

'I can't address that yet.' He slumped in the chair but maintained his easy-going façade. 'Farley has always said you're a good woman, and if we had met any other way I know we would have been friends. But for now – just for now – I have to put you off until later.'

'Why?'

'Because I need to talk to some people.' He clasped his hands around the back of the chair. 'I owe them that.'

'Do you really think I can just sit around until you're ready to tell me?' Kit said. 'Assuming you ever are.'

'You're going to have to.'

'No, I'm not.' She stood up and pushed the chair against the wall beside an open roll-top desk covered with sheets of music. 'I'm going to start looking for the camp now. I know it's around here and there can be only so many roads that are close to both this place and the fruit stand.'

'You won't find it,' he said. 'And you could put yourself in danger by looking for it. Please wait until I speak to those in charge.'

'What do you mean by put myself in danger?' she asked him.

'That's all I can say right now, and it's more than I should.' He pointed at the door and its smashed lock. 'I didn't break into my own cabin. I didn't burn the guitars in my own barn. Please don't take any chances. I promise to get back to you right away.'

'I'm still going to look,' she said. 'I can't help it.'

'I wish you wouldn't.' He started toward the door. 'If you do, it could be worse for Farley.'

'Worse how?'

'That's all I can say.' Jonas stood up wearily. 'But I wouldn't lie about something this important.'

THIRTY-FIVE

Even though Jonas said he wouldn't lie, she wasn't certain. Someone had broken into his barn and now his home. Yet he claimed the group at the camp was peaceful. Maybe he was just trying to keep her from one more day of searching. If so, he had failed.

As she drove through the narrow road to the forest and the farmhouse, she hoped she would see John Paul's truck when she turned into the dirt drive. Only a camper, a motorcycle and two cars were parked there. John Paul's truck was gone. Although she wasn't surprised, she felt a stab of loss. Then she told herself that he probably was just looking for an excuse to avoid working with her. That had been their problem from the start. He wasn't comfortable working with anyone – especially a woman – who wasn't a cop.

She looked in at Virgie, who was still asleep, glad that they had keys to each other's rooms. A tray outside Virgie's held a cup of coffee and a covered platter. Room service, but Kit wanted to go downstairs. She closed the door slowly behind her and locked it from the outside.

The free breakfast that came with the room was probably long from coming, but the tiny kitchen had a basket of rolls on the counter and a cooler of soda and bottled water. She grabbed one of each and sat on a comfortable lounge chair. With a live signal, she could search for maps of the area and she might have a better chance of finding the Lavender Fields camp. It had to be close to both the fruit stand and Jonas's school. She began searching and soon realized that the school and the stand were almost across from each other with only forest between them. The camp must be there, maybe even walking distance from the fruit stand.

Kit continued checking, trying to narrow in on the location, trying to focus. The smell of coffee filled the tiny room. She heard the rustle of noise in the kitchen and someone pulled open the heavy drapes. Early morning sunlight and the scent and sound of sizzling bacon warmed her at once.

The French doors opened and someone sat down on the settee beside her. The rattle of a newspaper drew her attention from her phone.

She glanced up at the guy on the loveseat, who had moved the newspaper and was looking intently at his own phone. Although a baseball cap covered his dark hair, the blue eyes were the same.

'I can't believe this,' he said. 'Good to see you again.' The same doctor guy from the country store smiled over at her.

'How was your party?' she asked.

'Overdone, like everything else my mom does. And fun. I'm on my way back. I thought you said you were passing through.'

'I am.' She felt herself color and glanced down at her phone as if to say she didn't want to talk anymore. 'Something came up so I'm going to stay a little longer.'

'Not much to do around this place,' he said. 'It's beautiful, though. A walk might be nice.'

'I'm not really looking for anything to do.'

'Working?'

'Yes.' She lifted her phone. 'I'd better get back to it.'

'Looks like you have some kind of map there.' He squinted at her screen. 'Are you looking for directions for anything? I might be able to help.'

Kit was tempted. Still, the guy was too friendly for this and maybe any time of day. If she asked him for help he might pretend to know more than he did just to keep hanging around.

'Not really,' she said. 'I just like having an idea of where I am.'

'Not always easy out here unless you are as familiar with the land as I am. My dad was a forest ranger. I could find anywhere from here to Mendocino in my sleep.'

'Do you know where Ananda Free School is?' she asked.

'Not far. Maybe two miles.' He leaned back in the settee as if to give her space. 'Probably the best private school in the area. They're closed now, though. Spring break.'

'Good *morn*-ing.' An older woman in an apron greeted them with practiced cheerfulness and started filling the chafing dishes lining the wall along the windows. Kit glanced up, both wanting to ask this guy more questions and afraid to take the chance.

'Is anyone at the school right now?' she asked. 'Someone must be in charge.'

'That would be Jonas.' He made a face. 'Nice guy, but when school's on break he could be anywhere. Last I heard, some friend of his was visiting and they were hanging out.'

'Hanging out where?' Kit did her best to pretend disinterest.

'I'm not sure. As I said, I only stay here going through to visit my parents.' He inhaled the breakfast scents filling the room. 'I don't know about you but I'm ready to eat. Can I get you a plate?'

'Thanks, but I can do it.' Still something not quite right. Kit just couldn't figure out what it was. Two couples came through the French doors as if led by the scent of the food. Kit let them go ahead and motioned to the man to do the same. Instead, he stood back with her.

'You go first.' He stepped aside and Kit realized how hungry she was. So much for the yogurt and granola. She picked up a spatula, then a warm plate from the stack, and slid an omelet onto it. Then two pieces of toast. Then what looked and smelled like freshly fried hash browns. And cream-drenched berries – either blackberry or huckleberry. Virgie would know. In fact, Kit needed to fix a plate for her.

Out of the corner of her eye, she watched the blue-eyed guy do the same. At the end of the line he looked at the pile of fragrant waffles. 'I dare you,' he said with a grin.

'This is all I can manage.' He was starting to annoy her. 'You go for it, though.'

'I will.' He lifted an empty coffee cup to the espresso machine and handed the cup to Kit. Then he took another one for himself.

The cheerful woman returned and opened the sliding glass doors leading to the patio. Kit headed that way.

'Want to share a table?' He was already there, pulling out a wrought-iron chair.

What would it hurt? Maybe he would tell her something about the area if he really did know it as well as he said he did.

They sat across from each other at the table, and Kit realized she probably ought to get back to Virgie. First, though, she needed to ask him some questions.

'So tell me about Jonas,' she said.

'Just a guy who likes teaching kids,' he said. 'People around here are a little weird, so he has some of that. I'd never stay here if I didn't have to visit my parents.'

Kit gripped her cup and finally remembered. 'What did you say your father does?' she asked.

His smile didn't move but his skin flushed. 'Doctor,' he said. 'Like me.'

'Didn't you just say he was a forest ranger?'

'No way.' He cocked his head. 'That would be my grandfather. What an amazing man he was. That's how I learned my way around this place.' He took his coffee cup in both hands. 'Anything you want to find around here, I can show you where it is.'

Just another pick-up line. Kit sipped her coffee. No reason to push this, especially since she no longer believed he knew anything. 'I'll be leaving soon,' she said, 'and I'm sure you will be too.'

'Right after check-out. You and your friend will probably be doing the same.'

Kit nodded and took a second sip of coffee. It was as bitter as the first. Then she remembered the coffee Virgie had poured out the day before at the country store – and the cup on the tray outside the door to Virgie's room.

'I'll be right back.' She put the cup down on the table. 'Wait right here, please.'

She got up, ran outside and took the stairs as fast as she could.

The door to the room stood open, and when Kit stepped inside she saw why. Virgie lay face-down on the floor, her arms stretched out and her breathing shallow. The coffee cup was tipped over on the nightstand beside her bed. Kit reached for her, felt cold flesh and headed for the stairs, shouting for help.

'What's going on?' John Paul's door flew open and he stood there.

'Virgie. I think she's been drugged.'

'Call for law enforcement. Don't let anybody leave the premises.' He shot orders at her as he ran to Virgie's room. 'Now, Doyle!'

Somehow, her legs moved. She called for help again and everyone in the kitchen, including the woman in the apron, crowded around her at the foot of the stairs.

'Someone here poisoned my friend.' Her lips trembled and she tried to imitate John Paul's tone of authority. 'A police officer is with her now.' She didn't bother to say former police officer. 'No one can leave here. No one.' She took one wild look at the stunned faces in front of her and rushed to the patio. No one sat at the tables. Everyone who had been outside was now inside. The blue-eyed man had gone.

THIRTY-SIX

Virgie sat propped up in bed and sipped from a large mug of broth the woman who owned the farmhouse had brought her.

'Same guy, isn't he?' She looked up at Kit, who sat on one side of the bed. 'From the market?'

'What guy?' John Paul pulled a chair up beside Kit.

'A man who approached us at the grocery store yesterday,' Kit said.

'Approached *her*,' Virgie said. 'And showed up here when I went downstairs for a soda. He was coming down the stairs at the same time. I should've known.'

'He gave you the coffee?' John Paul asked.

She shook her head against her pillows. 'It was outside the door. Stupid me. I thought it was room service. I should've known after yesterday.'

'What did he do?' John Paul tensed.

'Chatted Kit up. Brought her a coffee. I thought he was just interested in her – you know. Can't believe I didn't see through him.' She turned her head away. 'I'm too soft now. That's all.'

'You're fine.' Kit took her hand. 'It's a good thing you didn't drink much of it.'

'Guy sucks at his job.' Virgie squeezed her hand and turned back with a grin. 'If you're going to drug someone you'd better do a taste test first.'

There was a knock on the door and John Paul got up to open it. The gray-haired woman in the apron stepped inside.

'I'm so sorry about this,' she said. 'We've never had the slightest disturbance in our little inn.'

'Understood, ma'am.' John Paul stepped aside so that she could approach Virgie.

'Someone tried to kill me,' Virgie told her. 'I'd sure like to know where he is.'

'I wish I could tell you.' The woman shook her head. 'We've gone through the guest logs and everyone who checked in is accounted for.'

'What about the motorcycle?' Kit asked.

The woman shook her head again. 'No motorcycle. It would be noted.'

'Are you sure you don't remember him?' Kit asked. 'Long dark hair? Bright blue eyes, probably contacts?'

'No.' She turned toward the door. 'Do you mind if I leave now? I have guests waiting.'

'We can't keep you here.' John Paul stood at the door, as official and unyielding as when he had let her in. 'The officers investigating this will need to talk to you, though.'

'Officers investigating?' She paused. 'Was the man you're describing a doctor?'

'He said he was,' Kit said. 'Why?'

'Because a doctor from Mendocino stopped by today and asked about what it would take to set up a party here. He said he had just graduated from medical school and wanted to surprise his parents with a weekend away from home.'

'That's the man.' Kit's stomach knotted. 'Do you remember his name?' she asked.

'Now that you mentioned a motorcycle, I think his name might be like that.' She shoved her teased hair behind her ears. 'Harley? Yes, I think that might be it. Harley Black. I didn't write it down. We get a lot of inquiries.'

'Farley Black,' Kit said.

'Right.' She started to back out of the room.

'Wait.' Kit followed her. 'What color was his hair?'

'Black.' She turned to John Paul. 'I'll cooperate in any way, of course. I just hope the investigators will be discreet.'

'Of course.'

'And now I really do need to get back to my guests.'

'We'll be in touch with you soon.' John Paul moved toward the door. 'Just be watchful.'

'So,' Virgie said once the woman had left, 'we need to find this guy.'

'No we,' Kit told her. 'As soon as you're able, you're going home.'
John Paul nodded. 'You both probably ought to head back.'

'No,' Virgie said. 'We've seen more than you have. We can find out what's going on and who's doing it.'

'Except . . .' John Paul stood, '. . . one of you has been drugged and the other one could have been. Tell me everything you know. It won't be the same, but at least it will get you away from this guy.'

'This guy who probably harmed Farley or knows what happened,' Kit said. 'That's why he used his name. He's playing some kind of crazy game. I'm not going, John Paul.'

'Neither am I,' Virgie said. 'I'm not leaving Kit.'

'And I'm not leaving Farley.'

He turned his back to them and strode to the window overlooking the pond. When he turned to face them, he stared into Kit's eyes and said, 'OK. I have no jurisdiction here and I can't make you leave.'

'I think we're close,' she said. 'Jonas asked me to wait and then he's going to tell us where Farley is.'

'He knows?' John Paul sat on the edge of the bookcase.

Virgie cleared her throat and looked at Kit.

'Are you with us?' she asked him.

'I've always been with you.' He glanced out the window again. 'Right now, we've got to stay together, though. That guy got too close today.'

'Do you know about the guitars in Jonas's barn?' she asked.

'Only about the fire.' He met her gaze. 'I still have contacts.'

'Do you know who set it?'

'I don't have any idea. I don't even know why he was making them. All Farley said was that Jonas had a gift for woodworking and was teaching him.'

'He never mentioned the guitars?'

'Never specifically. He just talked about how smart the guy is and how his only weakness is . . .' He paused. 'Women.'

'Farley told me the same.' She got up, walked toward the window and slid the glass open so that fresh air could fill the room. Then she glanced at Virgie, who nodded and pushed herself up in bed as alert as always, or at least pretending to be. 'The guitars were for kids Jonas tutored in an off-the-grid community.'

'Commune?'

'Permaculturists – people who have had it with technology. The woman at the fruit stand is part of it. Jonas is part of it.'

'And Farley?'

'I think he knows about it and always has,' she said. 'Now it's your turn.'

'I did find a lead, but first tell me who set fire to the guitars.'

'Maybe Megan. That's just a wild guess, and it doesn't feel right even though she's impulsive enough. Maybe it was this guy who tried to drug Virgie and me.'

'But why?' He paced the room. 'There's always a reason.'

'True.' For the first time in a long time, Kit remembered how it felt to work *with* John Paul and not against him.

'Now,' she leaned against the cushion of the chair, 'what do you know that Virgie and I don't?'

'Mind handing me Farley's phone?'

Virgie glanced at her but Kit knew John Paul wouldn't try anything weird at this point. They needed each other as they never had before.

'Virgie?' Kit said.

She pursed her lips at John Paul. 'It's in my bag. Charged last time I saw it.'

He started for it and then smiled at Kit. 'We're working together now,' he said. 'You do the honors.'

Huddled with him on the window seat over the phone, Kit pulled up the photo of Farley and Mickey and handed it to John Paul.

'Farther back. Farley took other selfies.'

'Virgie and I already went through them,' she said. 'Just bar shots of Mickey and him.'

'And this guy.' He tapped on a photo of a man who seemed to be leaving the bar.

An average-looking, dark-haired man, somewhere between thirty and forty with a winery logo on one side of his blue shirt, waved at the camera as he passed.

'Who is he?' Kit asked.

'You told me about the camp so I'll tell you about Rudy.' His eyes lit up but his unsmiling expression remained the same. 'First thing I did was ID everyone in the photo. The bartender, Mickey. He knew this guy.'

'How'd you get a copy of the photo?' she asked.

'Off your phone. Sorry.'

'I should have known.'

'Mickey told me that this guy had some kind of relationship with the girl from the fruit stand. Megan.'

'What kind of relationship?'

'He didn't tell Mickey anything except that the guy who died is a friend of his, and Rudy isn't certain that his friend's death was an accident.'

'Then let's go visit Rudy,' Kit said.

He glanced at Virgie and shook his head. 'First thing this morning.'

'That would be now.' Virgie flipped off the pale blue quilt covering her bed. 'Let's go find Rudy.'

THIRTY-SEVEN

John Paul made some calls and Kit sat on the bed next to Virgie, feeling grateful that they were finally working together. It wouldn't be easy for the two of them. John Paul would never understand her friendship with Farley. They would have to deal with their personal relationship later.

Only one problem with that. Kit watched as he sat beside her on the bed and lifted a water glass to Virgie's lips. She watched his face as he talked about how much they needed to find Farley.

After he went downstairs to check out, Kit and Virgie sat overlooking the pond outside.

'You look much better now,' Kit said.

'You too.' She paused. 'He's not a bad guy. John Paul.'

'If he leads us to Rudy, he'll be stellar.'

'You know what I'm saying, Kit. Don't act like you don't.'

'We'll talk about it later.' She pulled their bags to the door. 'At least we travel light.'

'Depends on how you define travel.' Virgie pulled herself up.

'You know you can stay here,' Kit told her.

'What would you say if I said that to you?'

'Probably what you're ready to say to me.'

John Paul returned and Kit put her hand out to Virgie. 'Come on. Go slowly.'

'I'm fine.' Virgie started for the door and grabbed Kit's arm. 'Whoa,' she said. 'I'd better sit for a minute.'

'Why don't you sit for an hour?' John Paul told her. 'You've got your phone in case you need us. We'll talk to Rudy and come back for you. Then we can all go looking for the camp.'

'What if the guy comes back here?' Kit said.

'He won't.' Virgie sat on the edge of the bed. 'Think about it. He tried to drug you and did the same to me. He's moving onto whatever he's doing next, whatever that is.'

'If he's the one who burned the guitars Jonas probably knows who he is,' Kit said. 'He hinted that someone in the camp might be breaking the law. In the meantime, we'll talk to Rudy and get back as soon as we can.'

The other guests stood in the patio area speaking in worried tones. Kit climbed in John Paul's truck and they pulled away from the parking lot.

'Do you think she's safe?' she asked John Paul.

'Virgie nailed it. This guy is moving ahead to carry out whatever plan he has. I don't think he'll backtrack. Besides, the hotel staff know him.'

They drove past a small group setting up a classic-car show in a park. A gold-trimmed red train moved north on overhead rails.

'I wish we'd compared notes sooner,' Kit said. 'I made the mistake of thinking the group Farley is with was breaking the law in some way.'

'We don't know they're not.'

'Jonas said they're not. He insisted.'

'That doesn't mean he's telling the truth.' He glanced over at her and said, 'Why are you smiling?'

'Because I've missed this. Even when we argue, you make me think.'

'Same here. I've missed working together as well.' He reached for her hand. 'I've missed *you*.' They held onto each other like that for a moment. 'And I'm still going to buy you flowers,' he said.

That broke the tension. They both laughed. He let go of her hand and took hold of the steering wheel again.

'You do that.' She pointed to a field of lavender. Some of the bushes were almost as tall as she was. 'That's my absolute favorite.'

He put down the windows so the smell of it could fill the truck. 'I wish I could stop right here and pick you a bunch of it, Kit.'

'Soon,' she said and then realized how callous that must sound. 'Once Farley is safe and this is behind us.'

The road signs directed them to sustainably farmed vineyards, redwoods overlooking natural gardens and the green-and-yellow blur of canola fields.

'This is the place.' John Paul parked in a redwood grove perched above a sweep of vineyards. 'Cabernet,' he said. 'I might as well tell you the rest of it. I've been here before and Rudy refused to speak to me.'

'I figured.'

They got out of the truck and walked toward the wine bar, a simple, rustic arrangement of a counter of wooden planks and a few stools.

'It's really beautiful,' Kit said. 'No wonder people come here to escape from technology and everything else.'

'Could you do that?' he asked.

'Probably not. Remember, I was practically born in a radio station.' They walked farther. 'Could you?'

'I don't think it's realistic.' He looked down at her and for a moment Kit thought he might take her hand again. 'The bad guys are still out there. They're still out *here*. If you go off the grid, give up technology and whatever else these people are doing, you have no control over your destiny. They can walk in and take everything from you. You and I wouldn't know this much about what happened to Farley without our phones – or his!'

She wanted to ask more but they neared the wine bar and a dark-haired woman polishing glasses with a spotless white cloth that matched her apron smiled at them.

'We don't open until later.'

'We need to talk to Rudy.' His brisk, official tone seemed to work.

'One moment.' The woman picked up a phone and spoke into it. Then she pointed at a tiny structure surrounded by more rough planks. 'He'll meet you in the office.'

Wearing the same spotless blue shirt as he had in the photo

John Paul had showed her, Rudy strode in, taller and better looking in person.

'Hey, man.' He nodded at John Paul. 'I got to get to work, so make it fast.'

'Understand,' John Paul said. 'We need to find that woman you were with and we need to do it today.'

'No can do.'

'My friend Farley is probably with her.' Kit stepped closer to him. He glanced away from her gaze. 'You know Farley. You heard him play at the pub, didn't you?'

'Yeah.' He shifted. 'I heard him and I don't want no trouble, OK?'

'What about Chuck?' she asked.

'I'm not even going there with you.'

'The man was your friend and you aren't talking about him?'

'Hey, how do you know that?' He jerked around and poked a finger at John Paul. 'If Mickey turned snitch, I need to know that.'

'Kit asked you a question.' John Paul moved closer to her so that Rudy was forced to look at both of them. 'What about Chuck?'

'I don't know, man.' He turned up empty palms. 'One minute we were buddies and the next, he was dead, drowned, with his head bashed in. I didn't do it, if that's what you're thinking.'

'We know that.' Kit lowered her voice so as to offset John Paul's commanding tone. 'But Rudy, you were at the pub the night Chuck died.'

'You can't prove that,' he shot back.

'Actually, I can show you a photo of you there,' she said, 'but I'd rather you just tell me the truth.'

'I got nothing to say.' He turned away from them and paced the room. 'I told you he was my friend. We worked together. Had a drink sometimes.'

'What about Megan?' Kit asked.

He sucked down another sip from his water bottle. 'I don't know who you mean.'

'Sure you do. You spent time with her.'

'Mickey will pay for this.' His voice shook. 'He's the only one who knew.'

'How well did you know her?' she asked.

'I would've seen her again,' he said. 'Hell, I would have dated her. Will, though. He was just too much trouble.'

'Will?' Kit asked, and remembered the guy at the grocery store.

'He set me up with her.'

She remembered the photograph on Farley's phone. A selfie with Mickey and him. Yet behind them, Megan stood with a man holding onto her, a man she denied knowing when Kit confronted her at the fruit stand. It was a photograph that was now on Virgie's phone, her phone and clearly John Paul's phone as well.

She reached for hers and pulled the photo onto the screen. Her hand trembled as she looked at it. Although the man's features were blurred and his hair was pulled back here, he was the same one in the photograph – the same one they had seen in the store. Will.

'Do you know what this man does for a living?' she asked.

'No ma'am.' He glanced over at John Paul. 'I'd like to go to work now.'

'We appreciate your honesty,' John Paul said. 'We know you had nothing to do with what happened with your friend. Did you see anything else after you left that night?'

'Tell you the truth, I didn't want to see anything.' He clenched his hands together. 'I liked the lady and thought she might like me. When Will asked if I had any friends who might, you know, be interested, I told him Chuck.'

'Why?' Kit said.

'I don't know. Maybe because Chuck was the most decent guy I knew. Maybe because I thought he would be nice to her and then she might be nice to me.'

'I understand, man.' John Paul clapped him on the shoulder.

'I'm ashamed. I never did anything like that before. Never will again.'

'Do you know where she lives?' Kit asked.

'No, and I don't even want to think about it. Probably with him.' He sighed. 'Now, I've got to get to work.'

'Will's the guy,' Kit told John Paul as they left. 'I talked to him in the store. He's the one who drugged Virgie and tried to drug me.'

THIRTY-EIGHT

Later that day, Farley seemed to stir.

'Where?' he mumbled. 'Where.'

'He's coming out of it,' Jonas said and hugged Megan, even though Michael and Priscilla stood in the room near the piano.

'You know why, don't you?' Megan slid her arm around his waist. 'Whatever Will was giving him wasn't helping him at all.'

'That's not your fault.' Priscilla hugged her.

'I know he saved Callie,' she said.

'Now that we know what a liar he is we'll never know what really happened.'

Megan felt her eyes fill with tears. 'Please let me stay here with you.'

'Of course.' Priscilla hugged her again. 'We decided that a few days ago.'

Jonas gave her a short nod and returned to Farley's room. 'I'll contact Kit Doyle,' he said. 'She'll figure a way to get help out here. And we're going to need help for Farley now that he's coming around.'

Megan and Priscilla sat on the window seat in front of the side window.

'I'm sorry I wasn't honest with you sooner,' Megan told her. 'Will knew you had money stashed and he wanted to steal from all of you. I never would have gone along with that.'

'We trust you.' Priscilla squeezed her arm. 'Let's just sit here until he comes back. It won't be long.'

'He has clothes here,' Megan said.

'No longer. They're in the barn in bags, totally intact. We haven't harmed any of his possessions.'

'He won't care.' Megan felt tears squeeze out of her eyes. 'You were kind to us.'

'It's all right.'

They sat there on the cushions lining the window seat and Megan felt herself calm down.

'You and Jonas.' Priscilla nodded and met her eyes. 'That just might work.'

'I don't know.'

'You're in love with him, aren't you?'

She felt herself flush. 'I just don't know how we're going to figure it all out.'

'You will.' Priscilla said. 'You know why? Because Jonas is in love with you too.'

'I hope you're right.'

'I know I am.' She rubbed her large belly. 'Now, let's try to figure out if our home is still safe or if we need to move.'

'I hope we don't,' Megan said. 'But if we have to, I'll do everything I can to help. I feel as if I've brought all of this on.'

'You didn't know what you were involved with. People like Will have no conscience. They can't keep their own lies and their own desires straight. I'm glad he brought you to us, though.' She squeezed Megan's hand. 'And to Jonas.'

Megan knew she was blushing but finally she no longer had to hide her emotions.

'I know he's ready to leave everything behind but his music,' she said. 'Would you allow him to join us full time?'

'We have discussed that in the past and, although we had some reservations, yes. I will need to speak to Michael and to the other families but I think this might be a good time for that.'

They sat there as the sun warmed them. Finally Megan said, 'Why did you have reservations about Jonas before?'

'Nothing to do with you.'

'What then?'

'This life isn't right for everyone. We love Jonas. He's wonderful to our children and to us, for that matter.' She stood. 'And you know what? If we're ready to accept him now, I think that's the only explanation anyone needs. The rest is between you two.'

Megan rose as well, thinking how easy this was. No hiding. No pretending. 'He's shared with me,' she said. 'As I have with him.'

The sound of car brakes interrupted them. Megan ran to the window in front of the cabin and Priscilla followed. Dust billowed up around a dark green van. Will got out from behind the wheel. On the passenger's side a woman sat with her back to them.

'This is what I've been waiting for,' Priscilla said. 'We need to get him out of here right now. Finish it.'

Megan squinted though the sunlight coming through the window. 'Who's the woman?'

'No idea.' Priscilla cupped her hand over her stomach. 'Michael, Jonas. You might want to join us out here.'

They walked outside the cabin as Will marched up the path. He wore preppy-looking off-white pants and a matching polo shirt under a reversible quilted navy vest which, in spite of the weather, he hadn't zipped. No longer did Will resemble anyone at this camp. He looked like the doctor he now probably believed he was.

'You don't need to come, Megan,' Priscilla said.

'I want to.' She eyed the woman in the van, who was turned so far around, the collar of her white coat pulled up so high that they couldn't see her.

Megan had been that woman once. She had been that submissive, that afraid.

'I came for my things.' Will dipped his head as if greeting strangers.

'What about Farley?' Priscilla asked.

'That's your problem.' The wind blew his dark hair straight up, baring his high, narrow forehead. 'Quite frankly, it was never my idea to bring him back here in the first place. The minute he recovers – and he will now – he'll tell Kit Doyle and his cop friend where you are, and your shabby little paradise will be invaded by law enforcement, media, you name it.'

'If that happens we will deal with it,' Priscilla said, 'but not the way you dealt with Farley.'

'Hey, I got coerced into that one.' He pointed at Megan and grinned at Jonas. 'And for the record, buddy, don't be too quick to think you have a prize there. There's a lot about her that you don't know.'

His words stung and Megan knew he was enjoying watching the burn spread to her face. 'Oh, he knows, Will.' She walked up to him, past Jonas, who tried to hold her back. 'Everyone knows everything.'

'Including your plan to steal our funds,' Priscilla said and moved beside Megan in front of the men who stood before the door of the cabin like a barrier between Will and Farley. 'That's sad because if you had needed something we would have done our best to provide it.'

'Typical of you to take the word of this tramp.' He motioned Priscilla aside. 'I'm going in to get my stuff, including some valuables you better not have touched.'

His windblown hair emphasized his piercing eyes, and even though his manner was pleasant, Megan felt cold all over.

'I know what you came for.' She stared at his empty wrist.

That's what he wanted. The watch that had belonged to Chuck – the proof that he had probably killed him.

'Let's keep this friendly, all right?' He reached into his vest pocket and pulled out a pistol.

Megan drew in a sharp breath.

Priscilla didn't move. 'There's no need for that,' she said.

'My point exactly.' He put the gun back in his pocket and smiled at all of them as if nothing unusual had just taken place. 'All cooperative now? That's how it ought to be, right? Now, I'm going inside. I'll be out in a moment.'

'There's no reason for you to.' Priscilla stood perfectly straight as the icy breeze brushed strands of her pale hair across her forehead.

Megan inched back and took a step toward the van.

'I promise you I won't kill the patient,' Will said. 'I did nothing to harm him anyway, only heavy painkillers. He should be himself in no time. Maybe in the future he'll think twice before he interrupts two men having a private conversation in a parking lot.'

'That was no conversation,' Megan said. 'You murdered Chuck and would have killed Farley if I hadn't come outside when I did.'

'In that case, it's pretty generous of me to let both you and Farley live, isn't it?' He turned from her to Priscilla. 'You said there's no reason for me to go inside. I showed you a gun. How do you suggest we proceed?'

'To the barn,' Priscilla said, her voice calm. 'You can check everything there. We'll wait here until you're ready to leave.'

'Excellent.' He took a step toward the path that led back to the barn, then stopped. 'Wait a minute. Why did you put my things out there?'

'Why do you think?' Priscilla asked.

'Because of her? Because she's told you so many lies about me

that you actually think you can tell me to leave?' He patted his
vest pocket. 'Lucky for you I'm already bailing because, believe
me, lady, if I wanted to stay, I would.'

'I'm sorry it turned out this way,' Priscilla told him. 'I appreciate
your saving Callie's life. Doctor or not, you're the reason she's
here and I'll always be grateful to you for that.'

'You know Megan's crazy, right?' He laughed. 'Of course you
do, and that's why you've taken her in with the rest of the losers.
You think you can heal her, and I truly hope you can. Still, you
shouldn't have shoved my possessions in your barn like garbage.'

'We didn't feel comfortable going through them.' Priscilla let
out a breath she seemed to have been holding for some time. 'As
I said, we'll wait here until you're sure everything is in order.'

'It had better be in order.'

Will walked toward the barn and Michael and Jonas looked at
each other.

'Jonas, you get back to Farley,' Michael said. 'Are you OK,
Megan?'

'I'm fine.' But she wasn't. She had something else to do, her
last chance to make any of this right. 'You go in,' she told Priscilla
as Jonas closed the door behind Michael and him.

'Oh, no. I'm waiting right here until Will comes back from the
barn.'

'Then please understand what I'm doing right now,' Megan said
and started toward the van.

'That's not a good idea.'

'It's the best idea I've had in a long time.' She glanced back at
Priscilla and Michael. 'I have to.' And then, because she didn't
want to hear any other objections, she ran to the van and spoke
against the window. The woman didn't turn around. Only the white
collar of her jacket showed. 'I know you can hear me,' Megan
said.

The woman seemed to pull even farther away, toward the steering
wheel and the driver's seat of the van.

'I know Will has told you I'm some kind of tramp or crazy
lady or both. I was like you once and no one told me that this
man makes up lies as easily as he breathes.' She spoke slowly,
clearly, the way she wished someone had spoken to her. 'He makes
you feel like dirt and he picks you carefully enough to know that

you're wounded enough to believe whatever he says and accept whatever he does.'

The woman jerked around. 'Get out of here.'

She might have been pretty but Megan wasn't sure because her features barely registered. All that did was the anger that barely hid her fear the way the collar barely hid her long blonde hair.

'He killed a man,' Megan said. 'He's not a doctor. He flunked out of college in Berkeley and he has no parents in Mendocino. There's a man inside he would've killed if he could have. Will's been drugging him, keeping him barely alive, and he tried to drug me too. What else do you need to hear?'

'You're lying.' The blonde turned her back again.

'Check out Farley Black from Sacramento,' Megan said.

The woman faced her again, her shocked expression like a mask in the window of the van. 'Farley?' she mouthed.

'He's inside.' Megan pointed at the cabin. 'He's going to be all right now, but you won't be if you don't get away from Will as fast as you can.'

THIRTY-NINE

Kit and John Paul considered going back to the farmhouse, but when Kit called Virgie she said she was fine. 'Except for the law crawling all over the place,' she added in a dry voice that pleased Kit because it sounded much more like her than the weak one had earlier.

'Good,' Kit said. 'Stay safe. We got a good lead and will be back soon.'

Once they ended the call, John Paul asked, 'Back to Mickey's?'

'Absolutely.'

'What do you think we'll get out of him?' he asked.

'We've got to find Will. He's behind this.' She glanced over at him. 'What do *you* think we'll get out of him?'

'He's pretty tight-lipped. This is his business, after all.'

'Is he a decent guy?'

'Seems to be. Let's go find out.'

Kit and John Paul drove to the bar. Mickey was sweeping the front path, his long hair hidden under a cap.

He looked up as they pulled in and squinted, as if trying to decide whether or not to head inside. Instead, he walked over to the truck.

'Hey, man,' he said. 'You're a little early.'

'Need to ask you some questions.' John Paul opened his door and Kit did the same.

'I remember you.' Mickey flashed Kit a nicotine smile and glanced at her hand. 'I told you that stamp would fade in a few days.'

She and John Paul had headed around from opposite sides of the truck and they now faced him, side to side.

'You didn't tell me about Will, though,' she said.

'Will?' He choked out the word.

'Will as in Will and Megan,' she said. 'Megan as in Megan and Rudy and then Megan and Chuck.'

He heaved out a sigh. 'You might as well come inside,' he told them. 'I need a drink.'

'Last time I was here you didn't drink at all,' Kit said.

'That's the best way when you own a pub.' He leaned his broom against the side of the building and motioned to the back. 'Come on. I really don't want anybody to see me talking to you out here.'

'Why not?' Kit asked.

'It's just better. Enough people are gossiping about what happened already.' He managed a nervous laugh. 'Besides, I don't want to end up like Chuck.'

'No one wishes you any harm.' John Paul stood where he was and Kit didn't move either.

'I could end up there.' He glanced back at the moss-covered creek. 'Come on. I'll buy you a round.'

'Only if you tell us why you think your life's in danger,' John Paul said.

'That's a no-brainer.' The door stood open and they walked inside. The bar at midday was chilly and quiet in a disturbing way. The three of them sat in one of the three booths in the back. It still smelled faintly of whatever disinfectant Mickey had cleaned it with.

'What are you worried about?' John Paul asked him.

'Someone got killed after leaving my bar.' He shook his head.
'I still can't believe it. Can I get you some drinks?'

'No,' Kit said, 'but what you can do is tell us about Will.'

'I don't know anything about him.' He took off the cap and the
skinny braids fell over his shoulder, making him appear vulnerable,
almost frail. 'And you may not want a drink, but I'm having one.'

He went to the cooler and came back with a beer.

'When was the last time you saw Will?' Kit asked.

'I don't remember.'

'After they found Chuck's body out there?'

'I'm not sure. Maybe.' He stared down at his untouched beer.
'Actually, he's been in a couple of times.'

John Paul leaned across the table as if this were a friendly chat.
'Was he with anyone?'

'Yeah, he was. A woman who has been in here earlier. Just
don't say you heard any of this from me.'

Kit felt a chill from her skull to the back of her neck.

'Tell me about the woman.'

'Not much to tell.' This time he took a long swallow of the
beer. 'Good looking. She was trying to find anyone who had seen
Farley. Was in here the night they found Chuck, same as you.
Really upset.'

Kit and John Paul looked at each other and Kit reached for her
purse.

'Would you recognize this woman if I showed you a photo of
her?'

'Maybe. Maybe not.' Mickey pressed his hands on the table as
if ready to get up. 'Most of all, I don't want any trouble around
this place. We've had enough.'

'Just let me show you.' Kit pulled out her phone and found a
photo of Monique online. 'Does this look like the woman who
asked you about Farley?'

'What happens if I tell you?'

'Nothing,' John Paul said. 'Only that we stick a little closer to
you from now on.'

He set his bottle of beer on the table with a thud. 'That's the
woman.'

'We have reason to believe that this man Will is extremely
dangerous,' John Paul told him. 'If he comes in here again, contact

the police at once.' He pulled a card out of his pocket. 'I'd also appreciate it if you would contact me.'

'You think Will killed Chuck?' He reached for the bottle again.

'All I can tell you for sure is that he's committed crimes and he is dangerous.'

'And the blonde?' he asked.

'As I said, if you see her, contact us.' John Paul slid out of the booth.

At the truck, he called his friend at the Willits Police Department and sent a photo of both Will and Monique.

'Another reason why we need to learn how to live with technology,' he told Kit. 'Dropping out isn't the answer.'

'Not for you and obviously not for law enforcement, but Jonas shared with me what the final straw was with Priscilla and her husband. She and her daughter were trapped in their car and would have been killed if not for a Good Samaritan. Everyone else who stopped was too busy taking photos with their phones to help.'

'No different than the people who would have just driven on by in the past,' he said.

'I think it might be different. People's senses are dulled in a way.'

'Yet it was the technology of television that brought the realities of the Vietnam War to American families.' He opened the door of the truck for her. 'For the first time, they saw what war really looked like, and that did anything but dull their senses.'

'You make a good point but somehow something happened along the way. I'm not saying I could live like Priscilla, Megan and the others but I can understand why the idea would be tempting.'

He took her hand and helped her into the seat. Still holding onto her, he said, 'Earlier, you told me that even when we argue, I make you think. That works both ways, Kit. Not that I agree with you or anything.' He let go of her hand and closed the door, yet she still felt the warmth of his touch.

For a moment, they looked at each other through the open window of the truck. He moved closer. She pulled back. He nodded. She managed to find her voice.

'Are you still going to buy me flowers?' she asked.

'Absolutely.' He paused for a moment and then headed for the driver's side. 'Lavender – a whole bunch of them.'

Once he started the truck, she told him, 'We need to find the camp, and before Jonas gives us permission to.'

He glanced over at the pub. 'I'd bet that Mickey doesn't know where it is.'

'But Nickel does. He makes the straps for their guitars and he and Jonas are friends.'

'Nickel's a vault when it comes to sharing information, not to mention a drunk. He won't tell us anything.'

'He's also a good person,' she said. 'He might tell me.'

'With Will out here somewhere, you and Virgie can't be going off on your own anymore.'

'I'm not suggesting that,' she said. 'I'm suggesting that I go in and talk to Nickel while you wait outside. Nothing will happen to me in there and I might be able to convince him.'

'I don't know.'

'It's the only way to find the camp and find it fast.'

'Let's give it a shot,' he said.

'First, though, I've got to warn Monique about Will.'

He pressed his foot on the brake. 'Do you think that's a good idea? The woman followed you, Kit.'

'Only because she was trying to find Farley.'

'Who obviously didn't want her to find him.'

'I get that.' She paused, trying to figure out how to make him understand. 'John Paul, she's a stalker, she's insecure, but I can't believe she's a killer. Will is, and she connected with him only because she'll do anything to find Farley. Believe me, Will is a charmer. Hypnotic, almost.'

'Speaking from personal experience, are you?' He studied her face and she shifted in her seat.

'Yes.'

He nodded slowly. 'Still, if you warn her, you warn him.'

'Not necessarily.'

'You could also put her in greater danger.'

'She's already in danger.'

'It's still a gamble.'

'Better than doing nothing.' She picked up her phone and called Monique's number. Voicemail answered, as she was certain it would. After the beep, she said, 'Monique, it's Kit. This guy you're with is dangerous. You've got to get away from him. I'm with

John Paul and we can help you. Most of all, get away from Will. He may seem charming at first but he's not any of the things he says he is and he has probably killed at least one man – the one we saw being pulled out of the creek.'

She ended the call and hoped that Monique would believe her. 'I hope I did the right thing,' she told John Paul.

'Me too.' He turned onto the main road. 'Now, let's go find Nickel.'

FORTY

A
s they drove to Nickel's campground, the redwood forest grew closer, yet its thin roads felt easier because of the thick fragrance of the trees after the rain.

'We'll find him,' she told John Paul. 'I feel it.'

'I hope so.' He stared straight ahead at the road. 'I know how much you care for him.'

There it came again, and Kit hated it. 'No, you don't.' She scooted around on the seat so that he would have to look at her. 'I doubt that even he knows how much I care for him. Or what that means.'

He raised an eyebrow. 'Like men are too stupid to get it?'

'It has nothing to do with stupid and a whole lot to do with not getting it. I love Farley and he is my friend. That's all, and that's everything.'

'You sure fell apart when you thought that was his body,' John Paul said.

'He's my friend,' she repeated. 'Of course I fell apart.'

'Sometimes feelings change. Ours did.'

Kit felt a flush she couldn't hide. 'I should hope so. We didn't even like each other.'

'Didn't trust each other,' he corrected her. 'That was before I knew how brave you are and what a good person.'

'And before I knew you weren't a jerk.'

They both laughed. Then he grew serious. 'I just want you to know that I'll do anything I can to help you find him, even if you discover you have feelings for him you didn't know you had.'

'Didn't hear a word I said, did you?'

'Just trying to make you understand.' He sighed.

They didn't discuss it further and Kit realized that, like many, John Paul didn't understand that a woman truly could care about a man as a friend. Once this was over, she would try to explain to him once more that she had been attracted to Farley briefly but that they both quickly moved past that into a caring friendship. Yes, she would try to have that conversation with John Paul again. But only once Farley was safe.

Within the hour, they pulled into Nickel's campground. Everything looked the same. Somehow the weathered campers, trailers and cabins seemed more appropriate to the rustic setting than new ones would have been.

'Are you OK with staying out here?' Kit asked John Paul.

'No.' He pushed back the seat and stretched his legs. 'But I know the guy won't tell me anything. If you're not back here in ten minutes, I'm going in.'

'Fifteen,' she said. 'Nickel doesn't have a weapon. I'm sure of that.'

'Ordinary things can become weapons if someone is panicked or angry enough.'

'Good point.' She squeezed his hand. 'I'll be careful.'

She got out of the truck and walked up to Nickel's cabin. As usual, the door stood partially open. Kit pushed it the rest of the way and stepped into an empty room.

Now what?

She looked around at the fanatically neat desk and the pristine sink, and then she saw an opened bottle of Gallo Hearty Burgundy on the counter. Good. Nickel was here. He just might be passed out. Afraid to go down the narrow hall to his bedroom, she moved farther into the room. The front door closed behind her and she realized it had been held open by a large rabbit carved from stone. She started to go back to open the door but heard a noise from the back patio and ran to the door.

Nickel sat out there, holding a glass of red wine and mumbling to himself. She glanced around, saw no one and stepped outside.

'Hey, Nickel. How are you?'

'Well,' he said. 'Isn't this *déjà vu* all over again?' He laughed at his own joke.

'I need your help.' She sat on the foot rest in front of his lawn chair.
'I can't help you.'

'You need to show me where the camp is.' His eyes widened
and she could almost see the wall he was building between the
two of them. 'No, listen to me, will you? I'm going to find it
sooner or later, but I need to find it now. Jonas already said he'd
try to get me in but I can't wait because of Will. He killed Chuck,
that guy who drowned in the creek outside the pub. He drugged
Virgie and he tried to drug me.'

Nickel looked up at her with watery eyes. 'And they wouldn't
let me in,' he said in a precise southern accent. 'Because I drink.'

'Their rules are their rules, but I've got to find that camp because
I know Farley's there. I've got to get him out.'

'Maybe he's too sick to get out.' He leaned back in the chair
and folded his hands over his stomach. 'Will's his doctor. At least,
he's supposed to be.'

'Will's a killer.' She jumped up from the stool. 'Call them.
They'll tell you.'

'I can't,' he said. 'No phones.'

'Then trust me. Show me where they are. We might be able to
save Farley's life.'

'You think they'd let me in if I did that?' He sneaked a glance
at the glass of wine on the table beside him.

'That's not the point,' she told him. 'Please, Nickel. I know you
want to do the right thing.'

'I don't have a vehicle.' He looked over at the glass again. 'I'm
not supposed to have a phone.'

'But you do, and so does Jonas,' she said. 'You let him know
that Virgie and I were heading there after we arrived here.'

'It's not breaking rules to do that. Jonas is a tutor and I'm a
friend. We're not official members, but we do try to limit our use
of and dependence on technology.'

'Let Jonas know we're heading there,' she said. 'I'll go in first,
but also tell him that John Paul will back us.'

He squinted at her and she wondered if he were already too
drunk to direct her. 'So Will's really dangerous?'

'I already told you that.' She forced herself to slow down and
focus. 'Let Jonas know we're on our way. Let him know right now.'

'Hang on just a minute.' Nickel navigated toward his garden

and lifted an upside-down flower pot. He put a phone to his ear and said, 'It's time, man. I'm bringing her there.'

Kit exhaled and bit her lip to keep from crying.

'Ready?' she asked.

Nickel nodded. 'Ready.'

They walked out the door together.

John Paul waited just outside Nickel's cabin.

'Oh, no. Not him.' Nickel started back inside. 'I said I'd take you inside. I didn't say I'd take the law.'

'He's not the law,' Kit told him. 'Not anymore. He cohosts a radio show in Sacramento. He's OK, Nickel. I promise.'

'Not taking him,' he said.

'Do you want Farley to die?' she asked.

'Of course not.'

'Then tell us how to find him. Where are these people?'

'So close we could walk there.' Nickel ruffled his hair with his fingers and looked at John Paul again, just as Kit's phone chimed.

She looked down at it and could barely breathe.

'Monique,' she said. Then she answered it and put the call on speaker phone.

'You were right,' Monique whispered in a voice Kit barely realized. 'He's doing crazy stuff, talking about going back there and killing all of them.'

'Where are you?' Kit asked.

'At the cabin where he and Megan lived. I'm hiding outside.'

'Stay where you are. We'll get there as fast as we can.'

'Hurry.' Monique sobbed into the phone and ended the call.

'I'm heading to the cabin,' John Paul said. 'You be careful.'

'You too.'

'Once I get her out of there I'll come back for you two.'

'Please give him directions.' Kit nudged Nickel.

'It's a bit tricky.'

Pointing, Nickel began explaining in a detailed manner, as if suddenly sober, and Kit made her way into the woods. As she suspected, the camp wasn't that far away. None of these people had automobiles. Nickel stumbled behind her, shouting directions. They must have walked for most of an hour. Every tree, every bird call, every breath of forest breeze looked, sounded and felt like the last one.

Kit's jacket grew too heavy. She yanked it off and tied it around her waist.

Finally Nickel led her past a grove of redwoods, into the core of them. Together, they moved closer as the tiny shelters between the trees became cabins. Laughter beyond the trees led her gaze to the children sitting on logs, their hair flowing as they played musical instruments and sang into the breeze. They were performing some kind of play. A taller girl with long blonde hair spotted Kit and Nickel, stood and moved toward the house. She looked enough like Priscilla, the pregnant woman from the fruit stand, to be her daughter and probably was. She was also probably going to warn Priscilla that visitors were approaching.

This was the camp and Farley had to be here. Beyond the children, partially hidden by a tree, Kit spotted a flash of silver – a silk car cover hiding a vehicle.

'Farley's car!' She pointed and Nickel nodded. 'Where is he?'

'Inside. You wait here.'

She ran ahead of him to the front door. If Farley were in here, if he were alive, she wasn't about to wait.

Priscilla opened the door. Megan stood behind her, eyes wide.

'Let me in,' Kit said. 'Please.'

They looked at each other and then stepped outside. 'We'll let you in shortly.' Priscilla motioned to Nickel.

'I just want to see Farley. That's all.'

Priscilla stepped back and studied Kit in a way that made her feel that the woman was trying to see inside her. 'And you promise that you won't bring attention, media or otherwise, to our home?'

'You know I can't promise that, but if I can help you, I will.'

She put out her hand. 'Then, welcome.'

Nickel caught up and Priscilla closed the door behind them.

The cabin was similar to Jonas's but larger. Simple and warm, it was filled with handmade pillows, stacks of books and the deep, sweet smell of jam. Now Kit knew where the fruit-stand jars came from. A row of empty ones lined the kitchen sink next to a wood stove and a stand holding what looked like antique brass fireplace tools.

Jonas came out from a narrow hall in khakis and a plaid shirt open at the throat. His face lit up when he saw her, and he flashed her the first genuine smile she had seen from him.

'Welcome, Kit.' He hugged her tightly. 'He's doing better, much better. We're getting a real doctor out here today and then he'll have the care he needs.'

'What happened to him?'

'From what was said and what we can observe, heavy painkillers. We thought Will was one of us.' He took her hand and led her down the hall. The others waited in the main room. 'I'm sorry about not being forthcoming before,' he told her. 'I was wrong.'

'You were scared. You didn't know me.'

'I'll wait outside.' He motioned to the open door and Kit rushed inside.

There, on a blanket-covered pallet, Farley lay. His hair, darker blond than the last time she had seen it, was swept back from his pale face. His rhythmic breathing sounded more like a person asleep.

She dropped to one of the pillows on the floor and touched his face.

'Farley,' she whispered. 'It's Kit.'

His lids drifted opened and he seemed to stare into space. 'Hey, Kit.' Then his eyes shut again. She looked at the door, where Jonas stood, tears in his eyes.

'I'll be in the main room when you're ready,' he said, and turned away.

FORTY-ONE

Farley was alive. He was going to stay alive. Kit wanted to hug him but she didn't dare. Instead, she needed to find out what Jonas knew. She leaned down, kissed Farley's forehead and said, 'I love you and I'll be back soon. You rest.'

He responded with something that sounded like a hum.

When she stepped out of the hall into the warmth of the main room, she composed herself as well as she could.

Priscilla motioned her to a wooden table much like Jonas's.

'Nickel and Michael have gone to help John Paul find his way here,' she said. 'I made lavender tea and scones.'

Kit knew she couldn't eat but she sat beside her, across from Jonas and Megan, their hands joined on the table.

'Do you think that's a good idea?' Kit asked. 'Nickel's not all that reliable.'

'He's reliable enough to have led you to us. He's reliable enough to make guitar straps for our instruments and carve toys for our kids. We're even starting to sell some of them and he wants none of the money.'

'But you won't let him join you because of his drinking?'

'We love him but it's too big a risk right now,' Priscilla said softly. 'I keep hoping, one day, he'll be able to overcome his demons. I pray for it.'

'How did Farley get here?' Kit asked her.

'Megan?' Priscilla said it as graciously as if offering her a scone.

'Because of me.' Megan clutched Jonas's hand and he placed his other one on top of hers. 'Will set me up with a man. More about that later.'

'I know about Chuck,' Kit said.

Her cheeks turned red. Jonas put his arm around her. 'Chuck was a good man. He wanted to help me. Will attacked him and Chuck told me to make sure no one in the pub saw what was happening. When I came back outside, Farley – he was the guitar player to me then – was fighting with Will on the ground. Will grabbed a wrench out of the saddlebags on his motorcycle and hit him over the head.' Tears filled her eyes.

'Why didn't you call the police?' Kit demanded.

'I was afraid that he would die and that I'd get blamed.' She met Kit's gaze. 'I was a different person then, under Will's spell in a way.'

'Why didn't you at least take Farley to a hospital?'

'You don't understand Will.'

'I've met him,' she said. 'He tried to drug me at the general store.'

'But you don't understand what it's like to be on that merry-go-round that he can be,' she said. Jonas and Priscilla chuckled. 'No, it is like a merry-go-round,' Megan said. 'Music and movement and crazy stuff behind the scenes. I knew he was planning to kill Farley the first night because he told me to get rid of his phone.'

'And you hid it in the fruit stand,' Kit said.

'I didn't want any part of what Will was planning.' Megan

turned to Jonas, who looked almost as pale as Farley. 'I thought if I kept his phone I'd have proof of who he was.'

'In case Will killed him?' Kit didn't bother hiding the anger in her voice.

Megan jerked up from the table. 'You have no right to judge me. I did the best I could for Farley, and when I could get away from Will, I did.'

'I'm not judging you,' Kit said.

She nodded and pulled her black ponytail out of the clip. 'Maybe I'm just tired. I haven't had much sleep and I think I just need to rest.'

'I didn't mean to snap at you.' Kit sipped her tea and forced herself to remain calm. 'It's just emotional for me to find him here, and I am grateful to you for saving his life. I can't tell you how grateful.'

Megan had started across the room. Kit stood, went to her and hugged her. 'Thank you.'

Megan's stiff stance felt more natural, softer, and she took a deep breath. 'There's something I haven't told you. Will came by here today driving a dark-colored van with a blonde woman in it. He said he came for his things.'

Monique. That's who it had to be. 'Did you see the woman?' Kit asked.

'She turned her head.' Her voice broke and she took a deep breath. 'But when he was in the barn getting his stuff, I told her she needed to get away from him, that he was a killer.'

'Interesting,' Kit said. 'I called her not long ago and told her the same thing.'

Megan gasped. 'You know her?'

'Her father owns the radio station where Farley works. She was his girlfriend.'

'But he wanted to get away from her.' Jonas stood, pulled his chair around and stood behind it. 'I've shared this with Priscilla and no one else, not even you, Megan. She had decided she and Farley were in love and she was doing things like logging into his email, even checking out his bank account to see where he was having lunch and what kind of stores he frequented.'

'I knew it,' Kit said. 'Considering that her dad owns the radio station, her job was pretty vague but she excelled at the technical stuff.' She looked from Megan, to Jonas, to Priscilla. 'Monique was stalking Farley. He never invited her to go surfing with him, I'll bet. He just told her he was going surfing.'

'And he told me he was coming here to get away from her.' Jonas shook his head. 'Once we know Farley is getting the right care, I'll tell you more. For now, I'll just say, she approached me and pretended to be you, Kit.'

'She did?'

He nodded. 'Megan knows all about it now. Monique was obsessed with finding Farley. I'm sure that's how Will found her. I hope he doesn't harm her.'

'John Paul will get her away from there,' she said. 'I think all we can do right now is wait.'

'In a minute.' Megan took Jonas's hand in hers. 'The night I met Chuck – the night Will set me up with him – Chuck was wearing a watch that had been his father's. I commented on it because I had never seen a watch like that and because it seemed kind of off for a guy like Chuck to be wearing it.'

Kit's stomach clenched. 'Was it a curved band?' she asked. 'Rose gold?'

Tears sprang to Megan's eyes. 'You saw it, didn't you?'

'On Will,' Kit said.

'That's one of the reasons he rushed in and out of here so fast,' Megan said. 'I'm sure there were other things that would have incriminated him but the watch was the big one.'

'Of course,' Kit said. 'Why did you let him take it?'

'I didn't.' She reached into the pocket of her smock and lifted out a gleaming rose-gold watch. Then, she burst into tears. 'Take it.' She shoved the watch into Kit's hands. 'There's your proof that he killed Chuck. I can't tell you anything else right now.'

'Come on, now.' Jonas put his arm around her. 'You've done the right thing. It's time for your guitar lesson, so let's not let what's happening keep us from what matters. Farley's going to recover. Finally we're all going to be OK.'

'We are.' Megan smiled up at him.

'Amen,' said Priscilla.

Kit hoped John Paul would get there soon and that Farley would continue to improve. She headed down the hall and decided to stay there in the room on a cushion beside his pallet.

She slid down beside him and whispered, 'I'm here, Farley.'
He mumbled something she couldn't understand.

As Kit looked around the small room filled with his steady breathing and the screeching laughter of the children outside, she realized how incredibly lucky Farley was that Megan had insisted that Will bring him here. She felt lucky too. John Paul would get help and join her any minute. Farley would get the right care until he was well again. She didn't want to deal with the rest of it yet – what would happen to Monique or what Kit and John Paul could salvage from their uncertain relationship. All she wanted was to stay here with her friend, breath by certain breath.

FORTY-TWO

Jonas and Megan leaned against the pillows on the floor of Michael's and Priscilla's screened-in sunroom. The earlier mist had ignited the scent of the clumps of lavender growing outside and the entire porch was drenched in the heady fragrance. Megan's guitar rested beside her. The glistening crystal rose stones of the strap looked almost effervescent in the afternoon light. She ran her fingers over them while Jonas strummed his guitar.

'*La Catedral*. I love it.'

'Very good. And what do you love about it?'

'Well,' she said, 'the way it moves from one mood to the next – from serenity to exhilaration. And the fact that you're playing it.'

'All good reasons.'

'Thanks, teacher.' She rested her head on his shoulder and cradled the guitar she was supposed to be playing.

'Once we're married,' he said, 'we can move into a cabin here. I'll give mine to Farley. He's totally capable of taking over the school.'

'Do you think he'd leave the radio station?' she asked.

'He's not happy there and, after what happened to him, he might have the same kind of wake-up call I did.' He kissed her forehead. 'I hope one day he finds a woman like you.'

With her cheek against his chest she could feel his heartbeat, and Megan wondered how she had ever gotten this lucky considering the dangerous path she had traveled to this man's life.

She looked up into his eyes. 'I love you, Jonas.'

'This was supposed to be a guitar lesson,' he said, yet his eyes were focused on her lips. 'Once we're married, we'll teach the kids, the two of us. Maybe have some of our own. You're a natural. Besides, you have great compassion and empathy. The kids here already love you.'

He took her into his arms and Megan kissed him with all the hope she felt. 'From now on,' she whispered against his cheek, 'we're together.'

'Excuse me.' Will stepped through the screen door. 'I believe you have something of mine.'

They pulled apart and Jonas jumped to his feet. 'We don't have anything of yours, Will. How did you get in here?'

'You forget you idiots don't believe in keys?' He laughed, and Megan realized he was wearing new clothes again – a yellow ski sweater and chalk-gray pants.

He knelt down beside her on the floor. 'That wasn't nice what you did, Megs. You shouldn't have scared my new woman like that. She's turned against me too.'

'I didn't.'

'I heard the message you left.' He shook his head as if scolding a child. 'You told her I was dangerous, which was pretty ridiculous considering that I didn't harm you when I had every chance.'

She stood, pressed her back against the wall and thought about how fast she would have to move to get out the door. 'You tried, Will. You put pills in the tea I was taking to Jonas.'

'That wouldn't have killed you.' He moved closer to her. 'They were just painkillers. Same as I was giving Farley. I saved his life, Megs.'

Only after you almost killed him. She didn't dare say that, though. Will's talk and the jerky way he moved were much more reckless than he had been all of the time they had been together.

She inched herself along the wall, closer to the door. 'I don't want any trouble, Will. Tell me what you need from me.'

'First of all.' He stabbed a finger at Jonas but his voice remained calm, almost professional. That terrified her more than if he had shouted at them. 'This gentleman needs to leave the room. This is between you and me. '

'I'm not leaving her,' Jonas said.

Will smiled, too calm for what was happening.

'You can have the watch,' she told him.

'It's too late for that.'

She needed to get him out of here before he tried to hurt Jonas and the others. The screen door stood open.

'Don't even try that.' He took a step toward her.

She screamed and ran through it, into the woods.

Dry branches crashed underneath her. She slid around the muddy base of one large tree and then another, heading deeper into the branches that scratched and bloodied her arms.

Finally she stopped and rested her forehead against the thick, gouged trunk of a pine tree. As the cool air filled her lungs, Megan could feel her frantic heartbeat slow down. Shouting came from the camp. Good. Jonas was on his way, maybe even John Paul. Once they had Will she'd let them know where she was hiding. Tonight she would sleep beside Jonas without fear.

The voices blended into the sounds of the forest. She thought she heard her name called but she didn't dare move. Something hit the tree and she jumped. Sweat covered her face. No, not a gunshot. Just a pebble. Then another.

She jerked around. Will leaned on a tree behind her, holding a handful of small rocks, smiling.

'Hey, Megs.'

She screamed and tried to run. Will grabbed her by an arm, yanked her around and shoved her against the tree.

'Let me go. Please.'

'Sorry, Megs. I gave you chance after chance and you lied and cheated at every turn.' He slid his hands up her throat and squeezed. She kicked and struggled with everything in her but his fingers kept tightening. 'I've always wanted to do this.' His voiced sounded dreamy, blurred. 'You have such a perfect neck.'

'Get away from her.'

Megan tried to make sense of the words, of the shouting, but she was sliding too fast now down the trunk of the tree as each breath exploded in her chest.

FORTY-THREE

'I said get away from her.' Kit clutched the fireplace poker and glanced over at Megan's body on the ground. Her chest still heaved. She was alive.

After shouting to Priscilla that Will was back, Kit had grabbed the closest weapon she could find and run from the cabin. She followed the voices and found Will strangling Megan. She swung the poker but he heard her, jumped away and it barely grazed his head.

Now a strange calm controlled her as she focused her gaze on him.

'Hey.' Will grinned at her and lifted his palms. A thin trail of blood made its way down the side of his face and he wiped it away. 'Looks like you have the upper hand. You wouldn't really drive that thing into me, though, would you? It would make one gruesome mess out here in the middle of all this natural beauty.'

'I'll do whatever I have to.' She clenched it tighter. 'John Paul is on his way right now. So are the police.'

'And you really think I'm going to stand out here with you two women and wait for them?'

'I don't care what you do.' From the corner of her eye she saw a flash of blue fabric before it disappeared behind a tree and knew Jonas had found them. 'I just want you out of here and away from Megan.'

'Figures.' He made a face. 'You're no better than she is.'

In a sudden lunge, he grabbed her and Kit tried to hang onto the poker as it slid from her grasp.

'Now.' Will shoved her against the same tree where he had pinned Megan. 'What am I going to do with you, Kit?'

'You won't be doing anything.' Jonas picked up the poker and stood beside Megan, who moaned and sat up from where she had fallen. 'I'd be happy to use this on you,' Jonas said.

'I get it.' Will grimaced. 'And you can put that thing down, man.' He lifted his arms in a calm gesture of surrender and Kit saw the sweat stains under them imprinted on the pale yellow sweater.

'Don't put it down,' she told Jonas. Then she went over and helped Megan to her feet.

'I'm not about to,' he said. 'You killed a man, Will. It's not up to me to decide what happens to you but I'm going to protect my woman until the police get here.'

'*Your* woman?' Will laughed. 'Your woman who stole the watch from the guy I pimped her out to?'

Megan gasped, and Kit grabbed her arm and eased her onto the ground.

'She didn't steal it,' Jonas said. 'You did.'

'Pretty hard to prove with him dead and all. For all you know, maybe she killed him.'

Kit's text dinged. 'John Paul,' she read aloud. 'Just pulling in.'

'Good to hear.' Will grinned and began pacing back and forth in front of them. 'Cops coming, sad ending for me. What would you do if you were in my place, Jonas?'

'I'd keep my mouth shut.' Jonas kept the sooty black poker pointed at him.

'Good answer.' He turned back in the direction of the cabin. After a couple of steps he stopped and glanced back at them. 'I will tell the police all about Megan. She'll probably be arrested for soliciting.'

'I told you to shut up,' Jonas said. 'Get moving.'

'Excellent idea.' Will yanked a gun from his jacket. Jonas charged him and the gun fired before dropping to the ground.

Kit screamed.

Megan, her face stark white, jumped up, grabbed the gun and fired it at Will. Then, still holding it, she knelt down beside Jonas's still body.

Kit ran toward the shouts of those coming for her. John Paul was the first one she saw.

'Will shot Jonas,' she told him as he grabbed her hands. 'Megan's out there. She shot Will but I think he's still alive.'

'Get inside and call nine-one-one,' he said as he headed into the dense curtain of trees.

Will had killed Jonas. There was no way that still body on the ground had a breath of life in it. Now, Kit walked inside, knowing that John Paul and the police would handle the rest.

Farley was out of danger. Priscilla had gathered her children close to her and was speaking to them softly in the sun room. Kit went past them, down the hall and into the room where Farley lay, his eyes open and his expression startled.

'Kit?' He tried to sit up against the wall. 'How did I get here?'

She ran to him, crouched, and threw her arms around him. 'Oh, Farley.' For that moment, they held each other tightly. 'You're going to be fine,' she said. 'I'll tell you everything as soon as you're stronger.'

Someone walked into the room. She let go of Farley and jerked around toward the door.

John Paul stood there, arms at his side.

'Just wanted to be sure you're all right,' he said. 'They took Will in. He died on the way to the hospital.'

'And Megan?'

'She'll be staying here with Priscilla's family and she's pretty messed up. Jonas didn't make it.'

'Jonas?' Farley's voice broke. 'What do you mean? Where's Jonas?'

Kit put her hands against his shoulders and pushed him gently back into the pillows. 'We can talk later. You need to rest now.'

'No.' Tears filled his eyes and ran down his cheek. 'He just said Jonas didn't make it. You have to tell me, Kit.'

She could tell he was alert enough to hear her now, and what she had to tell him tore her apart. 'Will shot Jonas, Farley. He murdered him.'

'I'm sorry, man,' John Paul said.

'God.' He shut his eyes and seemed to retreat.

Kit put her arms around him, trying to pull him back. 'It's horrible but Will's dead now. Everyone here can try to start over.' She felt as if she were chanting, saying anything that came into her mind. '*You* can start over, Farley.'

'Monique?' He tried to say more but retreated to silence again.

'She won't bother you anymore, I promise. You're going to be OK – better than OK. You can do this.'

'Love you,' he said, eyes still squeezed shut, damp hair shoved back from his face.

'Love you too. Stay strong.'

'Don't leave.'

'I won't. I'll stay until you're better.'

'Don't leave,' he said again. 'Oh, Jonas. Oh, God.'

Kit didn't know how long she held onto Farley's hand like that. In the hours that passed, he occasionally called for Jonas, pushed her away and, later, held her close to him, squeezing her hand in his uncertain sleep.

Finally Kit relaxed and straightened up, but still kept his hand in hers. Early morning sunlight filtered into the room. She had barely closed her eyes all night. Each time she tried, violent images appeared again – Megan's body on the ground in the forest, the horrible thunk of the fireplace poker as it grazed Will's head and the easy, thoughtless way he'd shot Jonas.

Someone knocked softly and Virgie stepped inside the bedroom.

'I'm helping Priscilla cook breakfast,' she whispered and leaned against the door. 'If you don't want the toast to get burned why don't you come on out?'

That wasn't like her. Kit knew something else must be going on.

'Is Priscilla all right?'

'She's doing better.'

'So is Farley.'

She followed Virgie down the hall and into the kitchen, where Priscilla stood at the woodstove.

Kit looked at the empty table. 'Where are your children?' she asked.

'In the sun room.' She rested her hands over her belly. 'Tea's on and I toasted some oat bread. You shouldn't travel hungry. There's fresh jam too. Take whatever you like back with you.'

In spite of her easy manner and the mixed smells of food coming from the stove, something about the room didn't make sense.

'Where's John Paul?' Kit asked.

'He's taking off,' Virgie told her and motioned toward the window. 'Going back.'

'Leaving this early?' *And without saying goodbye?*

'He left these for you.'

Kit glanced over at the kitchen counter where a bunch of dried lavender lay. Then she turned and rushed to the window in time to see him walk down to his truck, lean against it and look back at the cabin. As she watched, he stared as if he could see her. For a moment, Kit considered running out there to him but she couldn't.

She had nothing to say. Instead, she watched as John Paul climbed behind the wheel of the silver pickup and drove away. She stood at the window until the truck was only a small shape, a shadow on the horizon.

FORTY-FOUR

Although Virgie and Kit didn't discuss John Paul's sudden departure, Kit knew Virgie hadn't missed its significance. 'I'm going to fill up the gas tank for the trip back.' She zipped up her vest and took a final swallow from her coffee.

'Thanks.' Kit watched her leave and then stared at the dead flowers on the counter.

Wearing an apron as soft and pale pink as her skin, Priscilla cleared her throat and motioned to a kettle on the stove.

'Onion soup.' She hugged Kit so hard that several strands of pale blonde hair fell down from her ponytail. 'I'm glad we got to know you.'

'Me too. And I'm sorry about Jonas, sorry you had to go through any of this.'

'We allowed the wrong person in but we're determined we won't judge the next one more harshly because of it.' She brushed back the hair from her eyes. 'We will probably have to move on, but we will continue to live as we believe.'

The sound of classical guitar music came from the sun room and Kit felt a chill.

'I understand,' she said. 'You have my word that I will never tell anyone about your camp.' They hugged again, quickly this time, and Priscilla walked back toward the sun room.

'Got to get the kids involved in an activity.' She motioned toward the source of the music. 'I don't want Farley to hear that, and frankly, I can't bear to hear it right now either.'

Too late. Farley stood in the doorway, head bowed, and Kit knew he was mourning Jonas.

Priscilla disappeared into the back and the music stopped as suddenly as it had started.

Kit went to the stove, ladled some soup into a bowl for him and poured a cup of tea for herself.

Farley had put on a wool shirt that fit him loosely over his T-shirt. Pale stubble covered his face but his cheeks had a little more color in them. He was going to be all right. He sat down across from her and lifted a spoon to his lips.

'Lucky to be alive,' he said and patted his hair. 'I must look like hell.'

'I've never seen you look better.'

Sitting in the warmth of the kitchen, with John Paul's dried lavender on the counter, all she wanted was to be sure that Farley was well enough to return, not just physically but mentally. She knew both sides of that now and she wanted to help him.

'How does it taste?' she asked.

'Fine.' He sighed and pushed the bowl away. 'Strike that. It's delicious, but we can do better than this conversation we're having.'

'Such as?' Then she thought about the guitar strap and Farley's name in Nickel's book. It was time to really talk and to say what she had been suspecting. 'When you faked that surfing trip, you weren't just coming up here for a visit with Jonas, were you?'

'I wasn't sure.' He paused and then added, 'I needed to get away from Monique and the way she invaded every part of my life.'

'And you blamed it on technology,' Kit said.

'That's exactly what it was. She was good at it, and she could trace everything I did.'

Kit reached across the table and squeezed his hand. 'Monique won't bother you now, I promise.'

'Just because Will tried to kill her? I wouldn't bet on that.'

'I would,' she said. 'John Paul said she was terrified when he found her. She's on her way home now.'

'If you say so.' He shook his head. 'But I have a feeling I'll still be looking over my shoulder for a while.'

'If you had joined this group . . .' She took a sip of the tea and felt her throat tighten as she swallowed.

'What?'

'Would you have told me?'

'Of course. You're my best friend. I planned to ask you to help me get rid of my things, help me sell my place.' He looked down at the table and back at her. 'I hope you will.'

'So you've made up your mind?'

'It was pretty much made up, and not just because of Monique. Now I can stay on here and teach music to the kids, even with this messed-up hand.'

She struggled with the idea of fun-loving Farley settling down with a camp of peaceful permaculturists escaping the dehumanization of society by technology. Yet she had always sensed there was more to him than surfing and radio. She had known there was something missing too.

There was no point in gushing out that she was happy for him, or that she hoped he'd stay in touch. No words could erase the reality of Jonas's murder.

They sat for a moment in silence as she sipped her tea.

'You will always know how to find me,' he said. 'I promise you.'

'I can't ask for more than that.' She stood and moved toward the front window.

Outside, on the path before the cabin, Virgie parked the car. Its white paint sparkled in the sunlight.

Farley started to rise but she shook her head.

'Don't walk me out.' Instead she went back to the table and hugged him tightly.

Then she walked over to the counter and lifted a handful of lavender blossoms – nothing left of them but their scent. She crushed them in her hand and the smell brought tears to her eyes.

After closing the front door behind her, she stood on the porch and looked into the woods, the sunlit green-on-green that faded finally into black, the scarlet streaks in the cloudless sky, the narrow path that led to places she couldn't begin to imagine.

Virgie stood in front of the car, arms crossed over her vest. She looked up at Kit and said, 'You ready to go home now?'

'I am.' She walked down the old wooden steps, every creak like the sound of a door opening and closing. 'And Virgie,' she said, 'I'm driving.'